DEADLY DECEPTION

DEADLY DECEPTION

Andrea Johnson Beck

Text copyright © 2012 Andrea Johnson Beck

Published by Montlake Romance, Seattle

www.apub.com

ISBN-13: 9781612184562
ISBN-10: 1612184561
Library of Congress Control Number: 2013915255

To "my" Leonard and Sheldon

He who has made it a practice to lie and deceive his father, will be the most daring in deceiving others.

—Horace

Seeking to forget makes exile all the longer; the secret of redemption lies in remembrance.

—Richard von Weizsäcker

CHAPTER ONE

"Ten…nine…eight…." The deep voice lulled Dr. Anne Jamison out of the darkness that surrounded her subconscious. "Seven…six…five…four…three…two…one. Come back to me, Anne."

Her green eyes fluttered rapidly as she attempted to focus on her stark white surroundings that were layered with a post-hypnotic haze.

"How do you feel, Anne?" Dr. David Lindsey asked, perched across from her in his leather chair.

Her mouth was dry and she felt disoriented but oddly calm. Dr. Lindsey adjusted his wire-rim glasses as he began to jot something down on his steno pad.

"I don't feel any anxiety," Anne finally replied, looking toward the skyline backdrop.

She stood and began walking toward the wall of windows. She straightened out her black pencil skirt and placed her flushed forehead against the wintery glass. Anne gazed twenty-two stories down at the bustling morning traffic, watching the cars maneuver through the maze of downtown Minneapolis. Her hot breath fogged the glass, clouding the image; she began playing with the string of pearls draped across her slender neck.

"That's great. I know that you want to remain off your medication. How are you feeling today?" Dr. Lindsey asked.

"Today," Anne repeated in statement form, exhaling deeply.

"Anne? I know that you haven't had any nightmares in some time. Have they returned?"

Anne could feel Dr. Lindsey's question burn in the back of her skull. She left the pearls alone and turned back to him. His salt-and-pepper hair reflected the harsh fluorescents that beamed above them. He reminded Anne of her psych professor in college.

"No, I haven't had any nightmares since." Her long blonde strands had become entangled in the necklace. Wincing, she pulled the knotted piece free. "Since Adam."

"You must be quite ecstatic about your recent engagement," Dr. Lindsey said, smiling.

She stroked the three-carat princess-cut solitaire with her index finger and watched the ballet of colors dance inside the diamond with illuminated grace as her fiancé, Adam Whitney, came to her mind. Warmth radiated throughout her body.

"I'm quite happy indeed, Dr. Lindsey, though I do at times feel that uneasiness, that lack of closure." Anne felt the emotions rising just below the surface of her flushed skin.

"You must remove yourself from that liability. Carter led a reckless lifestyle. He was obsessed with proving to people that he was more than just his father's son. Carter wanted to show the world that he was the best at everything and that included dangerous activities like rafting a down a river in inclement weather. You can't blame yourself for his actions."

Before Adam came into her life, Anne had been in a whirlwind but passionate relationship for nearly a year and a half with Carter Leeds. Three years ago he had vanished and was presumed dead. His death had broken Anne not only mentally but physically. Despair riddled her body like cancer, but her best friend, Casey, hadn't given up on her. She had forced Anne to see Dr. Lindsey, and when she met Adam, it was like breathing in a new life. They helped pull Anne from the darkness and self-torment.

"I know, but how do you truly have closure when there's no body? How do you say farewell to a poster-sized picture draped with sympathy bouquets?"

"Anne, Carter is gone. He's not coming back and you need to start focusing on the future. Focus on you and Adam. He's good for you."

Dr. Lindsey's expression softened as he placed the steno pad down on the wooden coffee table between them.

Anne glanced at her watch. "I need to cut our session short today. I have a full patient load." She stood up, smoothed out her maroon cardigan, and reached for her black purse. She picked up her trench coat, draping it over her arm.

Dr. Lindsey walked over to Anne. "Maybe you should take the day...."

Anne raised her hand in protest. "Absolutely not. I'm a big girl, and these children need help. I can handle it. They can't."

Without further argument, Dr. Lindsey stepped out of her way and toward the door. He opened it to the reception area, ushering Anne through.

"Take care, Anne." He squeezed her arm and turned toward the young man who was his next appointment.

3

Anne walked over to the reception desk where she was greeted with warm brown eyes and an upturned oval face. "Would you like to schedule your next appointment, Anne?"

"I'll just call in, Claire. Thank you."

Claire was Dr. Lindsey's daughter, and Anne had grown quite fond of the bubbly brunette over the past couple of years.

"Great, then you are good to go. Have a super day, Anne."

Anne smiled. "You too." She turned, walked out of the glass door, and into the narrow hallway. Her heels clicked against the tan tile, echoing off the vintage walls. Her own self-produced breeze flowed through her loose curls as they bounced with her quickened step. Anne took her final turn and there stood Casey Adler, best friend extraordinaire and colleague, with one hand on her hip and the other holding a latte. Her hourglass shape filled the grey-and-white leopard sheath dress perfectly, evoking the style of Marilyn Monroe. She raised an eyebrow at Anne.

"Where the hell have you been?"

"Well, good morning to you too," Anne replied.

Casey yanked Anne's phone from the open pocket in her purse and held it up.

"I called and texted you a dozen times. Where have you been? And don't lie to me, Anne. We've been friends since college and I know when you are lying."

"I had an appointment with Dr. Lindsey and, before you even start white-couching me, I am perfectly fine, okay?" Anne snatched her phone back, throwing it into her purse.

"I promise I won't, but I'm just worried about you. You stopping your anxiety medication makes me nervous," Casey said as she brushed her flaxen bangs to the side.

"I know, but I feel so much better, freer of all those self-loathing emotions. The hypnotherapy is working. Adam deserves a fiancée who doesn't need to take a pill to bury all that unnecessary baggage."

"You shouldn't have to bury anything. What happened was not your fault."

A brief flash of sorrow circled Anne, as her best friend was giving her the same look that she had the day she confirmed Carter was dead.

Anne shook her head. "Enough of this, let's talk about *this*." She beamed as she held up her brand-new, stunning accessory. Casey grabbed her hand to examine the rock.

"*Gorgeous, darling!*" she said in her best British accent. "You know how much I adore Adam. He's a magnificent guy and perfect for you. I'm so happy for you both."

Casey's approval meant the world to Anne. She smiled and opened the door to their practice. They entered their office in a lighter mood. Their assistant Shelly sat prepping moss-green patient folders while twirling a piece of loose white hair that had fallen from her bun. Anne and Casey chimed "good morning" in unison, which made all three of them laugh.

"Good morning. Here are your messages. Dr. Jamison, I have a package here for you. It was next to the door when I arrived."

Shelly passed the large manila envelope to Anne over the chest-high ledge. Anne examined the envelope to locate some clues of its sender. In bold black on the front, it read:

Dr. Jamison
Confidential

She could feel rectangular contents inside as they slid under her fingertips.

"It's probably from someone in the building." Anne tucked the mystery envelope under her arm and headed to her office.

"Dr. Anne Jamison—soon to be Dr. Anne Whitney," Anne whispered, running her fingers along the indented gold letters of her name plate before stepping into her space and putting all the contents that were in her arms on the lavender plush couch. Anne was one of the youngest neuropsychiatric doctors in Minnesota and had been dubbed the "female Doogie Howser M.D." in the psychiatric world. All Anne had ever wanted was to help the one person who needed her the most, but she had been unable to do so. She shook the grim memories and looked over at the black-and-white canvas prints of Stone Arch Bridge and Cowles Conservatory against the exposed brick wall. Adam had bought her the two canvases after their third date when she had told him those were her two favorite places in Minneapolis. It was where she would go to think and clear her mind. She took in a cleansing breath and let it go. She was now ready to psycho-analyze the children of the city.

~

Anne finished her session with thirteen-year-old Alice Harper and began vocalizing her notes into a mini-recorder.

"Alice is bipolar and has been on and off various medications over the years. She is the perfect candidate for the Mayo Clinic's brain study on genetic factors of mental disorders. Can they be suppressed with direct injection of medication to the brain tissue?"

The study stemmed from Anne's own family history of mental illness. She didn't want to become another statistic. Though her "modern-day lobotomy" study had many critics, Anne knew what this could do for children who needed help. Casey saw what it could do for their practice but for Anne, it was never about notoriety or money. Over the years, Anne discovered that genetics played a crucial role in mental illness and she wasn't the exception to the rule. *If only I had someone wanting to help me when I was growing up in a house of madness....* She dismissed the thought, not wanting to travel down that road right now. She realized that her phone was still on silent, retrieving it from her purse. Besides missed calls and texts from Casey, there were a couple from Adam.

**Good morning, darling. I missed you.
Why did you leave so early?**

Anne blushed. She'd snuck out of Adam's townhome like a wham-bam-thank-you-ma'am.

**Are you ignoring me?
Is this about last Friday night?
You aren't answering your phone so I called your
office and Shelly said you are with a patient. At
least I know you are alive. Please call me.
I love you, Anne.**

Anne tapped his name in her contacts.

Adam picked up on the first ring. "Anne, are you alright?"

"I'm fine. I'm sorry, I forgot that my phone was on silent," she replied as she ran her fingertips over a picture of Adam that sat on her desk.

"I was worried that you were panicking about our engagement."

Anne could hear the tension in his voice. "No. Absolutely not. I wouldn't have said yes if I wasn't one hundred percent certain. I love you, Adam."

"Why did you leave so early? You didn't even say goodbye." Adam sounded wounded by her disappearing act.

"I had a new patient this morning, and I wanted to go over her chart; plus, you looked so peaceful I didn't want to disturb you." Anne felt warm inside as she pictured her fiancé lying next to her, exposing his flawless muscles.

"Do you have time for lunch? Say in an hour?" She heard a faint soft voice in the background. "Tell him to wait, Victoria. Anne, I have to go. See you at noon here?"

"Sure, see you soon." Anne tried to keep her tone neutral. She couldn't stand Adam's assistant, Victoria Cameron, the law firm succubus.

"Great, I love you."

"I love you too." Anne replied, tapping to end their conversation and still seething over that woman. She felt that Victoria would try to deepen her claws in Adam now that he was engaged. Her prey of choice was unavailable men. Anne had caught them on a few occasions in heated conversations, like they were having a lover's quarrel. She didn't want to accuse Adam of cheating without any evidence, but it was hard to ignore the situation since Victoria was always around.

Anne stretched her neck muscles as they tightened at the thought of Victoria. Her attempts to shake the green-eyed monster were ineffective, so she turned her attention to the mystery envelope waving its secretive arms, enticing her to open it. She picked it up and walked over to her mission-style desk for her envelope opener. Anne took the silver blade, slicing through the glued seal. The contents trickled out and onto her desk. Colored photographs fanned out in front of her, and a white note with red writing stared at her.

For My Anneliese

"No."

She gasped, her hands beginning to numb. The one person in the entire universe who ever called her by her given birth name was Carter. The room lost all focus and quickly became dim. But then Carter's face became clearer, like a luminous apparition pulling her subconscious in deeper.

CHAPTER TWO

Her final memory of Carter floated around her, replaying like an old movie...

"Please stay with me, Carter." Anne stood in the threshold of Carter's bedroom while he continued to pack his navy-blue camping sack.

"It's only for three nights. You worry too much."

"I have a bad feeling about this. The weather is going to be terrible for rafting. Why do you have to do such dangerous things?"

Carter stopped what he was doing and walked over to Anne. She was so envious of his perfect olive skin and his wavy russet hair that accentuated his mesmerizing sapphire eyes. He laced his arms around her small waist. She leaned into his chest. Carter's smell was so comforting and the softness of his fleece pull-over made her want to curl up in his arms and stay there for eternity. He squeezed her gently, and she could feel his strength. Anne tried to ignore the knots in her stomach. He placed his lips on her forehead, kissing her tenderly, and then gazed at her.

"My sweet Anneliese. I have to go," he whispered against her mouth. Carter closed his eyes and pushed his eyebrows together...

A horrendous buzzing noise ripped through Anne's memory. She gasped for air as her body lunged forward, her ribs smacking into the wooden desk. She blinked rapidly as she found herself back in the present. Anne looked around her office and saw that her intercom light was flashing. Her phone buzzed once again.

Anne scrambled to reach for the button on her phone but saw the pictures now lying on the floor next to her chair. Bending down to retrieve them, Anne quickly examined the glossy photos. They appeared to be of Carter's last camping trip with his friends, Sam and another friend of theirs, Ryan. They were standing next to their orange tent, and Carter had a paddle in his right hand. There were a few other guys in the photo but no one that she could make out.

"Who left these here?" Anne whispered still thumbing through the photos.

There was a soft knock at the door. Quickly she hid the photos under a stack of papers on her desk. Anne composed herself and opened the door to see a troubled Shelly.

"Dr. Jamison, you didn't answer the intercom and I was worried."

Anne swallowed hard. "Is Casey busy?"

"Dr. Alder's in with a patient, but I believe she will be available in about twenty minutes. The Mayo Clinic is on line one in regards to your inquiry about Alice."

Anne knew that she couldn't speak with them right now. Her mind was out of focus.

"Shelly, please tell them that I'll call them back and inform Casey that I had to leave on an urgent errand."

Shelly nodded with a worried expression and exited the office. Desperately, Anne tried to collect her thoughts.

Using the back door to her office, she quietly stepped out and walked through a set of double doors that led to the main hallway. Clutching the manila envelope, she peeked around the corner to make sure no one was watching her skulk around like a thief in the night. Anne made it to the bank of elevators and frantically pressed the down arrow. She tapped her black heels on the tile as if the elevator would be aware of her urgency and fly up to the twenty-second floor without further delay.

"Come on." She impatiently scanned the hallway.

Finally, she heard the sound she had been waiting for. She practically lunged inside the metal box. Her breathing was irregular, and sweat began running down the nape of her neck. She leaned her trembling body against the back of the elevator. Anne stared at the black-and-white-checked floor, trying to figure out what was going on. Her mind raced in hundreds of directions. *A code is necessary to access the building on the weekends. The delivery drivers can't even get in without permission. So how did this envelope reach my office door?* Anne rested her gaze on the key panel, as a wave of nausea swept through her.

An eternity later, the doors opened to the dimly lit parking garage. She walked through the intimidating space, the car fumes and harsh noises echoing off the concrete walls and pillars causing anxiety to shoot up her spine.

She reached her black VW Jetta and before opening the driver side door, she glanced about the parking garage, feeling like she was being watched from somewhere in the ominous corners of the darkness. It was a sensation she had felt often. Quickly, she hopped in, tossing the contents of the envelope on the passenger seat, before driving off into the bustling downtown streets.

It had been lightly raining for some time now, forming sizable puddles on the streets and sidewalks. Traffic was always a mess, no matter what time of day it was. While waiting at a stop light, Anne searched for her cell phone.

"It's Anne. Are you busy? I need to see you right now."

"No, I'm free," the woman on the other end said, complying with her request without hesitation.

"I'll come to you. Be there in twenty minutes."

Anne ended the call and pushed a little harder on the accelerator. She made her way onto Interstate 94, which would lead her right into St. Paul, where Carter's family business, Leeds Imports and Construction, was located. His father Steven had wanted Carter to take it over in the future. Anne was on autopilot. Her mind drifted to the past, when she'd first encountered Carter Leeds.

～

Casey's twenty-seventh birthday party was being celebrated at the incredibly posh d'Aubinge Wine Bar and Restaurant. Her husband, Tony, had reserved a private room filled with expensive food and wine. Fifteen of Casey's closest friends filled the room with laughter and stories about Casey's wild days in college. The restaurant had a beautiful French singer who had sung "Happy Birthday" in her native tongue.

"Joyeux anniversaire!" the singer belted out and then kissed Casey on both cheeks.

Anne thought it was superb. She could have sung "Do your ears hang low" and it would have sounded exquisite. With glasses in the air, they all toasted the woman of the hour.

"Can I just say one thing?" Anne stepped up on one of the chairs. "Casey, you are my very best friend and I love you so much. When you hit the ripe old age of thirty, I will think of you as I enjoy an extra year in my twenties." Casey stuck her tongue out at her as the guests sympathetically groaned and then broke out into laughter.

Anne held up her glass as everyone followed suit. "To Casey!"

She was getting down from the chair when she noticed a dashing man standing at the edge of the room, grinning at her. Anne politely returned the gesture and walked over to Casey, whose sleeveless, sequined silver dress reflected off the lights. Casey always loved a flashy dress.

Casey wrapped her arms around her neck, squeezing tight. "I love you, Anne, thank you!" Anne pulled back. "I think it's time to refill everyone's glasses." She tapped her wine glass, smirking. "I'm going to head over to the bar area and see what I can find."

"Good idea."

Anne made her way through the barrage of friends and out of the gold rococo room. Her crimson heels clacked against the hardwood floors, sounding more like a Clydesdale than a petite woman. She reached the lounge, which was blanketed in darkness, creating a romantic ambience that was enhanced by a woman's sultry jazz voice that floated amidst the moving bodies in the room. Anne adjusted her little black dress and glanced down at the end of the bar. The man who had been standing in the threshold while she was giving her toast was walking in her direction. The bartender approached her, breaking her gaze.

"May I help you, mademoiselle?"

"Yes, the Alder party is running low on wine. Could we please get a few more bottles?"

Anne shifted her stare and saw that Mr. Tall Dark and Handsome was now standing right beside her. Instantly, she felt a twinge flit through her hips.

"Yes, mademoiselle, right away."

She peered up at the man, who gave her a stunningly wicked smile. Anne thought his lips looked delicious. He was under-dressed for the venue but didn't appear sloppy, outfitted in a black short-sleeve polo shirt tucked into fitted dark wash jeans and paired with white-on-black Skechers.

"Are you checking me out?" he asked with a smug look on his face.

"No! I'm waiting for the bartender to come back."

Anne was quite taken aback, even though she was in fact checking him out, but he didn't need to know that. She took a slight step away from him and then began twisting the stem of the empty wine glass, keeping her hands busy.

"Well, that was quite a toast. Hop up on furniture often?"

He lessened the space between them. Anne could feel his body heat prickle her bare arm.

She narrowed her eyes. "What is this? Twenty questions?"

"Actually that was only two questions but I'm sure I can find eighteen more."

"Super."

An awkward silence moved in between them, and Anne could feel beads of sweat starting to form at the nape of her neck.

His arm brushed against hers. "What's your name?" he asked.

Anne noticed how his eyes twinkled, reflecting the soft pendant lighting that hung above them.

"Anne. And yours?" She raised her voice over the music that had changed into more of an upbeat jazz melody.

"Carter. Nice to meet you, *Anne*."

He extended his hand to her. It was warm and enveloped hers, causing that twinge to sprint not only through her hips but also through her arms, legs, and spine. But she couldn't help but notice how he soured his tone when he said her name.

She yanked her hand from his. "Why did you say *Anne* like that?"

"You don't look like an Anne."

"Well, my full name is Anneliese."

"That's an exquisite name," he said, donning a come-hither grin and leaning toward her. "Anneliese."

The second he repeated her name, she felt dizzy. No one had called her Anneliese in some time. Quickly, she sat on the leather stool; all the blood began flowing to her cheeks and neck. He held her gaze with ease as he sat beside her. She couldn't deny that the attraction was instant and intense.

After an hour of conversation, she had completely forgotten about the wine and about the birthday festivities across the room.

"Shit."

She looked over her shoulder and saw Casey standing in the cove of the dining room, smirking.

"Will you excuse me for a moment?" Anne asked. She placed her hand atop his. His skin was smooth and magnetic.

Carter stood. "I should really let you get back to your party. I've held you hostage long enough."

"No…really…don't leave yet."

Anne hurried over to Casey.

"I am *so* sorry, I met this guy and we started talking…."

"Don't you dare worry about it." Casey peeked over her shoulder. "He's hot, Anne."

"His name is Carter, and there is just something about him—I don't know how to explain it. I mean, at first he came off really arrogant."

"Men." Casey quickly interjected with a roll of her eyes.

"But he listens to me, it's not all about him. It's weird. We have this instant chemistry." Anne placed the palm of her hands on her cheeks, feeling the flush engulf them.

"Wow, maybe it's love at first sight," Casey nudged her. "Why don't you have him give you a ride home?"

"Why? I drove here."

Casey planted her hands on her hips. "Really, Anne? Lie and say we brought you here. We'll pick up your car tomorrow, unless you're too exhausted to go anywhere."

"No. That's way too desperate," she whispered.

"Oh honey, you need desperate. When was the last time you went out on a date?"

Anne actually had to think about that. She tapped her finger on lip. "I've been busy and besides, I wouldn't count sitting at a bar with a complete stranger for an hour as a date."

"You better come into the twenty-first century. Trust me—he's into you."

"I'm doomed." Bemused, she rested her head on Casey's shoulder.

"He's looked over here at least a dozen times so head back over there and just go with it. Stop over-analyzing everything, even though that's your job," Casey spoke quietly in Anne's ear.

Anne lifted her head. "I'll try."

They hugged and exchanged kisses on the cheek. Anne took a deep breath, turned, and walked back to Carter, who was coolly leaning against the bar, flashing his irresistible smile. *God, he's gorgeous. Stay calm, Anne. He's just a man. You can do this.*

Carter pushed away from the bar. "Did you blame me for your absence at the party?"

"Absolutely. I threw you right under the bus." She smiled, feeling her body flush with heat once again. "I really should get home. It's late." Anne was uncomfortable and out of practice.

"Would you like to meet for coffee in about—" he paused to look at his watch, "eight hours? I didn't get all my twenty questions in."

Anne laughed. "Sure. Where?"

A fiendish look graced his face. "How about my place?"

Anne cocked her brow. "Presumptuous much?"

"Not at all, Miss Dirty Mind. I'll pick you up and bring you back to my house and cook you an amazing breakfast. I'll even give you my social security number and date of birth so in the meantime you can run a background check on me."

"That's not a bad idea."

Smiling, Anne pulled out one of her business cards and wrote her address on the back of it, and Carter did the same. They swapped the cards and walked to the front entrance, stepping out into the sultry summer night air.

"Are you parked close by?" Carter looked up and down Eighth Street.

Anne pointed up the street. "Just a few cars that way."

"Let me walk you."

Their arms brushed against each other. Anne bit down on her lip, stifling a schoolgirl giggle. A pang of disappointment hit her when they reached her car.

She turned to Carter. "Thank you for the escort. It was wonderful meeting you."

Anne backed up, feeling the car push against her spine. Carter bent down, his lips touched hers. They were soft and warm; Anne could barely keep her legs from folding underneath her. The palms of her hands pressed flat against the car window as her body pushed more into his. His kiss was bringing out her desire. Carter's lips moved from hers, brushed her cheek, and stopped just inches from her ear. She could feel his hot breath run down her neck, giving her goose bumps.

"Goodnight, *my* Anneliese."

CHAPTER THREE

Anne bit down on her bottom lip as she came out of the bittersweet memory. She slowly pulled into the sea of cars that stretched the length of a football field. In big bold letters, the sign on the front of the ancient, three-story brick building read **LEEDS IMPORTS & CONSTRUCTION**.

She pulled into Carter's old parking spot that sat between his mother's Cadillac and his father's Mercedes. Anne grabbed her purse and the envelope and walked toward the front entrance of the building and opened the heavy tempered glass door.

Standing before her, with a polished appearance, was Carter's mother, Rita Leeds, the matriarch of the family. Her beautiful, thick, black hair fell over her collarbone. She always looked fresh from the spa, skin flawless, make-up applied perfectly, with not a single hair out of place. Rita's green knit dress hugged her curves as she walked toward her. "Hello, Anne." She pulled Anne into an embrace. "You sounded so urgent on the phone. What's going on?"

She stepped out of Rita's arms. "Can we go someplace private?" Anne looked around the reception area.

"Sure, let's go up to my office."

Rita and Anne walked up an open grand staircase to a mezzanine that overlooked the colossal warehouse. Anne hadn't seen Rita in months. She felt weird being there without Carter.

Turning left, they entered a spacious wood-paneled office. Rita had pictures of Carter everywhere, making the office seem like a shrine to her son. The smell—a mixture of musty air and pungent floral perfume—was enough to unsettle Anne's stomach.

She sat down in a stiff blue wingback chair across from Rita's desk, which was covered by a mountain of paper work, file folders, and pink message slips. Rita shut the door, walked over to Anne, and sat down opposite her.

Rita gave Anne an expression of concern. "So what's going on? You had something important to discuss with me?"

Anne pulled out the envelope and handed it to her. Rita paused to examine the envelope before she slowly opened it.

Rita shuffled through the photos. "Are these from Carter's camping trip?"

"Yes, they are. They were left in that envelope outside my office door sometime over the weekend. But that's not the craziest part of it. Read the note."

Anne watched Rita open the creased paper with trembling hands. "And you said this was waiting for you at your office?"

"Yes, and there's no return address." Anne pointed to the note. "That's Carter's handwriting. He was the only one who called me Anneliese. Have you heard from him, Rita?"

If looks could kill, Anne would have been dead on the spot. "No. Do you think if I had heard from him, I would be sitting here so stunned by this?"

"I'm sorry, I'm so confused and I—I don't know what to do with this."

Anne swallowed hard, trying to keep her composure in check.

"Did you take this to the police?"

"Not yet. I wanted to come to you first. I thought maybe you knew something...."

Rita shot up. "This is crazy! Carter has been gone for three years. I have had to accept the fact that my son is dead. This is some cruel joke."

She threw the note and pictures back at Anne, scattering them across her lap. Anne put everything back into the envelope and stood up.

"Rita, I'm not trying to hurt you. You know me better than that. I mourned him too. A lot of people did. I'm going to find out what happened that day. Something doesn't seem right."

Rita shook her head at Anne's words and darted for the door. "You need to leave. I can't do this right now."

Anne halted in front of Rita, whose face was covered in fierce red blotches.

"Maybe someone forged this note, maybe Carter is dead, but why would they do this? Why now? Don't you want to know?"

Rita looked away as her lips quivered. "I miss him so much."

"I do too, but I want the truth. I deserve that much." Anne choked back emotion.

She hurried from Rita's office, keeping her head down, not wanting people to see her tears. Rounding the corner she heard a voice behind her.

"Anne?"

Shit. She swiped her fingers under her eyes, took a deep breath and turned around. Steven Leeds, Carter's father, was rolling his sleeves up as he walked toward her with his Humphrey Bogart swagger. His cleft chin jutted out but was covered by a coat of granite scruff. Anne had never seen Steven with facial hair before. His crown of dark hair laid perfectly with a layer of gel. He had always been so put together, but Anne never saw Steven in Carter.

Her mouth felt like it was filled with cotton. "Hi, Steven. How are you?"

He bent down, placing a kiss on Anne's cheek. "I'm great. How are you? What brings you by?"

The envelope burned under her arm, but Anne didn't want to say anything to him. She had stirred enough emotion in the building for one day.

"Oh, I'm collecting donations for the upcoming mayor's ball. Leeds Imports and Construction has always been a huge donor."

"Yes, Rita does enjoy giving money away."

This is awkward. Anne glanced over to the warehouse and back at Steven. His expression seemed distant but annoyed.

"Well, I better go. It was nice to see you."

He squeezed her arm. "You too, Anne. Take care and don't be a stranger."

She nodded and turned back to the stairs. Quickly she made her way back to her car, feeling defeated and weak. The winds were starting to pick up and there was a vicious chill in the air, matching the one she had just left behind. Getting back into her car, she sat for a moment peering toward the building. Rita's silhouette stood hovering in the window. *She's definitely hiding something.* She took out her phone and saw that she had missed many calls from Adam. Inhaling deeply, she dialed his number, knowing he would be upset about her ditching their lunch date.

"Anne."

"I'm so sorry. I had an errand to run, and I left my phone in the car."

"I called your office and Shelly said you left looking quite ill. When you didn't answer your cell, I started to get worried. Are you alright?"

"Yes, I'm heading back downtown now. No worries, I'm fine. I'm sorry about lunch. Are you still coming over after work?"

"I have to run but yes, I'll be over the moment the trial is done."

"Okay. I love you so much, Adam." Her tone dripped with desperation.

"I love you too, darling. I'll see you soon."

Anne placed the phone in her lap and tried not to burst into tears. She couldn't keep this secret to herself but she knew she couldn't say anything to Adam—not right now, anyway. As she pulled out of the parking lot, she dialed Casey.

"Hey, you. Where are you? Shelly said you were sick or something."

Casey must have been in the hallway. Anne was having difficulty making out the echo of words.

"Yeah, um, do you have a patient right now?"

"Not until one o'clock. I was heading down to get a coffee. Why? What's up?"

Anne glanced at the envelope sitting on the passenger seat. "You know that envelope that was mysteriously left by the door?"

"Yeah."

"There are pictures of Carter at his last camping trip and a note with his handwriting in it."

Anne could hear Casey gasp.

"What? Are you serious?"

"So, let's meet at the coffee shop. I don't want to talk about this at the office. I should be there in about twenty minutes."

"Are you sure coffee is going to work with this conversation? Maybe a cocktail?"

"I don't think seeing patients after cocktails is a good idea."

"You win. Coffee it is. See you in a bit."

Hanging up, Anne continued back onto the interstate. She began to think about the motives behind this sudden revelation. *Why now? Three years have passed so why would anyone want me to have these photos?* Anne racked her brain for answers. She lost her concentration on the journey back downtown and nearly missed her exit.

She parked her Jetta in front of the quaint coffee shop that was about a block away from her office building. She searched for change in her purse and fed the meter. With a heavy gust of wind another set of somber clouds rolled in, showing signs of late-season precipitation.

She pulled open the thick wooden door and instantly an aroma of coffee and pastries filled her senses. She drew in all that sweet caffeine goodness. Casey was sitting at a small wooden bistro table in the back corner, already armed with mochas and scones.

"That was fast." Casey stood up and hugged her visibly shaken friend.

"Traffic wasn't too bad. Thanks for getting me this."

They sat down. "I knew you would need it. So tell me what's going on."

Anne took out the envelope and handed it to Casey who looked through the pictures and read the note while Anne dove into a blueberry scone, carefully watching her face.

"What do you think?" Anne asked.

"I don't know. I just don't understand why now." Casey stared at her. "Do you think Carter is alive?"

Anne pondered the question.

"It's crazy for me to say yes to the possibility but then that little sliver of hope that sits dormant inside starts to awaken. I mean, the note could be forged. Maybe one of his friends had these pictures and wanted me to have them—I don't know."

"So where'd you go this morning?" Casey asked and took a sip of her coffee.

"I went to see Carter's mother." Anne picked at what was left of the scone.

"What? How'd that go?"

"Not so well. I wanted to see if she knew something, but it just made everything worse and more confusing. I know that I'm reading a lot into this but it's this constant, open-ended event, you know? Where did he go? Did he really drown?"

"Anne, it's been three years." Casey spoke in a soothing tone.

"I know, I know, I know."

Anne placed her index fingers onto her temples, trying to rub away the headache that had been plaguing her since early that morning.

"Are you going to tell Adam?"

"Not right now. He has enough going on without dealing with his nutty fiancée receiving notes and pictures from her dead boyfriend."

"Dead boyfriend?"

"Don't start over-analyzing this. In my head he's dead but in my heart…."Anne swallowed hard.

"Maybe we should ask to look at the security tapes from over the weekend," Casey suggested.

"Do you think they'll let us?"

"Why not? If there is some random person breaking in, wouldn't they want to know that the building isn't as secure as they thought it was? I'll go to the security office and ask. In the meantime, why don't you go home, relax, maybe take a nap, and I'll call you later."

"Thanks, Casey."

For as long as Anne could remember, Casey had been her voice of reason even when there was nothing but darkness in her life. She never gave up on pulling Anne out of the abyss.

Casey patted Anne's hand. "We'll get to the bottom of this."

Anne nodded as they stood and walked out of the coffee shop and onto the busy sidewalk. They said their goodbyes, and she was once again in her car.

Anne's apartment was just a few miles from her office. She adored her place. It was modern but cozy and had all the amenities of the downtown culture. Art galleries, shopping, and theaters were all within walking distance.

The brick and concrete façade towered six floors and had iron-scroll balconies. Anne was ready to toss her heels off and relax for a bit. The elevator ascended to the main floor so she could retrieve her mail. A wall of mailboxes lined the right; she stopped at 507. Feeling that familiar pull of someone watching her, Anne surveyed the surroundings but saw no one.

"I'm becoming paranoid," she whispered and began to insert the key into the lock.

A section of a white envelope stuck out of the corner of the rectangular box. Anxiety pushed through her and with a quivering hand, she slowly opened the door and let out a huge sigh of relief when she seized a crumpled cable bill.

Get a grip, she rolled her eyes at her irrational reaction to the simple retrieval of her mail. She made her way back to the elevator, feeling a slight twinge of embarrassment.

Anne threw her mail on the stone island that sat in the contemporary kitchen. Carter's family had been the construction company for the apartments; beaming with pride, Carter had eagerly flaunted their work. She fell in love with the apartment's design and had moved in two weeks later.

It still had that "new" smell. The maple cabinets and floor complemented the black granite countertops flawlessly. She and Carter had picked out the bronze glass pendant lights that had coffee swirls etched around the oval shape and all the stainless steel appliances.

Anne changed out of her work attire and threw on some black yoga pants and a fitted pink t-shirt. After throwing her blonde locks up into a loose ponytail, she began thumbing through her mail. Nothing but bills and junk. She grabbed the manila envelope and stared at it for the longest time. She entered into her walk-in closet that was sandwiched between the bedroom and bathroom.

At the very top of the three levels of wooden shelving there sat a black-and-purple shoe box. While on the tip of her toes, she pulled the box down then placed herself in the center of the closet, sitting cross-legged like a young child. Her entire life with Carter fit in a simple size seven shoe box. Anne pulled out newspaper clippings that told of his disappearance and death, photos of the two of them together at the park and out with friends, little mementos that he had given to her over their intense but passionate time together, and beautiful notes he had handwritten just for her. His words were always filled with such adoration. Opening one of his many notes to her, she read the sweet words slowly.

My Dearest Anneliese, how my life would be filled with emptiness if I didn't have you. You give me such hope and promise. I have never known love like this. I have never felt desire like this. Please my love, never leave my side.

Yours Faithfully, Carter

Anne inhaled the scent of the paper; vanilla and sandalwood still lingered on each weaved fiber. She compared the handwriting of the note she received this morning to the one that Carter wrote right after they had met. They were a perfect match. *But how can that be?* she thought. *And what was so significant about these photos? What am I missing?*

There was something familiar about a man who stood in the background of one of the photos. He wore a bright yellow ski jacket, but his face was blurred. He also had on black gloves with a white symbol on them. She knew the symbol was one of an expensive clothing store, but she didn't know anyone who owned a pair.

She thought back to that day three years ago, when she received a phone call from Carter's oldest friend, Sam Goodman, informing her of Carter's disappearance.

"Carter's raft flipped in the river. He's missing! They think he drowned. He's gone, Anne, he's gone!" Sam had howled.

It felt like barbed wire was being pulled from her body; she had collapsed to the floor screaming Carter's name, begging God for the news to not be true. Her neighbors heard the commotion and feared a medical emergency; they immediately called the police, who were hammering on her apartment door within minutes. Inside, they found her unconscious in the middle of the living room, still gripping the phone.

Dr. Rasmussen had been her doctor, and once she started to wake up, he had explained to Anne that she had locked herself up in a comatose for nearly seventy-two hours. Time had been lost in her self-created hell. She had wanted to return to it once Dr. Rasmussen revealed to her the bleak and devastating news in what they called a "controlled environment."

Anne pulled herself from the flashback and looked over to her nightstand drawer, which contained various medications to make sure that her space stayed light and cheerful. Dr. Lindsey prescribed them to her, but she hadn't touched them in months. As of 9:30 a.m., Carter had been just a faded memory imprinted in her life so many years ago, but the writing on that note told of something different. She bent forward, unleashing an agonizing cry. Tears dripped down into the box of relics, expanding over the words that Carter wrote to her so long ago.

After regaining her composure, she could still feel her lungs burning from the tormenting trip down memory lane. She placed each item back into the shoebox ever so gently like it was a newborn baby. She walked over to the maple nightstand, taking out one of the translucent orange cylinders. Popping open the child-proof cap, she tapped out a single oblong white pill. Recalling how she felt when taking them caused a tremor through her spine. Anne would feel nothing, absolutely nothing. They desensitized her from all the hurt and agony. But before she could place the little oval of nothingness on her tongue, there was a knock at the door.

"Anne?" said a male voice from the hallway.

Quickly, she placed the pill back in the bottle and closed the nightstand drawer.

"Coming," she called to the man who rescued her soul from the darkness.

She opened the door, and there he stood, debonair and unapologetically handsome, her fiancé—Adam Whitney.

CHAPTER FOUR

Adam's dashing smile and childlike dimples sent a flutter of heat through her chest. His hazel eyes had a starburst of gold around the pupil. He bent down to find her lips. She reciprocated, running her hands over his taut chest that she could feel through his black tailored vest and white oxford shirt. Adam's hands wrapped around her waist, his fingers splayed across her lower back, pulling her against him and eliminating the space between them.

His kiss deepened as his tongue moved against hers. Anne welcomed the much-needed affection and moaned. Breaking away breathless from their impromptu make-out session in the hallway, Anne ushered him in. She tried to calm her heated breathing.

"That's my favorite kind of greeting," Anne touched her swollen lips.

Adam laughed as he walked into her apartment. "I won my case today so we are going to go out and celebrate." He stopped and examined Anne's face. "You've been crying."

Anne shrugged off his observation and walked over to the kitchen island. "It's nothing. I was watching this silly movie on Lifetime." Quickly she changed the subject back to his courtroom victory. "Congratulations! I bet Richard was thrilled."

Richard Morris was one of Adam's partners at the law firm. Anne had never taken a liking to him; he had been through half a dozen wives, whom he left high and dry. He was overweight, balding, with a halo of cigar smoke that followed him wherever he went, and he had an ego to match his size. Women only stayed with him because he was wealthy and bought them whatever their gold-digging hearts desired. The thought of him turned Anne's stomach.

"He was indeed thrilled, and he invited us out for drinks tonight to celebrate. Are you up for it?"

Anne crinkled her nose at the thought of sharing space with Richard and his bimbo of the week.

"I'll take that as a no," Adam replied as he strolled over to the refrigerator and pulled out a bottle of water.

He leaned against the counter and downed the water. Anne rarely ever saw Adam without one of his expensive tailor-made suits. Even on a casual day at home he wore fitted chinos with a buttoned shirt, a sweater, or a knit pullover. On occasion, he wore plaid shorts in the summer months. He was a walking Banana Republic ad.

Adam looked gorgeous in everything he wore. His squared-off chin and high cheekbones made him seem powerful and determined, something that had caught Anne's attention the first time they had met.

Anne walked over to Adam. "I was thinking we could order in, open a bottle of wine, and relax with a movie." She nuzzled against him, batting her long eyelashes.

Adam ran his finger down her jaw line. "You don't play fair, my angel."

"No, you're *my* angel, remember?"

The heat and heaviness from his body made hers shift with yearning. Without speaking another word, Anne began unbuttoning his vest, still holding his gaze. His hazel eyes churned black as she pushed the vest off, letting it tumble to their feet. His shirt was next. The chiseled glory that stood before her took her breath away.

Adam pulled her blonde strands down, watching the champagne cascade sweep over her shoulders and down her back. Tangling his fingers through her hair and arching her face up towards his, his mouth collided with hers in a fervent display. Their breathing was heavy but in sync, which made the kiss all the more arousing. Anne's body called to his, succumbing to his every touch. Pleasure gathered between her thighs the more he devoured her.

Clothing trailed to Anne's bedroom. Their bodies twisted harmoniously in sheets of white. Anne wrapped her fingers through the iron-gate headboard, arching her body into his. Adam raked his teeth over her collarbone then repeated the path with heated kisses down her neck and in between her breasts. Anne's lips trembled at the torrid sensation, as her breaths became gasps. The sweat between their bodies intensified Anne's hunger, and she dug her nails into Adam's back. He let out a small cry but kept with the needy pace. Anne's body escalated with every touch to the point of unimaginable bliss as every nerve ending imploded with euphoria. Her cries of pleasure filled her bedroom.

Anne nibbled at Adam's shoulder; she wanted to satisfy his rising desire. She wrapped her fingers around his bicep and quickened their pace. He kissed her lips hard; Anne teased his tongue with her own. Pulling away, Adam's face fell into the hollow of her neck; he growled against her skin as his climax roared through him. Anne smiled while running her fingers through his hair; she could never get enough of him.

They laid there in a most gratifying embrace. Adam gently stroked Anne's flushed skin and kissed her forehead.

"I'm madly in love with you, Anne, and I want you in my life always." Adam's baritone voice melted against her ear.

Anne ran her fingers over his chest. "You were meant to find me, to save me, to love me, and I can't wait to be your wife. And I'm not going anywhere. You're stuck with me,"

Adam let out a deep sigh as he lifted her finger where the diamond sat, kissing the inside of the platinum band. "You did the same for me."

"What?" Anne shifted up on his chest so she could see his face.

"Saved me."

Her eyebrows pushed together. "From what?"

Adam looked away for a moment and then back at Anne. "From the mayor's daughter that night at the charity ball."

Anne laughed. She remembered that night well. It was when she first laid eyes on Adam.

"She followed you around all night, fetching you punch and cake."

Adam laced their fingers together and laid them down on his chest. "I had my eyes on another woman. Too bad she shot me down."

"Hey, I eventually gave in. You're quite persuasive, Mr. Whitney."

Adam laughed. "There's a reason I win all of my cases, Dr. Jamison. Speaking of cases, I have one up in Duluth this week. What do you say we go up and stay at the cabin for a few days?"

Adam's family had an impressive cabin in Little Marais, which was a seventy-mile jaunt from Duluth. They had been up there with Adam's family during various holidays. It was a huge house and Anne couldn't imagine staying there alone while Adam was in Duluth. However, the quiet and seclusion would probably help her unwind and get her away from all this Carter nonsense.

"I think that sounds wonderful. I love going up there." Anne could see he was pleased with her response.

"Great. How about we leave Thursday morning?"

"I have a patient at nine but I can leave after that—does that work?"

"Works perfectly." He leaned over and kissed the edges of her flushed lips. "You have made me the happiest man in the entire universe." A darkness passed over his eyes. "I would do anything for you, Anne, you know that, right?"

Anne propped her head up on her pillow. "Of course I know that. You've been so patient with me. I know I haven't been the most compliant girlfriend in the commitment department but you are my life, Adam. No one can ever take this away from us."

"I would have waited an eternity. You're worth it and I'm not going to pressure you into setting a date. If you want to elope in Las Vegas, I will call Elvis right now, or if you want a luxurious royal wedding, I will buy you every inch of taffeta in the world."

His face softened as he leaned in eagerly for a kiss. Adam's fairy-tale words made her dizzy with delight. At that very moment, Anne felt like she was meant to be there, in his arms, feeling over the moon with joy and excitement. What she had with Adam she couldn't have with Carter— she never could. Their relationship had been passionate, yes, but it was also tumultuous and reckless. It became obsessive for both of them and dangerous. He was now just a ghost in the unseen room that lay deep within her subconscious.

Anne moved to untangle herself from the sheets. "I'm going to jump in the shower. Why don't you call Richard and tell him we'll meet him later."

Adam looked at her with surprise, watching her saunter naked toward the bathroom.

"Really? We don't have to if you don't want to," Adam replied while locating his clothes that were thrown on the floor.

"I know, but you won your case today, and that's something we should be celebrating instead of watching a sappy chick flick."

"I thought we just did celebrate." Adam wagged his brows.

"Funny," she sang.

Adam held his shirt in his hands. "I'll run home, change, and pick you up in about an hour."

"You know, you do have clothes here and we could celebrate more in the shower," Anne coaxed with a come-hither voice.

Having already turned the faucet on, Anne watched the steam from the shower begin to coat the mirror with thick condensation. Adam joined her as they washed away their sins from the day, stripping skin that had been tainted with memories of the past.

CHAPTER FIVE

The warm Thursday morning brought hope to the city of Minneapolis. It had been a long, blustery winter and with spring rapidly approaching, the temperatures slowly began to rise. The dirty snow that lined the city streets was melting into the sewer, which created more of a sloppy mess. Casey was still waiting for the security office to show her the surveillance videos, and they were continually coming up with excuses why they were unable to locate the correct video. Of course, this did not sit well with her.

"I mean, really, who do I need to sleep with to see those videos?" Casey demanded as she and Anne quickened their pace through the parking garage toward the elevator. "Honestly. This is why they're security guards and not real police officers. So incompetent."

"Casey, they have to get approval from their boss. They can't just hand them over to you."

She rolled her eyes in annoyance at Anne's response. "Well, I pay quite a bit for my space in this building. I have every right to see those tapes. You know I have left the owner of the building at least a dozen messages and he hasn't returned one of them, the little prick."

"Good grief, did you not have your Starbucks this morning?"

Anne grasped for some pleasantries from Casey, but her look shot them dead in the water.

Casey tugged on her red pea coat in disgust. "I did, but they are ineffectual and I don't deal with that very well."

"They will get it when they get it. Stop thinking about it."

"Why aren't you bothered by this? This is for you, you know?"

"I'm in vacation mode. I'm leaving for the cabin after my patient, spending the weekend by the lake, reading and drinking wine," Anne grinned.

After a couple of stops, the elevator finally made it to their floor.

"Is Adam going to be in Duluth the whole time?"

"I don't think so. He had to go up early so we have to take separate cars, which works out because I can explore while he's working."

Casey stopped Anne right before they entered their office. "Are you sure you're all right? The other day you were such a mess and now you are Miss Happy Go Lucky."

"I can't deny the fact that Carter was a huge part of my life, and I loved him more than anything but that's just it—*was.* Yes, I want closure and to know what really happened, but Adam is my life now. He's my future. It's not fair to him for me to be wrapped up in someone who isn't here anymore."

"I know this has been difficult for you," Casey took Anne's hands, "and we will get to the bottom of this, but I see how Adam makes you glow and how much he adores you. You have been through hell and back, no thanks to Carter. You deserve to have all the happiness in the world."

Anne's eyes misted over. "Thank you. I appreciate everything you have done for me but no more of this mushy talk," Anne nudged Casey with her shoulder.

Casey nodded, blinking away tears. They entered their practice and went to their offices to prepare for the day. Anne went through her messages and emails. Shelly brought in a patient folder for her to look over. Anne opened it up, grabbing her mini-recorder.

"Patient's name is Stella McGuire, age ten, experiencing social isolation and destructive behavior since the divorce of her parents last year."

Anne clicked the red stop button. She knew that feeling all too well, having grown up in a single-parent home, trying to cope in a tumultuous environment. *I never had a childhood, mine was held captive by lies.*

Shelly buzzed Anne and informed her that her patient had arrived. She gathered all her paperwork, her recorder, and two fabric dolls, one a boy and the other a girl. Children needed to be able to trust her and feel that they could open up to her, so she created a special room that was warm and inviting. Bright-yellow paint covered the walls and shelves of toys, dolls, and games reached toward the ceiling.

Anne walked out into the waiting room. She extended her free hand toward the slender, auburn-haired woman. "Good morning, Mrs. McGuire."

"Good morning, Dr. Jamison. Thank you so much for seeing us."

Anne knelt down to Stella's level, giving her a soft, friendly smile. "Hello, Stella, I'm Dr. Jamison, but you can call me Anne, okay?"

Stella was a miniature model of her mother, with curly, long, reddish-brown hair and fair porcelain skin.

"Okay," Stella squeaked out as she looked down at her scuffed sneakers.

"Please, Dr. Jamison, I'm at my wits' end. You're our last hope. I need you to fix my daughter." Anne looked up at Stella's mom who was wringing her hands.

She ignored Mrs. McGuire's pleas and looked back at Stella. "I have some fun toys in my play room. We can blow bubbles or play dress-up—whatever you would like to do," Anne spoke in a low, sympathetic tone. Stella seemed to be fond of this idea and placed her tiny little hand in Anne's.

"Let's go, shall we?"

The three of them entered the "play" room as Anne shut the door behind them. A silver-dollar-sized green light illuminated the room's entrance, indicating the room was in use and that others should not disturb the session.

~

Two hours later, Anne was wrapping up her dictation notes on young Stella.

"Stella blames herself for her dad leaving and divorcing her mom. Mrs. McGuire encourages her daughter's self-loathing emotions. I get the sense that Stella is protecting someone. Our next session will be one on one, without the presence of Mrs. McGuire."

A flash of Anne's childhood ripped through her brain. She was six years old again, swinging her legs under the hospital waiting room chair. A homeless man kept grinning at her. He was dirty and didn't have any teeth. Anne looked away from him and down at her hands. The blood had dried and felt weird and sticky to Anne. She just wanted to wash the blood off but the man wearing all blue told her no. *Why won't they let me wash it off?* Teardrops started to dot her red palms as specks of metallic sparkled off of the lights above her.

She heard her mother's voice and turned to see her talking to the man in blue. "I'm sorry about this; my daughter, Anneliese, can get a little wild. She didn't mean to break the mirror."

I didn't break the mirror, you did.

Anne's eyes filled with tears as she blinked the memory away and cleared the thickness from her throat. She placed the recorder down. *I'm not going to think about that, I won't let myself. She can't make me feel guilty anymore. She can't blame me anymore.*

Anne looked over at her clock and then at Adam's picture. *My angel.* She smiled and started to clean up the loose papers on her desk. Her goal was to arrive at the cabin before nightfall and hopefully shower and beauty up a bit before Adam returned. He had sent her a sweet text message before heading into court that morning.

I missed you last night. I didn't sleep well at all. I can't wait to move into our new place. Waking up without you feels wrong. I love you. Please drive safe and text me when you arrive.

Anne's lease was ending in less than two months and Adam was selling his townhouse. They had found a stunning classic colonial overlooking Lake of the Isles. Anne thought five bedrooms was a bit much for their first home but he assured her that they would fill the rooms with children's laughter. Adam came from a large, loving family, unlike Anne who was an only child and now parentless.

Anne locked up her office. "Shelly, is Casey still here?"

"Yes, but she is with a patient."

"Okay, well, I'm outta here. If you need me, call my cell. Sometimes the service isn't all that great, so if I don't answer, call the cabin's landline. I'll call and check in tomorrow, though."

Shelly tucked her pen behind her ear. "Have a wonderful time, Dr. Jamison."

Anne left the office and was officially off until the following Monday. She didn't want to drive for almost four hours wearing black trousers, a silk blouse, and heels but she couldn't wait to get to the cabin, open a bottle of merlot, and relax by the fireplace.

Traffic on Interstate 35 heading north wasn't too horrendous. A few pockets of clustered cars slowed her progress, but the farther away from the city she got the more open it became. She left Adam a voicemail letting him know that she was in the car and would be arriving around 3:30 p.m. The early afternoon sunshine beamed down on her engagement ring, setting off lively prisms that waltzed above her on the car's ceiling. Anne's phone began to ring, startling her out of her daydream. It was Casey; she placed the phone on her lap, putting it on speaker.

"Hey, what's going on?"

"I just saw the surveillance tapes, after shoving a Ulysses S. Grant down their throats, and they did catch someone."

Anne felt a rush of blood surge through her veins. "Who?"

"It was a guy but he had a baseball cap on so you can't see his face. He kept it hidden quite well," Casey replied.

Anne gripped the steering wheel. "Do you think...?"

"I don't think it was Carter. This guy looked too short and stocky, plus he had on a wedding band."

"Who could it be, then?"

"I don't know, honey. I wish I had more for you. You'll have to look at it when you get back. Maybe you'll recognize him." Casey's voice trailed disappointment.

"Thanks, Casey, for doing that for me. Just more questions, I guess."

"I'm sorry."

"I know. Well, I'm getting closer so I'll call you tomorrow," Anne tried to keep her focus on the road.

"All right, drive safe and please try to enjoy yourself. This changes nothing. Adam is still your future and whoever this guy is, he's just screwing with you." Casey's words were stern.

"I know, Dr. Alder, message received." Anne wanted to end this conversation before it became a white-couch session.

Every turn led to another dead end. *Whoever delivered the envelope didn't want to be known, but why?* Her excitement gave way to the mounting questions and to the realization that she was being watched. *But, by whom?*

CHAPTER SIX

Anne was about an hour away from the Whitney cabin. The splendor of the open wilderness in northern Minnesota was much more pleasing to the eye than the concrete jungle in which she resided. Though there was still quite a chill in the air, she still opened her windows to let the crisp breeze fill her lungs.

She slowed down to an upcoming gravel driveway on the right side of the road. She passed a large wooden mailbox and made her way down the long curved driveway. Ahead of her was the cabin in all its red-timber glory. It had been featured in *Midwest Home* last year.

It had two stories with a lower level that opened up to the cobblestone beach. The forepart of the cabin presented an infinite wrap-around porch, which in the warmer months was decorated with colorful potted flowers and hunter-green rocking chairs. Anne was ecstatic to finally get out of the car and stretch her legs. She inhaled so deeply that a wave of dizziness swept over her. Anne placed her hands on her hips as she viewed the hushed secluded property. Most of the trees were still bare except the thick pine trees that lined the front of the acreage.

Opening her trunk, she hauled out two pieces of matching luggage, then dropped them with a thud as small rocks kicked up under the rubber wheels. Anne pulled out the key to the front door, which Adam had dropped off before he left. At first he was going to have Anne retrieve it from Victoria but she quickly rebuffed that idea. Adam found his fiancée's jealousy charming but reassured her that Victoria had never made a pass at him. Anne knew better. Men were oblivious. She was positive Victoria had made a pass at him at some point. Her eyes were always on him.

The aroma of pine and apple-cinnamon wafted through the entry. It appeared much more open with all the Christmas decorations packed away. The grand staircase curved up to the second floor, showing off its polished wooden features.

She entered into the living room where a magnificent bay window featured the picturesque landscape of Lake Superior and its grey stony shores. The furniture, simple crafted pieces with red, green, and white plaid linen coverings, stayed within a typical cabin theme. The fireplace was the most impressive piece in the room, besides the view, with its multi-hued stones extending to the loft above her.

There sat a pyramid of firewood ready to go. Anne walked into the kitchen to check out the refrigerator and pantry. Adam had stocked it full. She took out a bottle of merlot and opened it. The wine glasses were stashed in the formal dining room hutch. Anne took a sip of the dry burgundy liquid, letting it envelope her throat with warmth. She sauntered out onto the three-season porch that connected to the deck. A shiver crept around her body as the feathered breeze bounced off the water and over her skin. She gave one last glance at the lake and made her way back into the warm cabin.

She managed to haul her luggage up the stairs and into the master bedroom, which was decorated in French country chic. The patina-metal bed was neatly made except for the yellow decorative pillows that sat stacked on the warped wooden chair next to the window.

Adam's clothes were hung in the walk-in closet and were filling the air with his fresh masculine scent. Stopping at one of his white dress shirts, she smiled slyly. She undressed down to just her pale pink lace bra and panties. She slipped her arms into his oversized oxford shirt and buttoned it mid-breast.

Anne walked into the bathroom, gazing at her reflection and giggling; a rush of crimson covered her cheeks. Adam's shirt hit mid-thigh, revealing her toned legs. She bent to the side and began fussing with her long blonde tresses. Anne sprayed a subtle amount of floral-laced perfume on her wrists and neck. Grabbing her phone, she saw that it was close to five o'clock. She tried calling Adam again but it went right to voicemail, which meant he was still in court; smirking, she left him an enticing message.

Anne spent the next couple of hours thumbing through magazines and sipping merlot. The sun was beginning to stroke the horizon. As it began to cast shadows amongst the rooms, an anxious feeling fluttered through Anne. She flicked on two lamps in the living room and the overhead Tiffany chandelier in the kitchen.

The cabin was beginning to cool down from the day's heat; Anne thought it was time to start a fire. She watched the fire-withered newspaper tickle the bottoms of the logs. Closing the metal frame, she gazed at the growing heat as it began to swallow the timber.

"Now that's a fire," Anne said, quite pleased with her fire-making abilities before brushing off a few stray pieces of bark that clung to the crisp shirt sleeves.

Clutching her glass of wine, she placed her iPod in the stereo that sat inside the built-in cove above the hearth. With remote in hand, she shuffled through her eclectic carousel of music until "Silver Lining" by Rilo Kiley crooned through the surround sound.

Anne sunk into the back of the plush couch, staring out into the pastel-swathed sky. The sun slowly lowered itself behind the earth, and the moon emerged ready to greet the night with enchantment.

The sky eventually draped itself in black. The fire roared with intensity, flickering with hues of blue and yellow; the firewood pulsed crimson. Anne walked back into the kitchen to pour herself another glass of merlot. Turning off the light, she took a slight step down into the three-season porch. In Adam's white button-down shirt, she walked out on to the deck. The bitter wood stung the bottom of her feet; the cold etched up her legs.

Anne gazed upon the blemished full moon that engulfed her in its light. It reflected off the still water and into her bright green eyes. But that wasn't the only thing in her sight. Down on the ebony cobblestone beach towered a dark silhouette. Adrenaline surged through Anne's entire body, awakening each and every cell.

After all the horror films she and Casey had watched, her subconscious was shrieking at her to run, lock the doors, and call the police. The figure began to creep toward the stairs that led up to where she was standing.

"*Run, stupid!*" her brain roared to the nerve impulses that were connected to her legs, but they remained unresponsive, as though some magnetic pull was holding her there. Her breathing ceased. Her heart pumped blood through her so quickly the cold she had felt earlier dissipated. Her chest was on the verge of splitting in two. The menacing figure grew closer, lifting up its hands, pushing back the black shroud that was covering most of its face, revealing its true identity. The moonlight unveiled the truth in those familiar sapphire eyes.

"Hello, my Anneliese." The baritone voice stung her ears.

The wine glass fell from her hand, shattering into a million pieces at her feet. This wasn't real; it was one of her crazy dreams. She would reach out to him and he would fade away into the night air. Then she would wake up to a tear-stained pillow and haunting memories.

Extending her hand slowly, she could feel her muscles become rigid. Her trembling hand reached the curve of his jaw. Her fingertips felt the heat from his skin. He was here, standing before her in flesh and blood. Tears sprung from her eyes and she launched herself into his outstretched arms.

"Carter, is this real?"

His arms enfolded around her as she wept in his embrace. "Yes, this is real. I'm here."

He kissed the top of her head as she clutched the back of his sweatshirt, practically clawing at him. She couldn't consume his presence fast enough. Her mind rapidly spun as his warmth enraptured her. But then reality snapped back into place. Pulling away, she peered up at him wiping her tears with the back of her hand.

"Oh my God, I can't believe this. What the hell?"

Carter bent down to kiss her lips, but Anne quickly backed away. When doing so, a shard of broken glass stabbed her right foot. Screaming from the excruciating pain, she began to lose her balance. Carter quickly grabbed her arm, pulling her up in to him.

"Let's get you inside." He cradled her quivering body into his arms as he opened the screen door that led into the dimly lit cabin.

Anne stared at Carter. "I'm losing my mind."

He placed her on the gleaming brown granite, putting the open wound into the sink. The gash was oozing blood into the steel basin, causing a small stream to flow down the drain. Carter grabbed a yellow dish towel and turned on the faucet. Anne let out a shriek, for her heart was pounding in her heel.

"I'm sorry. I'm trying to stop the bleeding." Carter held the dish towel to clot the gash. "Why the hell were you out there with just a shirt on and no shoes? It's thirty-five degrees out there."

Anne was in disbelief. He had been missing, presumed dead for the past three years. He showed up on her fiancé's deck alive and now he was going to stand there and lecture her about proper dress code?

She yanked the dish towel from his hands, holding it on the puncture wound. Carter moved closer to her. "W-what is going on? You're supposed to be dead."

"Sorry to disappoint you, Anneliese. I know this is confusing for you."

"Confusing? That's an understatement, Carter."

Tying the towel around her foot, she jumped down onto the hardwood floor. She winced at the pain that shot through her swollen foot and up her leg. "Where have you been?" Anne asked through gritted teeth.

Carter paused for a second, seeming to search for the right words, "I just couldn't stay away from you any longer. There's so much I want to say, so much I want to tell you. Once I heard you were engaged to Adam, I couldn't...."

Anne took a step toward Carter, holding his dark gaze. "You didn't answer my question. Wait, how did you know about that?"

"He's not who you think he is, Anneliese."

"That's ironic for you to say because I thought I knew you too, but I guess not. How could you do this to me? I was a mess when you disappeared, completely broken. I searched for you every weekend, praying that I would find at least your body. I didn't have any closure." Broken cries fell from her lips. "My heart died, my world came crashing down around me!" Her irises dilated with fury. "Do you even care? Do you?"

"Yes, I do. Why do you think I'm here?" Carter retorted, his face turning a deep shade of crimson.

Anne pounded her tightly clenched fists at his chest. "I loved you. And you left me. Why? Damn it, I want to know why. How could you do that to me? How selfish can you be?"

Carter grabbed her hands, securing them forcefully behind the small of her back. "Stop it, Anneliese. Listen to me."

Carter bent down and pressed his lips firmly against hers. Anne yanked away. "No. I want answers."

He looked down at Anne's exposed neck, releasing her hands. "You still wear the pearls I gave you."

She looked down and touched them with her hand, which revealed the diamond perched on her finger. Carter's face twisted with anguish as he backed up against the wall.

"You can't marry him. You don't know him like I do."

She shook her head. "What does that mean? How do you even know Adam?"

"Sit down, please," he motioned.

Anne hesitantly took a seat at the black bistro table, and Carter followed suit.

"Leed's Imports and Construction was heading into financial ruin. My parents tried everything but the banks wouldn't give them any more money so Steven became desperate. He went and asked the Montgomery family for help."

Anne's mouth dropped open. "As in Montgomery hotels? Montgomery Hotels Incorporated?"

"Yes, Simon Montgomery and Steven had been friends and business associates for years. Leeds Construction worked on quite a few of the Montgomery hotels. But what you don't know is that they are ruthless and extremely powerful. They don't play by the rules, and Simon always gets what he wants."

She looked down at the polished wood table. "I've seen their names in the paper before, mostly gossip columns, so I didn't pay much attention to them. But Casey showed me an article once, something about the heir to the Montgomery fortune being caught with some married celebrity. He had blackmailed her husband or something." Anne raised her eyes back to Carter. "Did he give Steven the money?"

"He did, but there were conditions. Simon wanted Steven to bribe the zoning board in Shakopee. Simon had plans for a new casino there, and he was being blocked. Steven was friends with a few of the members, and Simon had dirt on a couple of them."

"Why didn't Simon just bribe them? Why make Steven do it?" Anne couldn't sit still; the more questions she asked, the more uneasy in her own skin she became.

Carter's brows pushed together. "Simon Montgomery never gets his hands dirty."

"Steven did it?"

"He was going to but I found out about it. I threatened to go to the feds because the Montgomerys were already under investigation for extortion, credit card fraud, and bribery. They caught wind of my intentions and told my father that I was a liability and needed to be taken care of. Steven refused, so they decided to send over their own guy to take me out—Adam Whitney."

Anne couldn't believe what she was hearing. Bile rose from Anne's stomach and the room spun. *This isn't happening, this isn't real.*

"So you're telling me that Adam was contracted to kill you?"

"Yes. I knew too much and the Montgomerys knew who to send. I faked my death so they wouldn't come after us. That day I vanished, only three people knew I wasn't really dead—my parents and Sam."

Anne trembled. *I knew Rita was hiding something.* "I can't believe Sam knew about this. He's the one who called me and told me you were dead. I just saw your mother and she lied to me, right to my face. And what's this 'us' business? Why would they come after me?"

He leaned toward her, placing his hands on top of hers. This time she didn't pull away.

"Sam is the one who delivered the note and pictures to you. I couldn't take that risk of being seen. Once I heard Adam had made his move, I couldn't hide any longer from you. He has been using you the entire time. The Montgomery family suspected my death was a sham, even when my father showed them the death certificate. They sent Adam to you in hopes of luring me out. Simon thinks you knew I was never dead. To get to me, they used you and it worked. They think you know about some money that they are accusing me of stealing."

"Money from them?"

"Yes, but it wasn't me. It was Adam. He set me up. I'm telling you, he's dangerous and I'm not going to ever let him hurt you."

"Oh my God," Anne whispered looking around the room as it faded in and out of focus.

In the midst of Carter's shocking revelation, Anne's phone began to ring. They stood up simultaneously. It was Adam's ringtone. She didn't know what to do. *What do I say? Can I even believe anything Carter is saying? I can't think straight.*

Carter motioned her to answer it. "Don't say a word to him about me."

Swallowing hard, she tapped the screen that revealed Adam's gentle smile.

"Hey, babe," Anne pushed out in a tight exhale.

"Hi, I'm so sorry. I hadn't expected to be running so late, and I couldn't get away to call you back. I'm leaving right now so I should be there in about an hour."

Anne paused. "Um, it's all right. I've just been relaxing by the fire."

"Are you okay? You sound funny."

Clearing her throat, she continued to maintain her composure. Carter watched her, coaxing her to wrap it up. "I'm just tired, you know? That drive is exhausting plus I've had a couple glasses of wine." She awkwardly giggled.

"You don't have to wait for me. Just go ahead to bed and we'll have a nice breakfast in town tomorrow morning."

"Sure, that sounds great. See you in a bit."

Anne twisted the string of pearls around her shaky index finger.

"I love you, Anne."

She closed her eyes and blurted out those words that she knew would rip through Carter's chest.

"I love you too."

Choking back tears, she ended the call. Carter approached her, winding his arms around her whether she wanted him to or not. There would be no struggle. She gave in, sinking into his chest where she quietly sobbed. She studied his face; time had stood still for him. Same gorgeous wavy russet hair, same perfect olive skin, and eyes just as mesmerizing as ever. Even his smell was the same, sandalwood and vanilla.

Carter placed his fingers under her chin. This time his kiss was without force, full of eagerness and compassion. Anne backed against the counter, and Carter pressed his body against hers. Placing her hand on Carter's chest, she gently pushed him back.

"This is wrong. I can't do this, Carter, and you have to go." Anne grimaced.

"I love you, my Anneliese. I'm here for you." Carter's eyes burned into hers, confused by her rejection.

"I need to be alone. This is so much to process. You can't just appear out of nowhere and expect us to pick up where we left off. It doesn't work that way. I have my own life, a life that doesn't include you. I'm engaged to Adam."

Carter threw his arms up in frustration. "After everything that I just told you about him, you want to remain engaged to him? He's dangerous."

"He's never hurt me. I'm not afraid of him."

"You should be."

"I can't do this right now. You have to go. He'll be here soon," she moved further from his reach. "Don't think for a one moment that I'm finished with you. I want to know everything, and I mean everything, Carter."

"I'll tell you everything, I promise, but you must stay silent regarding my whereabouts," Carter warned, before walking toward the door that led to the deck.

"I won't say a thing, but when will I see you again?"

Deep down, Anne dreaded that her eyes would never fall upon his face again.

"I'll be in touch very soon. I love you."

And just like that, Carter vanished into the thick night air. Anne stood in the kitchen, breathless and bewildered. She was trying to make sense of what had just taken place. Her mind didn't even know to process it all. *Did that really happen? Carter's alive and tangled with the Montgomery family. Is their hotel business just a front? Who are they really? Is my fiancé truly a murderer and working for them?* She didn't know how she would act around him. In a daze, she quickly cleaned up, bandaged up her foot and got ready for bed. If she was asleep when he arrived home, she wouldn't have to speak to him.

Tomorrow, she would have to come up with a different plan. She drifted off, still feeling Carter's phantom hands. Her sweet dreams would be interrupted knowing that the man who was behind Carter's disappearance was sleeping soundly in the same bed with her. What would he do to Carter once he discovered that he was alive. Or worse, what would Adam do to her now that she knew he wasn't a mere defense attorney?

CHAPTER SEVEN

Anne couldn't help but stare in wonder at Adam who sat across from her at the white-on-red, cotton-draped table. They were having breakfast at a quaint little café in town. Adam read the newspaper and drank his black coffee. How could the man who had saved her be a killer? She remembered when she told Adam about her breakdown and how understanding he had been…

~

Anne sat on her couch, pulling her knees to her chest. The cushions sunk down as Adam sat down next to her, handing her a tissue. Anne took it and wiped her eyes.

"I'm sorry I'm such a mess tonight."

Adam tucked a loose blonde strand behind her ear. "Don't apologize. I'm just worried about you. You know you can talk to me about anything."

Anne laughed through her tears as she twisted the Kleenex. "If I tell you, you'll run and that scares the hell out of me. Because," she swallowed. "I'm falling in love with you. You've brought me back from a very dark place, and I fear I'll go back there if you leave. I know how crazy that sounds."

The thought of Adam leaving her pinched her insides. Anne was desperate to keep him, but he needed to know what happened to her.

"It doesn't sound crazy at all. Anne, I'm falling in love with you too, more and more each day, and it kills me to see you so upset."

His words filled her with courage and warmth spread over her heart. Adam's declaration of love flooded her soul with such radiant energy, casting out the demons that plagued her.

Anne took a deep breath. "A year ago…" she paused, trying to find the right words. "I-I had a breakdown because the man I had been with for a very long time drowned and his body was never recovered. I fell into a dark place. Casey gave me the name of an excellent therapist in our building, and I started going to him. I still have to take medication for depression and anxiety attacks." Anne fidgeted with her pearl necklace, trying to gauge Adam's reaction. She was used to people giving her the sympathetic look but he didn't. The dim lamp that sat behind him shadowed his face, but he looked right into her eyes. He took her hand and kissed the top of it.

"I'm not running. There's more, I can tell."

"There is more. My mother was sick, she was schizophrenic. I didn't have much of a childhood because she was always doing insane things to herself—or to me. It…it frightens me that I had a breakdown because I don't want to be like my mother and have mental collapses when something happens in my life."

"You said 'was'—is your mother dead?"

Anne pulled at the twisted tissue, which was also how her stomach felt talking about this. "Yes. I was in college.

She committed suicide. I couldn't save her, but by then, I don't know if I really wanted to anymore."

"I understand now."

She feared that she had revealed too much. "Understand what?"

"Why the Mayo Clinic study is so important to you. You're doing it to pacify your own guilt. You can't do that yourself. Hereditary or not, you aren't sick. I think everyone should have a yearly mental checkup."

Anne laughed and wiped her eyes again with the tissue. "Who's the doctor now?"

Adam slid closer to her. "Look, Anne, we all have our demons, but you can't allow them to control you. The darkness is scary, but you're good person who has helped so many children and you have so much love to give. You've chosen to be the opposite of your mother and that takes strength."

Adam pulled her into his arms. She sunk into him. She didn't tell him everything, but he didn't need to know her last secret....

∽

She looked at Adam as he flipped through the last of the newspaper. *No, I can't believe Carter. He was wrong, he has to be.*

The Friday morning air felt heavy, almost suffocating. There was a light layer of fog that hung low over the pine trees. It danced across the lake like a scenic ballet. Soft pink tones painted themselves through the watery haze.

Anne took a sip of her coffee and began fidgeting with her ring. Adam was always so gentle and loving with her. He would give her the world on a silver platter if he could. He looked so average reading his paper; he didn't look like a contract killer. Adam shifted his eyes toward her. She quickly looked away.

Closing his paper, he turned. "Okay, what's going on?"

"Nothing," Anne gave him a quick smile.

"You seem restless. Is this about the broken glass? Look, my mom isn't even going to notice, so don't worry about it."

If only that was the biggest of my worries.

"I know." She picked at the table cloth. "Will you be gone all day?"

"I don't know. I'll do my best to wrap it up so we can enjoy the rest of the weekend together. I'm sorry about last night, but you did look quite sexy wearing my shirt." The corner of Adam's lips lifted.

A flush of heat spread over the apples of Anne's cheeks. "Yeah, me and sexy don't go hand-in-hand all that well."

Adam enveloped her hand in his, kissing it softly.

"I think you're sexy no matter what you wear."

She smiled and looked out toward the road where she noticed a black Escalade parked across the way. Carter ducked down inside. Anne gasped, nearly knocking over her coffee.

"Whoa, what was that?" Adam steadied the coffee cup before it spilled.

"Um, just a chill. I shouldn't have worn a dress out today. It may be spring but the temperatures aren't quite that warm yet," Anne said, trying to recover from her spastic behavior.

Adam motioned to the waitress for the check. "So what are you going to do today, darling?"

Adam had many endearing pet names for her, which always caused a flutter in her chest. Until she knew more, she couldn't envision him as a cold-blooded killer.

"I think I'll just do some antique shopping and then head back to cabin and read."

"That sounds nice and relaxing. Just what you needed."

"Yeah," Anne replied quietly. There would be no relaxing for her.

They walked hand-in-hand to the gravel-spread parking lot. She kept from looking in Carter's general direction. Adam squeezed her hand as they stopped at her driver's side door.

"I'll call you when I'm finished, and I promise it won't be late like last night. I love you."

He kissed her on the lips. Anne had to remind herself to breathe.

"I love you too." She wanted to tell Adam the truth, tell him everything, but she withheld the notion.

"Stay out of trouble, my angel." He smiled and gave her a playful wink.

They both got into their cars and exited the parking lot. He went one way toward Duluth and she turned the other, waiting for Carter to follow her lead. About a mile away from the café, the black Escalade sped up behind her. She couldn't help but smile when she saw his face in her rear view mirror. They continued down the two-lane highway when Carter began to flash his headlights at her, motioning for her to turn left onto the upcoming dirt road.

Anne was unfamiliar with the road, but she did as she was instructed. Gripping the steering wheel with both hands, she guided the car carefully over the unstable, softening dirt. Up ahead on the right stood an old abandoned barn. Most of the once-vibrant red paint was chipped away and weathered by the many years of frigid northern winters.

They parked on the side of the barn that was not visible from the road.

Anne's instincts were to immediately run over to him and kiss every inch of his olive skin, but her open-ended emotions held her back. She walked over to him as calmly as she could while the tremors shook her core. Carter's tapered jawline was covered in light scruff and his hair was hidden under a navy blue baseball cap. Layered with a blue thermal was a red t-shirt that hung loosely over his dark jeans. *For someone who has been dead for three years, he sure does look good.*

He gestured toward the rickety barn door. "Let's go inside where we can talk."

"You mean hide," Anne replied snidely.

The inside of the barn was hollow. There were about a dozen stacks of hay left and a couple of bags of feed. The critters of the outside made their homes there during the cold winter months. Anne's knee high brown boots sunk into the pockets of mud and hay. The smell of horses lingered in the air.

"Did Adam suspect anything?" Carter asked, leaving an ample amount of space in between them.

Anne crossed her arms. "No, but you promised me you would tell me everything, so start talking."

"What do you want to know?"

She rolled her eyes. "Don't play dumb with me, I want to know everything. Hey, let's start with where the hell have you been for the past three years?"

Carter tucked his hands in his pockets. "I had a friend make me a fake passport, driver's license, and social security card. I took on a whole new identity then decided to leave the country for a while, just until things cooled down. I traveled all over South America and a little in Africa."

"Well, isn't that nice. You took a vacation while I spiraled into my own personal hell."

"Anneliese, it wasn't a vacation and you know it. There wasn't a second that went by by that I wasn't thinking about you. After a year, Sam returned to the States from Asia and became my watcher, if you will. I had to make sure you were all right."

Anne began circling the barn, absorbing Carter's explanations. *How much has Sam seen? What has he told Carter?* "I always felt like I was being watched. So you had Sam stalk me? Well, isn't that wonderful?"

Carter cocked his head. "I like the term *protect* better but then he informed me about your relationship escalating with Adam. I knew I wouldn't be able to stay away very much longer. God, I know I hurt you and I'm sorry. It wasn't easy for me to leave. I hated the fact that I was leaving you here alone."

Anne hurled daggers with her glare. "Hurt me? Really? I was devastated, Carter. I don't understand why you couldn't trust me. We could've left together, or you could've at least told me what was going on. After all the shit you put me through, I deserved the truth or least a goodbye."

Carter threw his hands up in the air. "What shit did I put you through?"

"You're kidding me, right? Helicopter skiing, paragliding, BASE jumping," Anne ticked off. "You were reckless. I was scared to death every time you left on one of your insane adventures." She walked over to the loose bales of hay and sat down as the tears flowed down her cheeks. "I was pregnant, Carter."

The words stung as they broached her lips. Anne rarely ever talked about her miscarriage. Carter moved closer, his mouth hung open. "Pregnant?"

"I was late but wanted to wait until I went to the doctor to confirm before I told you. I had dreams of a little wavy-haired boy running to me, pointing back at you yelling 'Daddy,' and you would scoop him up in your arms and kiss us both. I wanted the news to ground you a little bit. I was hoping to surprise you when you got back from the camping trip but...." Anne choked, feeling her heart ache with loss.

The pain was almost too much for her to bear. Falling to his knees in the muck and mud, Carter placed his hands on the sides of her legs. She removed his baseball cap and ran her fingers through his disheveled hair. Strands of auburn reflected the shaft of sunshine that peeked through the holes of the dry-rotted roof.

"When Sam called and told me that you had disappeared and were presumed dead, I blacked out and woke up three days later in the hospital. I had lost our baby."

Carter laid his head in her lap. "We were going to have a baby."

"So, Carter, not only was I mourning you but I was mourning our baby too. The last connection I had to you was gone."

Carter grabbed her, pulling her into his embrace. "I'm so sorry, my Anneliese. I'm such an idiot."

He wiped away the black mascara that streaked down her face. She tilted her head ever so slightly and kissed his lips. They both inhaled deeply, feeling the rush of air expand in their lungs like a vacuum. Carter ran his hands inside her dress and up her thighs, his touch was hot against her skin. The thumping of her heart thudded in her ears.

"I want you always, Anneliese," Carter whispered between breaths.

The palm of her hand pushed against his stalwart chest.

"What is it?" he asked, frowning and moving back from her an inch or two.

"This is…I can't…." Her voice trailed off. "But I don't want you to leave again."

"You have me right here, right now." He interlaced their fingers.

"What about tomorrow, Carter, and the next day? We have to figure something out. You can't keep running. We need to talk to Adam or go to the police."

Carter pulled himself away from her. "No. There is no *we* in this. I will fix it. I know who I'm dealing with and I'm not going to put your life at risk."

"Isn't it a little too late due to the fact I'm engaged to the man who was going to kill you? At least let *me* talk to Adam. I need to hear what he has to say."

Carter pointed his finger. "You need to keep quiet."

"Adam will figure out what's going on. He isn't stupid."

"I know, but in the meantime you need to play it off like everything is perfect."

Anne let out a scream. "I am so pissed at the both of you. This is something out of the *The Sopranos*. This kind of stuff doesn't happen here."

"You'd be surprised, and these people are dangerous. They will come after you, so let it be."

She picked up his cap that was lying on the ground next to her feet and flung it at him with such force he flinched.

"Let it be! Are you joking? To be honest with you, Carter, I don't know what to believe or who to trust. How do I know that you aren't lying to me? Looking me right in the eye and lying—it seems to come so naturally."

Carter's face flooded with anger. His movements toward her were swift and forceful. "How could you say that to me? You know me better than anyone. I'm risking everything being here right now."

"I'm so done with this." Anne attempted to walk away, but Carter grabbed her by the arm.

"I'm not playing with you. Your impulsive behavior is going to get us killed."

Anne yanked her arm away. "*My* impulsive behavior? You lurk around in the dead of night. You have your best friend do your dirty work for you and stalk me. Who the hell does that?" She looked him up and down. "I don't know this Carter and I didn't know that one either, I guess. Everything that I once believed in is gone. How can I trust you? When it all fell apart, you left me. You handed me right on over to Adam. You did that. If anything happens to me, it's on you."

Anne had nothing more to say as her heart crumbled inside her chest. Turning her back to him, she hurried out of the barn. Her senses were ablaze yet she felt so defenseless. No amount of medication would correct what she was feeling at this moment.

"Anneliese!"

She could hear Carter's footsteps pounding on the thawing earth as he ran toward her. She hesitantly turned to face him.

"Please, Carter, I need to go."

"Think only of the past as its remembrance gives you pleasure."

Anne turned her gaze to the bare cornfield off to the other side of the road, seeing exposed dirt fighting the elements of the unforgiving season—oh, how she could relate. He was exposing her to a corrupt world she was unaware existed. Carter's quote from *Pride and Prejudice* did not move her emotionally or otherwise. In fact, she felt insulted, as if one charming quote would entice her back in to his arms. At one time it would have, but things were now different.

"How can I let them bring me pleasure if they were nothing but fallacies?" She opened her car door. "And that's directly from me."

Carter stood there in defeat with his hands tucked inside the pockets of his jeans. Anne flattened the gas pedal, taking one last look in her rear view mirror. The scene of their rendezvous became smaller in dimension until it was no longer visible. Her mind was on auto pilot. She reached the cabin in what seemed to be mere seconds.

Anne wandered down the marked stone path that ran on the side of the cabin fortress and opened up to the cobbled beach. The bitter wind pushed the waves toward her. Guilt ran over her like the waves, as did the tiny stones beneath her feet, slowly eroding away her entire being. She grabbed a handful and tossed them into the gray water, watching the peppered ripples. Anne unleashed an unearthly scream that had lain dormant since late last night.

If Carter thought she was going to sit idly by and let her future be determined by lies and deceit, he was sadly mistaken. They were strangers to one another; it was not the reunion she had dreamed about so many times before. Now that she was aware of being of being stalked, she looked down the beach, assuming Carter was nearby, watching her. Walking back to the cabin, she went inside and secured all the doors and windows.

～

It was mid-afternoon; the winds brought thick dreary clouds that skirted deep in the sky. Anne sat in the club chair next to the fireplace with both legs draped over the arm, staring out into the colorless atmosphere. She knew confronting Adam would be haphazard, but what other options did she have? Taking off the diamond ring, she looked at it as a small smile brushed across her mouth. Adam's proposal was so beautiful; how could it all have been a lie?

On one knee he had knelt down, taking her hand in his. The room was aglow with candlelight, and the scent of fresh roses filled the air around them.

"Anne Corinne Jamison, I have loved you from the second I saw you in that ballroom. You opened your mouth and a symphony poured from your lips. I will spend the rest of my days on this earth bringing you nothing but happiness and love—that is, if you will let me. Anne, will you marry me?"

"Yes!" Without hesitation, she had accepted his proposal.

Sorrow crept in once the memory faded. She placed the ring on the side table next to the chair. How could she continue to wear a ring that promises love and devotion when she didn't know if his heart had been in it at all? Was she just a pawn in this lethal chess game?

Anne heard the lock to the front door unlatch. Adam was home. She watched him walk into the foyer and place his brown leather briefcase on the floor. Her hands fidgeted.

"Hey there." He wrapped his black knit scarf around the base of the railing.

"We have to talk. Please, come sit down."

His steps were slow and curious. He sat down on the couch across from her and noticed the ring sitting on the table.

Adam's eyes widened. "Why is your ring off?"

"Why are you with me?"

It pained her to ask the question but she needed to know. "What's this about?"

"Answer the question, Adam. Why are you with me?"

"Because I love you. Did something happen today?"

His expressions continued to change, but hers remained stagnant. Her head was slightly lowered, her eyes hooded.

"Do you have alternative motives for being with me? Are you truly in love with me and want to marry me or was there some other reason?"

Adam cleared his throat, appearing uncomfortable with where the conversation was heading. He gave her a sidelong glance.

"Are you truly in love with *me*? Let's be honest here. I compete against a ghost every day. So, are *you*?"

Anne promptly realized the tables were being turned. *Damn him.*

"You quickly forget that I'm the psychiatrist. I take plea-sure in mind games."

He stood up, loosening his navy tie and rolling up the sleeves of his crisp snowy shirt. He crossed the room to the rustic bar.

"How quickly you forget, I'm the attorney. I take pleasure in arguing my way out of tight situations." Pouring himself a brandy, he had a satisfied look on his face.

"I was just thinking if we're going to enter into a union of forever, don't you think we should lay it all out on the table? Honesty is such a lost art these days," Anne countered, jumping right into the game.

Adam finished off the amber liquid, putting the glass down with a thud.

"Something has apparently riled you up regarding my feelings toward you, so if we're going to talk about honesty, let's start with that. What happened?"

Anne began to open her mouth but was startled by her ringing phone.

"Saved by the bell," Adam motioned for her to answer it.

She grabbed it off the side table. "Casey?"

"Anne. You need to come back to the Cities." Casey spoke frantically.

"Why?"

"It's your patient, Stella McGuire. She's in the hospital with self-inflicted wounds."

"Oh my God. I'll leave right now. What hospital?"

Anne dashed the length of the living room then up the stairs to the bedroom.

"Regions Hospital in St. Paul. I'll stay here with her mother until you arrive."

"Thanks, Casey, I'll hurry as fast as I can."

Hanging up her phone, she threw it on the king-size bed. *Poor little Stella, so traumatized, so fragile.*

"What was that about?" Adam trailed behind her.

"One of my patients attempted suicide. I have to go."

She wasn't worried about folding or nicely placing her items in the suitcases. She just wanted to get to Stella.

"I'm sorry to hear that. Should you be driving?"

"I'm fine," Anne tried to dodge his body that seemed to continuously get in her way.

"We need to finish this conversation. Maybe I should drive back with you and we can talk in the car."

There was no way she was going to be trapped in a moving vehicle with him for four hours with the possibility of him dumping her body on the side of the interstate after she told him the week's past events.

"Not right now. I want to be alone. It'll give me time to clear my head."

He finally trapped her in the closet after all her efforts of dodging and weaving him.

His face was ashen and his hazel eyes had lost all vivacity. "The truth is this. I love you, Anne. I'm in love with you and I don't know who's been whispering in your ear but usually the one accusing is the one who is being dishonest."

"Usually the one being accused only becomes defensive when they have something to hide," Anne countered.

They could have gone several more rounds but Anne needed to leave this conversation for later.

She put the last suitcase in the trunk and turned to find Adam standing next to the driver's side door.

"Could you please text me when you get to the hospital so I know that you arrived safely?"

Anne looked down, Adam was holding her engagement ring. Her chest felt weighted; she was confused and needed to get away from him.

"Yes, I'll let you know."

He stepped away allowing Anne to get into her Jetta. Starting the engine, she drove down the gravel driveway. In the rearview mirror she saw Adam watch her car drive away. He disappeared once she rounded the corner of black evergreens.

In the past twenty-four hours, her life had been turned inside out. The mess and destruction was too much to handle. Anne wanted her medication, she wanted to disappear into the abyss, but she couldn't. Stella needed her.

CHAPTER EIGHT

Ten-year-old Stella McGuire had been sedated and brought to the pediatric wing of the hospital. Her arms were bandaged and an IV was running fluids into her delicate body. Anne and Mrs. McGuire sat in the waiting room while Casey ran to find a coffee vending machine.

Anne crossed her legs with a small notepad and pen in hand. "Mrs. McGuire, can you tell me what happened?"

Stella's mom stared at the beige tile floor. Her hair was up in a matted bun and she had smears of blood on her neck and collarbone. "I had been in the kitchen preparing dinner. I had just cut up vegetables for beef stew when I turned around and saw Stella standing beside the cutting board holding the knife I had just used. I was paralyzed. I didn't know what she was going to do but as I started walking toward her, Stella held up the knife and gouged it right into her arms. I tried to stop her but then she started cutting me."

Anne examined Mrs. McGuire's flesh-colored dressings that covered her hands. "Did Stella say anything to you before this happened?"

"No." Mrs. McGuire rubbed her red-rimmed eyes with the heels of her hands. "I can't do this with her. She's the reason my husband left. I can't do this. I'm exhausted."

Anne reached out and touched her leg. "You need to stop. That will not help Stella's recovery. She needs you right now."

Mrs. McGuire jerked her head toward Anne. "You were supposed to fix her, fix our lives, and bring my husband back. He won't come back now, not after this." She shot up and left the room before Anne could stop her.

Anne sat back in the stiff chair and tipped her head back. She realized that Stella was her all those years ago. Anne's mother blamed her for her father leaving them, verbally lashing out at Anne every chance she got. She felt Stella's pain; they were tortured kindred spirits.

She stood and walked across the hallway to Stella's room. Her chest rose and fell under the blanket. The blood pressure cuff inflated but Stella didn't stir. She had been sedated once she arrived at the hospital. Anne leaned against the metal doorframe, wanting nothing more than to bring Stella home with her. Protect her. Love her. Anne prayed that Mrs. McGuire would come around and not abandon her daughter. Her little lost soul didn't need to become entrapped in the system like so many others had. Casey and Anne walked through the corridors that led to the main bank of elevators. It was close to midnight, and the only people roaming around were the overnight medical staff.

"I'm going to have to make some phone calls tomorrow morning and find a facility close to their home that has room for a ten-year-old."

"She seems unattached to her daughter. Is the father around?" Casey asked, fiddling with her loose hair.

"No. He lives in Indiana with his brand-new shiny family."

"I see. Let me guess, the new step-mommy is a nice, perky, early-twenty-something-year-old with a forty triple-D chest but a brain the size of my pinkie finger."

"You got it. Love it how they all want the newest upgrades once they hit that mid-life crisis age. Men want to make babies but walk away when it gets rough." Anne knew that feeling of abandonment, feeling unwanted and unloved.

They exited the hospital to the front parking lot. Anne texted Adam when she had arrived. He thanked her and wanted to be clear that they needed to finish their conversation. Anne desperately wanted to tell Casey about her newest revelation; she needed to confide in someone.

"Are you heading back up to the cabin?" Casey asked.

"No," Anne swallowed down her hysterics.

Her hand suddenly ceased in motion as her body kept moving forward, throwing her off balance.

Casey latched onto her hand like a lobster claw. "Wait one minute. Where's your ring?"

"I left it at the cabin."

It wasn't a lie; she had left it up there but not by accident. Casey arched her thin, manicured eyebrow.

"All right, spill it; I know something's going on. I could tell the second you arrived."

"It's a really long story and I would rather not tell you out here." Anne scanned the parking lot as if she were on some covert mission.

"Wait, should I have a martini in my system first?"

Anne laughed. "Probably wouldn't hurt."

"Let's go to Nicollet's." Casey's eyes gleamed.

Anne agreed and they both returned to their cars to head back to downtown Minneapolis. Nicollet's décor was an inspired loft theme. It had an open concept with exposed brick and duct work, but the furnishings were glamorous and sophisticated. Each section consisted of ivory-covered seats with a small round black wooden table and rectangular ivory swaths that hung from the ceiling, creating a provocative partition. The ambiance was thick with conversation and excitement, even though it was nearing closing time. Anne and Casey found an empty table and sat down. A thin blonde waitress approached them.

"Two dirty martinis." Casey had to raise her voice over the parade of laughter surrounding them. The waitress nodded and headed to the bar.

Casey zeroed in on Anne. "I want all the details. Leave nothing out."

Anne took a deep breath. "Carter's alive. He followed me up to the cabin; he had Sam deliver the note and pictures. He claims that Adam was hired to play my doting boyfriend by the Montgomery family who also hired him to kill Carter because his father owes them a whole lot of money and Carter was going to turn them into the feds."

In the midst of Anne's confession, the waitress brought over their martinis but Casey's mouth hung open.

"You're telling me that both Adam and Carter are mixed up with the Montgomery family? The same Montgomery family that has been accused of every white-collar crime known to man."

Anne gulped the warm clear alcohol, letting it fill her veins. "Yes, one in the same. Apparently, Carter's father took out a 'loan' with hotel billionaire Simon Montgomery, but in return he wanted Steven to do his dirty blackmailing for him. Carter found out about it and threatened to turn them in. Simon ordered the hit on Carter, but he faked his own death first."

Casey leaned closer to Anne. "I assume the Montgomerys are more than just hotel owners. What else do you think they're into?"

"I don't know and I'm scared find out. Honestly, something doesn't feel right. It's not adding up for me. Why would they send Adam to babysit me? Carter must know more than he's telling me. He also said something about the Montgomerys accusing Carter of stealing their money, but really it was Adam setting him up." Anne could feel the warmth of the gin spreading through her blood vessels, erupting just below her fair skin.

"Yeah, there's absolutely more to the story than that. I mean, we are talking three years in the making…plotting, scheming. Did you confront Adam about it?"

Anne stroked the base of her ring finger where the diamond once sat. "In a roundabout way I did. But his defenses were up. I didn't get very far." Anne ran her finger over the stem of the glass. "Oh, and I told Carter about the baby."

Casey choked on her drink; a cough erupted from her mouth. "What? Wow, how'd that go?"

"He was upset." Anne shrugged. "I don't know, it was weird talking about the miscarriage with him. I never even told Adam about it." She placed her head in her hands. "I'm so confused. I don't know what to think."

"Remind me to never go on a getaway with you."

Casey's attempt to get Anne to laugh was successful. Anne finished off her second martini. As the last drop hit her tongue, the alcohol raced through her insides.

"They need to tell me the truth, stop sending me creepy notes, and stop prowling around like a lion stalking its prey."

Casey patted Anne's hand. "I guess, my dear, you are going to have to go get it yourself since neither one of them are up for the most upstanding citizen award. You're going to have to play both sides of the fence until you get your answers."

"That's one dangerous fence to be straddling,"

Even though playing private detective could jeopardize everything and possibly reveal information she wasn't quite ready to acknowledge, she knew Casey was right. She was going to mollify both of them to get what she wanted and that was the truth. Was one of these men worth saving over the other? If the answer was yes, then which one?

∾

In the wee hours of Saturday morning, a chilly seasonal wind whipped against the brick buildings and concrete skyscrapers as it howled through the exposed alleyways.

Anne unlocked the door to her apartment, which was toasty compared to the blustery conditions outside. Retrieving the two suitcases out of the hallway, she rolled them into the small alcove to the left where her desk and laptop resided. Most of the effects of the martinis had left her but exhaustion had begun to settle in. Before Anne could flip the light switch in the kitchen, she heard a faint voice come from the living room. Hearing only the beat of her heart, she took a slight step forward.

"Anneliese, leave it dark."

A volt of shock traveled through her body.

"Jesus, Carter, how did you get in here?"

Squinting, she could see a silhouette standing by the fireplace; the sheers on the patio door placed a soft orange glow from the street lights onto Carter's face.

"So, did you tell Casey all my dirty little secrets?" he asked, ignoring her question.

She choked on her own intake.

"Why do you assume we were talking about you?"

Even in the darkness she knew Carter was raising an eyebrow.

"Because you tell Casey everything,"

"She wanted to know why I wasn't wearing my engagement ring so I explained to her my conversation with Adam, and I guess your name came up a few times."

Only a couple of feet separated them.

"You are making this difficult. You know she can't keep her mouth shut."

"Listen, she isn't going to say anything to anyone. Your precious secret is safe and don't talk about her like that."

"I understand that I have put you in a precarious situation, and I'm sorry for that. I'm also sorry that you are in such pain. I love you so much and I'm just trying to protect you," Carter stepped closer. "Did you end your engagement to Adam?"

"Yes. I can't wear that ring knowing what he's done. And I don't need protection. I need the truth and not some construed version—the actual truth, because I know there's more going on." Anne's voice was beginning to tremble.

"If I tell you the truth, then you will need more protection. The less you know right now the better. Please, Anneliese, you need to trust me on this," Carter begged. "I need to touch you," he reached out for the curve in her neck.

His fingertips slid across her skin, running along the cotton collar of her dress. They stopped at the V hovering over the metal button. In the silence, she could hear uneven breaths, and she was certain he could hear the thunder that echoed in her chest, rumbling through her ribcage. Anne shuddered as the hair on her arms stood on end, tickling the already sensitive flesh.

Without realizing it, their bodies had molded to one another, and a familiarity shifted between their arms, chests, hips, and legs. Carter's heat seeped through the fabric of her dress, spreading a fever through her. Anne laid her head in the crook of his neck, tasting his aroma that engulfed her senses. She had missed his smell, his taste.

The more their limbs explored, the more the ache grew. She craved his kisses, his touch, and this made her a fool. In the darkness they stood feeling the fury gathering between their bodies. Restraining her desire was maddening; she feared she'd implode at any moment.

Her moral compass was spinning out of control, and before she could gain any type of willpower she was indulging in an all-consuming kiss. His lips formed to hers so perfectly; though it was wrong, she didn't want to stop his strong hands from undressing her right there in the middle of her living room.

Anne tore Carter's clothes from him with such frenzy, she could hear the threads from his shirt stretching and breaking. *I want him. I want him now.* She had waited years for this moment. Their naked flesh crumpled to the floor as they felt each other in pure rapture. Anne's pants and groans filled the still dark air while Carter's fingers roamed between her thighs. She remembered every stroke, every caress, and every grip. They clawed into one another, feeling the hunger and yearning of the past three years. They may have been thousands of miles apart but their hearts had never forgotten their unyielding passion.

"I belong here," Carter growled, filling Anne with his heat.

"Yes," she wrapped her legs around his waist.

Anne lifted herself into the desire, begging for it to never cease. Feeling her body surge high above the earthly lights, she allowed Carter to take her away from all the pain and confusion. The elation she felt was enough to bring tears; they trailed down into her hairline. Carter quickly placed his lips on each damp stream, transferring them to his satin lips.

"I've ached for you. Can you feel my love, Anneliese?" he asked.

"I can. Please." She gasped.

"Please what?"

"Please stay with me."

This simple request thrust Carter over the edge. His body tensed on top of her. Anne's heart called to him, pleading with him to never let her go but she knew better. She knew he would leave again. She just didn't know when.

Draped on her sofa they remained intertwined; the only movements were their shared breaths and small touches. They laid there embracing the quiet. Anne listened to the sweet symphony of Carter's beating heart. She smiled against his chest as she ran her fingers through the dark curls that dotted his Herculean chest.

He ran his fingertips down the sides of her arms, leaving a trail of heat behind them. "My sweet Anneliese, you're so beautiful. I've dreamed of your ivory skin draped across mine for so long."

"Look what you've done to me. You're positively evil."

She heard a soft chuckle echo in his throat. "You should try to sleep, Anneliese. The sun will be up soon."

She knew what he was trying to do. Once her eyes surrendered to the sandman he would creep out, leaving her alone once again. She tightened her arms around him, willing them to remain this way so he couldn't move, but a handful of hours later she would discover that that tactic didn't work.

While the hush of dawn filtered through the window casting a warm glow over her body, she shifted under the blanket, feeling nothing but cold fabric. *Damn him.*

~

Anne was caged in on Interstate 94. A sea of automobiles filled any empty space that was around her. This was typical Saturday morning traffic in the Twin Cities. She was actually starting to form a foot cramp from constantly tapping on the brake. She had just left Stella and her mother at the hospital. Anne began recalling the haunting words that came from innocent lips.

"I wanted to be with God. He's the only one who loves me."

The hairs on Anne's neck had stood straight up. Stella stared out the window and played with her blue hospital gown. She didn't go beyond that one horrid statement, and Anne didn't want to push her luck with such a fragile little girl. She was still looking into various mental health facilities for Mrs. McGuire but since it was the weekend, she had a feeling her search wouldn't get fully accomplished until Monday morning.

Mrs. McGuire had said nothing to Anne; she barely looked at Stella. Anne wanted to shake the woman, remind her of her commitments as a mother but she didn't. She sat next to Stella's bed, watching the innocence drain from her blue eyes. It was a transformation to which Anne could relate. The moment her soul calloused.

The car behind her honked, pulling Anne back to the clogged interstate. She heard her phone beep again. Adam had left numerous voicemails on her phone, pleading for a returned call. He didn't specify whether he was still up at the cabin or if he had returned to the Cities. Anne could feel the guilt rise in her throat, making her insides flutter and not in a good way.

She would step into that wasps' nest in due time but for now she was off to meet someone else, someone who could possibly shine some light on the precarious situation that Carter had shoved her into, one of the last people who had seen him before he disappeared—Sam Goodman. Their other friend, Ryan, had disappeared; she couldn't even find an address.

Sam had returned from Asia with a bride and a toddler. They resided in a quiet community in Woodbury. She cruised into Carver Lake Park, which also had a pleasant beach that was full of activity during the summer months. The sun's rays were bursting with warmth that soothed the once-hibernated public. The timber playground buzzed with children of all ages while parents conversed with one another about the joyous break of the winter blues.

Perched on a nearby bench hiding behind a black baseball cap and blue hoodie was Sam. Anne walked up to him guardedly but once he saw her, he jumped up and hugged her. Quite taken back by his enthusiasm, Anne returned the gesture. His blue eyes twinkled with the early afternoon sun.

"Anne. It's so good to see you."

She scanned the playground. "It's great to see you too, Sam. I heard you have a wife and daughter now. Are they here?

"I do. No, it's best that I keep them out of harm's way. I think I've done enough of that to last a lifetime."

"How was Asia?" Anne settled onto the wooden bench.

"Busy. Leeds Imports kept me on the go but I was thrilled to get back to the States." Sam rubbed the back of his neck.

Anne tilted her head. "You don't work for Leeds Imports any longer?"

"No, Carter needed me full-time."

I bet he did.

"Why, Sam? Why did you agree to follow me?"

A shadow etched over his fair freckled face. "Carter helped me get my wife out of Hong Kong minus the red tape so in return I kept a close eye on you. I'm sorry, Anne, I know I should've told you, but there are so many elements to this and he didn't want you getting involved."

"But you risked your family's life for him? For me? I know about the Montgomerys. That they gave Steven money and then went after Carter. But what I need to know is what's Adam's involvement in all of this?"

Sam shifted uncomfortably. "Wow, you just get right to it, don't you?"

"Look, whatever it is I can handle it."

His expression looked doubtful. "No, you can't, but I will say this: tread lightly. The Montgomerys have people everywhere and they mean business." Sam quickly glanced around the park.

Anne put her hand on Sam's. "What about Adam? I need to know the truth."

He covered his mouth with his hand, pretending to cough. "He has history with Carter and his family but Anne, you can't tell him about Carter. Do you understand me? Adam's expertise is elimination. That's why Simon Montgomery wanted him. Adam is more than an attorney. He's more than just a man who grew up in Minneapolis."

The seriousness of his manner made Anne feel anxious. She knew she was walking right into a minefield.

"I need more than this, Sam. Is he a killer?"

He shook his head in protest. "I have to go. Take care of yourself and remember what I said."

Sam patted the top of her hand, stood up and walked away. She watched him get into his teal Suburban and drive out of the parking lot. Not too long after he left, she noticed a silver BMW with tinted windows following closely behind him. Someone had been watching them. A violated sensation swept over her body, bringing a wave of nausea. Sprinting to a nearby plastic trash bin, she released all her distress with a large heave. The acid-laced bile burned her throat, bringing tears to her eyes. After searching for a napkin in her purse, she patted the corners of her mouth. She hurried to her car and sped out of the parking lot. It was time for her to face Adam.

CHAPTER NINE

S peeding down the interstate, weaving in and out of traffic, she exited onto the road that would lead her to the
uptown area near Calhoun's Square. Pulling up in front of
a row of three townhomes, she threw her car into park and
approached the covered walkway. Her brown ballet flats
made a slight echo on the wooden enclosure. Anne peeked
inside the garage; Adam's car was not there. With his house
key in hand, she slid it into the lock and opened the white
door. The shades were drawn and all was quiet.

"Adam?" she called out, just in case.

Closing the door behind her, she gently stepped into
the living area, listening for any sign of his or anyone else's
presence. Climbing the beige-carpeted stairs, she looked
around the corner toward the master bedroom. The king-
size bed had been untouched; the comforter, sheets, and
pillows were still neatly in place. Across the hallway was
his office. She knew where his personal documents were
located.

The two-drawer black metal filing cabinet was cold to
the touch. It opened with a slight squeak; she turned her
head toward the door. Still silent. All the multi-colored file
folders were alphabetically labeled. *Like he's going to label it*

C for Corrupt? She rolled her eyes at the thought. She didn't know what she was looking for except anything that linked him to the Montgomerys or to Carter.

Thumbing through piles of paperwork, she came across absolutely nothing. She sighed with frustration and rotated her head back to stretch out the muscles that had become tense. Anne looked off into the corner of the room and spotted a pair of gloves. Quickly she began opening doors to her memory vault, knowing those gloves looked familiar. All at once a picture of Carter flashed in front of her—the picture from the camping trip with Ryan and Sam. There had been a man in the photo who had hidden his face. The symbols on the black gloves were identical to the ones in the photo.

Adam was there.

"Find what you were looking for?"

Anne gasped, twisting her body, she backed up into the corner of the hushed office. "Adam, you scared me half to—" she suddenly choked, rethinking her choice of words. "Well, you scared me."

Adam's discontented expression said it all. "What are you doing here?"

A tremble in her throat made it almost impossible for her to speak.

"I…was looking for something."

He stepped closer to her. "I can see that," he said, examining the strewed papers that lined the floor. "Did you find it?"

Still clutching the gloves in her hand, she tried to inch herself out of the corner.

"I know the truth, Adam."

He smirked. "You know nothing, but for fun let's hear your version."

"You were hired to kill Carter, and when the Montgomerys suspected his death was phony they wanted you to watch over me in case he came back or he told me anything about their illegal dealings." She held up the gloves. "I know you were there the day he disappeared. I have a photo of you wearing these."

He took another step closer to examine her evidence.

"Hmmmm, so your theory is that I'm a contract killer on the side and was hired to kill your beloved Carter and now for the past three years I've been playing it off as your loving and adoring boyfriend and fiancé, so I could lure him out of hiding and finish the job. Did I miss anything?"

The calmness in his voice frightened her; it shook her right to her bones.

"It's not a theory, Adam—it's a fact. You should know that when there's evidence there's a warranted case."

"Beyond a reasonable doubt is my stance, and I'm not going to continue indulging in this psychological warfare. I'm more than willing to tell you the truth but not right now."

She shook her head and threw down the gloves. "You know, I'm becoming increasingly fed up with these games, Adam. I'm begging you, if I ever meant anything to you, please, tell me what happened."

This time, Anne moved closer to him, waiting for a reaction to her plea.

"You don't know how much it pains me to see you so hurt and confused. The truth will reveal itself in due time." He stroked her cheek but Anne flinched. "I'm not going to hurt you. I love you, Anne."

"If you loved me, you would admit to what you did."

"You mean what I didn't do. The death certificate read accidental drowning, but I guess that doesn't matter now, since I've been informed he isn't dead."

Without another word she pushed past him and flew down the stairs like he was chasing her, but he wasn't. Dashing from the house and to her car, she pushed the accelerator to the floor. A high-pitched sound echoed against the pavement. The smell of burnt rubber seeped into the car. Anne had no way of warning Carter of Adam's knowledge of his existence. She could only hope he would reach out to her before it was too late.

CHAPTER TEN

Anne tucked herself into the plush olive sofa, wrapping her fatigued body into a ball. Her eyes blinked heavily and wearily. The background noise of the television played in the distance as she drew closer to the dream realm. With all the madness circulating through her mind, the dreams quickly became nightmares....

Adam stood before her; his face distorted in rage, his shirt soaked with blood. He stepped closer to her and then pointed to his right. There laid Carter, dead, covered in blood. She screamed but nothing left her mouth and then Adam came toward her, placing his hands over her throat, choking every bit of oxygen out of her....

Anne threw herself up off the sofa as she was coughing, gasping for air. She clutched her throat and looked around the dim room. Shadows swayed along the walls from the vivid glow of the television. Anne stood up and made her way to the kitchen to get a drink of water, trying to steady her breathing pattern. Gulping down half a bottle of water, she inhaled deeply a few more times, gathering her composure. Almost hoping that Carter was lurking around, she peered out of the kitchen window but saw nothing except a couple walking toward the building, laughing, holding on to one another.

Early evening was setting in and the five o'clock news was starting. Anne placed her water on the table beside her and turned up the volume on the television. On the bottom of the screen it read **BREAKING NEWS**; a petite brunette news anchor was standing outside a two-story brick home that had been roped off by yellow police tape.

"Police say that thirty-three-year-old Sam Goodman was gunned down outside his Woodbury home shortly after four o'clock this afternoon. Neighbors say that a white or silver sedan stopped in front of the house while Goodman was outside. The gunman opened fire, shooting six rounds, and then sped away."

Anne could still see the anchorwoman's mouth moving, but it was all moving in slow motion. They flashed a picture of Sam on the screen with his wife and daughter.

"Goodman is survived by his wife and eighteen-month-old daughter. Police are still here at the scene, investigating and questioning his wife and neighbors, trying to find out who would want to brutally murder this quiet suburban family man in broad daylight. Back to you, Chris and Marsha."

Anne's breathing was labored. She struggled to stand on her unsteady legs, pushing them toward her bedroom. Tears ran down her face; whimpers ricocheted through the vague room. Fumbling for the switch on her small lamp, she fell in front of her nightstand. Shaking frenziedly, she attempted to read the labels on the prescription bottles.

Spilling out moans of frustration, she popped open the white ribbed cap and a dozen small pink pills dribbled out onto the floor. Her fingers grasped one and she shoved it down her throat, swallowing hard, praying for the little dustings of medication to flow through her veins and shut off the neurons that were causing her body to convulse with panic.

~

Lying face down on the hardwood floor, staring at the dust bunnies under the bed, her breathing began to slow; her pulse calmed. The darkness she once ran toward had now spilled out into her reality; that dark place was here, living and breathing like the self-destructive monster it was.

Feeling the vibrations on the floor of passing trucks and neighbors moving furniture soothed her. Then she heard what sounded like a tapping noise. Lifting her unsteady head to try to focus her hearing on the sound and realizing someone was at her door lightly knocking, she heaved her body up as carefully as she could. Her vision blurry, she reached out to the walls to guide her to the door as she heard the tapping noise once again.

"Anneliese, open the door or I'm coming in."

Coordinating her muscles to unlatch the locks took immense concentration, but once she swung the door open she fell right into Carter's arms, sobbing into his chest. He shut the door with his foot and pulled her further inside, stroking her tangled locks.

"Shhhhhh, my Anneliese. It's okay, it's okay," he kept repeating in a reassuring tone.

"Oh my God, Carter, it's my fault. Sam is dead because of me!" Anne's muffled scream sank into his wool sweater.

"It's not your fault. Stop saying that."

He continued to stroke her hair, placing kisses atop her head.

"It is. If I hadn't met him at the park, putting him in danger, he would still be alive."

Anne was near hysterics. Carter wrapped his fingers around her arms and pulled her back so he could see her agony-twisted face.

"He wasn't murdered because of you, so please stop blaming yourself. Sam was in a lot of trouble. He was associating with people he shouldn't have been."

Anne tried to focus on Carter's gorgeous sapphire eyes. They reeled her in like they had their own gravitational pull.

Carter examined her face. "Anneliese, did you take something? Your eyes look glassy."

"When I saw the picture of his wife and daughter on the TV, I lost it and—" Her voice trailed off as her body began to feel limp.

Carter tightened his hold on her, picking her up in his arms, cradling her like a small child. He walked into her bedroom.

"How many of those did you take?" He put her down on the bed and then kneeled down to the scattered pills on the floor.

"Just one. I was having an anxiety attack. They help me calm down."

Carter picked up the remaining pills, putting them in the bottle and back into the drawer. Her hunched body fell to the side, nearly missing her wrought-iron headboard. Her head sank into the plush down pillow. The room grew dark as Carter shut the lamp off and made his way to the other side of the bed. He lay down next her, and she moved closer to him, draping her arm over his stomach, feeling it rise and fall with each breath. He stroked her arm with the tips of his fingers.

Anne let out a weary exhale. "I am so sorry, Carter. Sam was your best friend and I...I just can't believe he's gone. Just like that. Now his daughter is going to grow up not ever knowing her father."

A rogue tear trailed down over her nose and soaked Carter's sweater. She knew that feeling all too well. Not fully knowing who you are or where you came from.

"Shhhhhh, my Anneliese, just close your eyes and rest. I'm here. It's all right."

Carter's touch caused her to melt into a deep, hazy sleep. Through the night there were moments when she felt awake and others as if she were in a trance, as though her body was disconnecting from her and floating around the boundaries of her bedroom. She heard Carter's voice out in the living room, it was one-sided. She assumed he was on the phone talking to someone. Not able to distinguish reality from hallucination, she tried to listen to Carter's harsh words.

"I don't care what the fuck she told you. Get the shit done."

Silence, then footsteps. She had never heard him talk like that to someone.

Anne turned in her bed. "Carter?"

"I'm here. How are you feeling?" he perched next to her and gently rubbing her arm.

"Who were you talking to?"

His spine stiffened.

"Oh that—well...I'm fixing the mess I got myself into. Nothing for you to worry about."

Anne ran her fingers through her snarled hair. "What time is it?"

"Close to midnight. You have been out for some time but you needed rest. You scared me, Anneliese."

"Why?"

"You seemed frantic. I've never seen you like that and you taking medication—that's new."

Anne sat up, still feeling the after-effects from the pink wonder. "I haven't taken one in a long time. After you disappeared I started therapy and he prescribed some medication to help me, but like I said, I haven't had to take any of it until…"

He looked down at his hands. "Until I came back, right?"

"Well, yeah, but when I saw Sam's face on television, knowing I just saw him alive, it shook me up. I saw that BMW follow him out of the parking lot. I should have done something."

"Like what? I told you these people were dangerous. You don't listen."

Anne shook her head. "I should have gone to the police. Sam was one of the good guys, Carter, and he was just doing what you told him to do."

Carter shot up. "So this is my fault?"

Anne was in no condition to involve herself in a spat with Carter, so instead of continuing the argument she rose from the bed and walked into the bathroom. Following closely behind her, Carter's reflection stood next to her in the mirror as she brushed her rat's-nest hair.

"Carter, I'm not going to fight with you. I'm exhausted."

Carter gripped the door frame. "I love you, Anneliese, and I don't want anything to happen to you."

She dropped her hand, the brush hit against the sink. Anne scanned his face. He looked the same, but she caught a glimpse of something different. She couldn't place it. But the fear of him disappearing again crippled her heart.

"I know Carter but I'm scared. I can't…" Anne rasped. Carter grabbed her, pulling her tight against his chest. She trembled, the thought of him dying like Sam frightened her, and she knew her mind and body wouldn't be able to handle the loss. No one would be able to pull her from the dark. Her mind was a terrible place to get lost in.

Carter brought her back to lie down. She felt his weight sink behind her. His arms circled her waist as he interlocked his fingers under her university T-shirt. Their skin-to-skin contact was enough to lull her to sleep.

~

"In the sweat of thy face shalt thou eat bread, till thou return unto the ground; for out of it wast thou taken: for dust thou art, and unto dust shalt thou return."

The elderly pastor, towering over the mahogany coffin, read from the book of Genesis while Sam's family quietly sobbed, holding onto one another, clutching white roses. Under the green vinyl tent, Anne could hear the soft pattern of raindrops falling from the ominous sky. The clipped wind bit through the mourners gathered around Sam Goodman.

His frail wife sat on a white metal chair, embracing their sleeping toddler. *She'll never know her father. As I have never known mine.* Anne didn't even know if her father was alive or dead. Her mother never told her. He could be roaming around the streets of Minneapolis and she would never know.

Anne could feel a presence beside her, and then she felt someone braiding her fingers through soft leather gloves. She shifted her gaze to the right; Adam was standing stoically, focusing his attention on the pastor. Not wanting to cause a scene, she retained his grip until the service concluded.

"And all of God's people said...'Amen.'"

One by one, people approached the casket and placed their long-stemmed roses on top of it. Some cried, some laid their cheeks to the cold surface, and some said a quick but quiet prayer. Anne attempted to break from Adam, but he tightened his grasp, guiding her to the casket. Controlling her breathing, she placed a rose gently on the casket, kissed her fingers, and touched his smiling photo. She would miss those peppered red freckles.

"This way," Adam bent down, whispering in her ear.

A shudder thundered through her spine. They walked away from the crowd of mourners and toward a black Lincoln Town Car. A burly man, who looked as if he just came from securing the president, loomed next to the back passenger's door. Anne yanked her hand away, rubbing her fingers that ached from being crushed in Adam's vice grip.

"What the hell are you doing here?"

The man opened the door, motioning for her to get in.

"Please, Anne."

Hesitantly, she slid into the spacious back seat. Adam followed suit. The windows were so heavily tinted she could barely see the world of gravestones around her. "You didn't answer my question. Why are you here?"

Adam kept enough distance between them so he could somewhat face her; their knees were nearly touching though

Anne scooted herself closer to the opposite door, feeling the cold leather against the back of her exposed calves.

"Anne, we have much to talk about. You can't keep avoiding me."

"So you stalk me at my friend's funeral?"

"You gave me no choice," he sighed.

"I'm not ready to talk to you yet."

"I know Carter is alive. He isn't who he says he is, Anne."

Anne crossed her arms. "Funny, he said the same thing about you."

"I'm sure he did, and I'm also quite certain you believed his every word."

Anne could feel her face beginning to flush with frustration; she turned her sights to the window. Droplets of rain were trickling down, distorting the grey scenery around them.

"He is putting you in danger by revealing everything to you. He's playing you for a fool, because he knows you would do anything for him."

Anne shot fury his way. "Again, he said you were playing me for a fool, lying to me every day, expressing to me your love and devotion, knowing it was a complete and utter lie. You will never understand what I feel for him."

Adam winced at her scathing words. "I do because that is how I feel for you. I vowed to protect you and right now you may not see it that way but you will. I knew one day I'd cross paths with Carter again and in my delusional thinking, I trusted that our relationship would triumph, but he has pulled you into his twisted world of lies."

Anne's face softened as she watched Adam's eyes fill with anguish.

She reached out to him, placing a hand on his thigh. "Adam, please tell me what's going on."

Adam lowered his eyes. "I can't."

"Then I will find out on my own."

Anne clutched the door handle with her free hand. He quickly trapped the one on his thigh.

"Anne, please don't or you will surely pay the consequences like your friend Sam did."

The threat sent volts of heat through her. His grip loosened; Anne departed the black vehicle and into the downpour. Giving him one last glance before she closed the door, she saw his expression was solemn and hard.

"Goodbye, Adam."

Anne closed the door and glanced over to Sam's casket, which had become one with the earth as four large men covered him with dark damp soil. Would she be next? Would she be laying there next to Sam while her friends mourned her? Anne shook the thought and picked up her pace through the eerie, silent paths of Lakewood Cemetery.

CHAPTER ELEVEN

Anne exited the main gate of the cemetery through flooded eyes; still feeling Adam's phantom grip, she rubbed her arm. His words tumbled around in her brain, burning through every cell and nerve ending. *Was he warning me or threatening me?* Adam had never been harsh with her before, but the hurricane named Carter seemed to send him into a desperate tailspin. Heavy emotions suffocated her while she drove through thick traffic, heading toward downtown.

She suspected Carter had been lurking behind a tree or mausoleum during Sam's burial, and she also suspected he caught the show between her and Adam.

The interrogation will commence soon from Carter. I never saw myself as naïve, but apparently I have been. I've been clouded by infatuation, duped by affectionate words and engaging promises that will never come to pass. I have believed nothing but lies.

Before entering the office suite, Anne stepped into the restroom to freshen up her make-up and hair. Between the tears and rain, her appearance was dreadful. Running a thick comb through her lengthy blonde locks, she twisted the damp hair into a loose bun that hung just above the nape of her neck. Dusting powder over her face, she tried to hide the lines where tears had streaked her pale cheeks.

Anne's black wrap dress was spotted by rain drops that had found their way through the openings of her coat. Shelly's face looked surprised to see Anne when she entered the office.

"Dr. Jamison, I hadn't expected you in today."

"I know, but I have some work I need to finish up. Any messages?" Anne needed to stay busy, plus she felt safer having witnesses around.

Shelly handed over a stack of pink message slips.

"Is Casey in?" Anne thumbed through the messages.

"She will be in around noon."

"Thanks, Shelly."

Anne walked to her office, closing the door behind her. The room had become increasingly disorganized. Green files were stacked on her credenza like a tower; a layer of dust covered her desk and keyboard. It reminded her of what Rita's office looked like—completely disheveled.

Anne sat down at her desk, turning on her computer screen. She accessed a database that housed records of every single person ever born in the United States. She typed in *Carter Steven Leeds* and his birth date. Scrawled across the screen in black and white, the result read:

No records found
Please try your search again

"That's odd," Anne sat dumbfounded.

She continued to click the tab that brought her to the medical information page; she entered Carter's full name once again. As the screen began to load, there was a knock at the back door of her office. Quickly, she flicked the screen black. Anne stood against the wooden door in apprehension.

"Wh-who's there?" Her voice shook.

"Anneliese, it's me."

Letting out a sigh, she unlocked the door.

"Why are you knocking on this door?" Anne closed and locked it behind her.

"I can't very well stroll into the waiting room, can I?"

Without further delay, he pressed his lips on hers and enveloped her, his arms wrapped around her waist. His lips were soft and moist. Anne's mind began to cloud but she remained focused.

"I've missed you. You don't know how badly I wanted to be at your side this morning."

Anne touched her lips, moving away from him. "Yes, well, it was extremely heartbreaking to see his family so devastated. I figured you were keeping your distance somewhere nearby."

"I was. It pained me to not be there to fully pay my respects."

The elephant in the room was beginning to grow, smothering them both.

"I know you saw Adam there with me, and that we had a discussion…if you want to call it that."

Carter approached her, running his finger down her jaw line. "Did he hurt you? Are you all right?"

She shifted her face away from his touch. "No, no, he didn't hurt me. He's just concerned and you know why. You both can't be playing on Team Good and in fact I suspect you are both playing on Team Very Bad, which leaves me to wonder ...Is this like picking the lesser of two evils?"

Carter looked to the ceiling. "Remember that first night we met. The hot summer night air can make you do crazy things and when I saw you across that room, I knew I had to talk to you. Even then I wanted to give you the world, the sun, the stars, the universe, and I knew I couldn't come close to that. Not then. Nor did you want any of that, my simple, sweet Anneliese. All you ever asked of me is to just love you...."

"It wasn't enough, was it, Carter? It still isn't. You've changed." His lack of response screamed at her. Her heart sank in the depths of her body. Carter pushed her numb shell against his dank cotton shirt, burying his face in the crook of her neck, soaking in her scent. Her arms remained weighted at her sides. "Always trying to prove yourself." Anne looked at him. "What are you trying to prove? And to who? Me? Steven?"

"Come with me, Anneliese, it will be just you and me. I'll give you everything you've ever wanted. Be with me. Let's leave this city and start a new life together."

She hated that he ignored her question. His plea electrocuted her senses. *I'm done playing the victim. No more damsel in distress.*

"No."

"Why are you staying here, in this mundane life?" he motioned around her office. "What's here? Nothing, that's what. You wake up, you come here, and you go home. Don't you want more than that?"

Anne ran her hands through her hair, tugging at the ends. "My life is not mundane. What I do is my passion, my love. These kids need my help, and I can't believe you would call my life that since you haven't been around in years. What I do changes lives, Carter."

"You need money to change the world, Anneliese. I can give you that."

"I don't want your illegal money." her voice waivered. "As much as I want us to be us again it can never be, don't you see that? Carter and Anneliese died together the day you disappeared. We have succumbed to such an entanglement of lies that there will never be a happy ending…not for us."

Carter embraced her with such might the air from her lungs escaped her mouth with a hiss.

"You will always be my Anneliese," Carter whispered in her ear, kissing her cheek.

Before she could blink, she was once again alone in her office, but his words lingered through the stale air. Anger rose from where her heart had plummeted. *Who is he to judge me?*

Returning her attention to the computer screen, she clicked it back on, gazing in disbelief. Carter Leeds never existed; no birth record or death certificate, nothing could be located. *What the hell? There should be something.* Anne clicked enter again, *maybe there's a glitch.* Nothing. She put her head into her hands, wanting to push out the throbbing that plagued her mind. Anne's email chirped. At first she planned to ignore it, but curiosity won in the end.

Anne,

I know you don't want to see me, but I need to tell you something before it's too late. I deceived you and for that

I'm sorry but I did it to protect you. I'm not sorry that I fell in love with you and I'm not sorry that I asked you to be my wife. I don't know how this will end, but it has all led to this. Remember, I promised I wouldn't run. I'll follow you to the ends of the universe.

I will be glad and rejoice in your love, for you saw my affliction and knew the anguish of my soul. Psalm 31:7

Forever Yours,
Adam

Anne could no longer find breath. Her lungs filled with heat. She had spoken this verse to him right after they began dating...

~

Without the presence of the moon, the skyline shone brighter in the darkness. Brittle leaves danced down the road, as Anne watched them spin and twirl with the wind. A chill spiked through her body, even the thick cotton blanket couldn't keep the cold at bay. Adam tightened his arms around her as they sat on the lounger five stories above the earth on Anne's balcony.

Her eyes remained on the outline of buildings with their speckled lights. "Can I ask you a question?"

"Absolutely."

"Do you believe in God?"

She felt his chest rise and fall, his breath thinned as if holding it inside his lungs. Anne had taken an anxiety pill earlier that evening, her brain typically tumbled into a morbid world of existentialism. Analyzing the life that was built around her brought forth Nietzsche's phrase: "God is dead." *Is He? If there was a God, why didn't He save me?*

"I believe there is something out there greater than you and I. I just don't know what that is. How about you? Do most psychiatrists believe in God or are you all science?"

"I grew up Catholic, read the Bible daily when I was little. I want to believe. I couldn't imagine believing in nothing. When I couldn't put my faith in God, I put it in science. When I see children who are so broken, I think, how could God do this to them? How could someone who claims they have a soul be so cruel, so evil?"

He stayed silent, a car alarm sounded in the distance. Anne waited for what seemed like an eternity for him to answer.

"Are we talking about your mom?"

Anne sagged against Adam. She couldn't speak; the scars she bared to her therapist were one thing but confessing them to the man she loved was troublesome.

"If we allow the darkness of the world to taint our souls then that is our doing, not God's or anyone else's."

She closed her eyes letting the emotion stream down her face. Anne hadn't cried in front of him, and she hated doing it now.

"Evil lies in us all." Anne spoke without emotion.

Adam leaned down close to her ear. "It doesn't in you, my angel."

No. He's my angel. He's taken away my nightmares, my darkness.

Anne twisted in his arms, she ran her fingertips along the side of his face and down his jawline. "I will be glad and rejoice in your love, for you saw my affliction and knew the anguish of my soul..."

~

"Anne?"

She grabbed her chest. "Jesus!" Casey had vaporized next to her while she had been deep in memory.

"Sorry, you didn't hear me knock. Are you all right? Looks like you've seen a ghost."

"I have—he was here."

Casey's cherry-red-painted mouth fell open. "What? Did Shelly see him?"

"No, he snuck through the other door, and then I got an email from Adam."

Anne could see Casey's bright eyes grazing over his bold words.

"What the hell does that mean—it has all led to this?"

"Adam showed up at the funeral. He was being vague. It's like this whole thing has been plotted out for the past three years."

Casey wrinkled her brow. "Gearing up for war."

Anne fidgeted with the pearls as she let Casey's words sink in. They made sense. Something had been building up all this time, and now it looked as if it was coming to a head with her directly in the middle of it all.

"I overheard Carter talking to someone on the phone the other night. He was harsh, I had never heard him speak like that toward anyone. He's changed, Casey."

"Well, your memories of him must be shot because he had a temper. Carter was possessive of you, he'd get pissed if another man even glanced your way. Maybe that hypnotherapy has messed with your brain. And, what the hell do you mean, 'when he was at your place?'"

Anne swallowed back the thickness in her throat. She was so confused. *He had a temper?* They had their arguments and the passion between them was intense, but he hadn't raised his voice or swore at her before.

"Stop, Casey, it was nothing. He came over after he had heard about Sam. I don't remember Carter being that way."

What was wrong with her? Casey stared at her like she had three heads. Anne's pulse was picking up, her palms were sweaty. *Maybe I should go see Dr. Lindsey?*

She threw her hands up. "I can't breathe. I need to get some air."

"Do you want me to come with you?" Casey watched Anne grab her purse.

"No thanks, I really need to be alone and try to sort it all out."

Casey hugged her and placed a motherly kiss atop her head.

The Riverfront District was a place of beauty. The downtown horizon of glass and metal reflected grandly off the Mississippi. Dreary rain clouds were starting to move out of the city, letting in peek-a-boo sunshine, which felt soothing against her skin. She inhaled the garden-fresh air.

Anne had stopped by Dr. Lindsey's office, but the office was dark and the door was locked. She assumed he and Claire were at lunch. *Maybe Casey's right, maybe the hypnotherapy was screwing with her memories.* Anne felt her thoughts freezing up one minute but then racing the second. How could these two men have lied to her for so long, and how didn't she see it? It was as if blinders had been placed over her eyes for the past four and a half years.

She settled onto a stiff wooden bench, observing a man and woman with two small children, grasping their father's legs, begging for piggy-back rides. Anne felt such sadness for Sam's little girl who would never share such memories with him. He would be absent from her first dance, her graduation. *Who would walk her down the aisle on her wedding day?* Anne knew that longing all too well and wouldn't wish it upon anyone.

Fury and heat burned through her stomach and entered her blood stream, oscillating resentment and disgust. All at once the wind ceased, and the distant noise of traffic and conversation were silenced. This would be the calm before the storm. *Hell hath no fury like a woman scorned.* Her stilettos clicked hard against the Stone Arch Bridge.

D'aubinge had a lighter feel to it in the afternoon hours. Anne sat at the bar where she had first met Carter. Realizing that she had been caught up in nostalgia, she found herself quietly smiling at the glass of merlot that sat in front of her. Anne shook it off and gazed around the polished brasserie. Sitting behind her in a small booth were two businesswomen and next to them was a man typing feverishly on his laptop. Anne twisted back toward the bar to discover she now had company.

"Hello, Anne," Rita slid onto the stool next to her.

The bartender approached them.

"Christian, I'll have a scotch on the rocks, and Anne will have another glass of merlot."

He nodded and went to prepare the drinks.

"Are you following me now?" Anne drank down the rest of her merlot.

"Anne, first let me apologize for my demeanor toward you the last time we spoke. I was having an off day, and I took it out on you. Second, I'm not following you, just simply making amends."

Christian placed the drinks in front of them.

"Thank you. I've got this, okay?" Rita gave him a wink; he once again nodded and returned to the other end of the bar.

"I know you knew that Carter was alive." Anne said.

"I swore I wouldn't say anything. I had to protect him. Lord knows his father didn't." Rita gulped her scotch.

"Why weren't you at Sam's funeral this morning? He was Carter's best friend and part of *your* family and business."

"I was there. I sat in the back of the church."

Anne narrowed her eyes. "You Leeds are sure good at lurking in the shadows."

Rita shifted her body toward Anne, radiating displeasure. Anne didn't care. "I know you are upset and you have right to be, but he did it to protect you. I'm in no way condoning what he has done, but, Anne, he loves you so much, and he is trying to get everything worked out with the appropriate people."

"I'm beyond pissed, Rita." Anne quickly lowered her voice; feeling eyes around the bar watch their exchange. "I've been lied to for God knows how many years. I can't trust a thing Carter says to me. And you, you knew and didn't say anything to me. I planned his memorial, and you came sobbing with your flowers and tissues. Was he there, Rita? Watching me? Watching my world fall apart?"

"Anne—"

"I've checked and there isn't any record of Carter even existing; your son was never alive, but I'm sure you already knew that. I want to know what Adam has to do with all this. Tell me now. And the truth would be great."

"First, Carter was not at the memorial. He had fled the country by then. Second, Adam's firm represented our companies. He was to escort Carter to Chicago to assist in the legal side of the investment with the Montgomery family. We had to make sure we weren't getting screwed in the deal. Long story short, the deal went south with Carter and Adam in the middle of it. Adam took the easy way out."

"No, I think Carter did."

Rita stiffened, finishing her drink. "Adam is nothing but a snitch, he held all the cards—there was nothing we could do. When he made his play for you, we knew the Montgomerys meant business and wanted Carter gone for good."

"Jesus, do you realize how insane this is? How do you just sit there and allow all of this to happen?"

Rita's face flooded with crimson. "I didn't have a choice. Steven wasn't going to do anything. He never protected Carter."

Anne slammed her hand down on the granite "I don't believe you. I know there's more, but you aren't telling me. Maybe I should call Simon Montgomery. I bet he'll tell me all about it." She put the wine glass to her lips and let the merlot flow into her mouth.

Anne watched Rita's eyes moved past her and toward Christian who was still standing at the opposite end of the bar, cleaning glasses. Anne sat the glass down as her vision blurred for a second.

"Why, Anne, you don't look so well." Rita pursed her lips.

Anne felt a rush of euphoria circulate through her veins, with every heartbeat thrusting the sensation more rapidly into her blood stream. Her mind thickened with haze, disabling all lucid thought.

"Here, my dear, let's go to the ladies room."

Anne could feel Rita's chilled arms wrap around her waist and guide her toward the back of the bar.

"What…was…in my…."

Anne's heavy head fell back as her eyelids fluttered. Through the heavy surge of whatever drug they had placed in her drink, she could faintly hear voices. Feeling her feet leave the ground, she was floating away into the shadows. Her breathing slowed and in one last exhale, Anne's world faded into nothingness.

CHAPTER TWELVE

"**E**verything will be all right, my sweet Anneliese." Carter's words swept into her consciousness like ocean waves. "Trust me, trust me...."

She could feel caresses glide across her cheek and then soft echoes. But quickly the nothingness pulled her back under.

Through her closed eyelids, she could see a peach glow; the rays of sun poured onto her still body. Anne moved her fingers along what seemed to be a leather surface, perhaps a chaise. It was dimpled with cold, circular buttons. The room was silent. She could hear her own breathing, which had returned to a normal rhythm.

Coaxing her limbs to reposition themselves, she moved ever so slightly. Her muscles ached from the tension she'd subjected them to as the drugs had entered her nervous system. Her recollection of what had taken place was hazy, as was her vision. Anne blinked several times to regain focus; her surroundings were unfamiliar.

An arched window that reached the top of the cathedral ceiling revealed the ginger sun and clear cerulean skies. Oak shelves covered the walls and some displayed thousands of antiqued books while others had sculptures and ornaments from faraway lands. The aroma of freshly brewed coffee and sandalwood filled the large study. Anne was alone, but only for a moment. The six-panel wooden door opened as Carter sauntered in, holding a newspaper.

"Good morning, sleepy head."

He spoke with an eerily cheerful tone. He strolled over to an iron cart that sat near the window and poured two cups of coffee from the sterling silver pot that reflected the morning sun into Anne's eyes. She sat up more but her head began throbbing wildly.

"Oh, my head." She rubbed her temples.

Carter placed the white porcelain cup on the table in front of her, along with two Advil.

"Here, the coffee will help."

"I think I'll pass."

She was fearful of drinking anything from him ever again.

"I'm sorry for that, Anneliese. It was the only way."

She cleared her throat; it was dry, but Anne ran her hands over her neck. It felt like something was constricting her breathing, but the only thing she felt was the pearl necklace.

"Why would you do this to me? I don't understand."

Carter sat in the leather club chair that faced her across the table. "You're safe, that's all that matters."

Anne was gaining her senses quickly now. "Why, Carter? Why would you drug me like that?"

"You wouldn't listen to reason and you threatened to go to Simon Montgomery. You were not only putting yourself at risk but me and my family as well, and I couldn't have that."

"This is unbelievable. You've lost your freaking mind. I wouldn't have had to be so intrusive if you would have just told me the truth." Anne looked down at the newspaper and read the date. "Shit, I've been out for two days! What the hell did you give me?"

"It was your own medication. Don't be alarmed—I knew the correct dose to administer, so you weren't in any danger." Carter's nonchalant demeanor was smug and irritating.

"You're a doctor now? Carter, you can't do this. You have to let me go. People are going to wonder where I am." Anne looked around the room. "Where the hell am I, anyway?"

"You're in a safe location and you *will* remain here until I feel everyone is protected or taken care of."

Carter's eyes were dark and hostile; Anne looked toward the window, biting down on her dry lower lip.

"Okay, you want the truth—you want honesty, correct?" Carter leaned her direction, pushing his fingers together to form a steeple.

"Yes. I think I made that clear some time ago," she snapped.

"Why don't you start? Tell me what Adam told you."

"Told me what?"

"His plans. His position in this game. Where is he?"

Anne was taken aback by Carter's accusations. "What game? What are you talking about? How would I know where Adam is? I've been here for the past two days."

Carter wrinkled his brow at her response. "Anneliese, please don't think I'm dense or unwise to his plot. I have a sneaking suspicion that you are in on it as well."

"I don't know what you are talking about. You are being paranoid. Adam hasn't told me anything. How could you think that of me? I gave his engagement ring back! Why

116

would I do that if I was okay with what he's done?" Anne swiftly changed her demeanor; the neuropsychiatrist in her knew she was dealing with someone who was not thinking clearly. Carter's allegations were absurd. "Carter, you are my only love. Why would I conspire to murder you?"

Carter stood up and made his way to her. As he sat down next to her, Anne placed her hand on his face to reassure him, trying to find some semblance of the man she once loved. His pupils grew, shutting out the blue, like an eclipse. "What happened to you? You've changed."

"You're right. I have changed. I was never good enough as Carter Leeds but...." He paused. She could see he wanted to tell her but the muscles in his jaw twitched. "Anneliese, I need to know you are on my side. Betrayal is something I don't take kindly."

Carter clutched her wrists, pulling her hands away from his face. She winced. Never in the past had he laid a finger on her. *Who is this man?* Fear broke the surface as the pain seared her skin while Carter tightened his grip. Her eyes filled with tears; she gasped for air. "I've always been one step ahead, Anneliese. That's my job. But I sit here and look at you and the past comes rushing in, how I love you. You can't ever leave me again, my love, and once I finish what I started, we can finally be together. It'll be just you and me."

Though his words were filled with adoration, they also contained an undertone of mania and covetousness. "Carter." She begged. "You're scaring me. Please let me go. Keeping me here against my will is not going to help the situation."

Ignoring her plea, he tightened his grip and pulled her body to his, placing his mouth rigidly on hers, forcing her to reciprocate. She could taste his hot breath; she endured the moment, praying for it to end quickly. Feeling the tautness in her lips, Carter pulled away.

"No. You're staying here and I don't want to hear another word about it."

Releasing her wrist, he removed himself from the chaise and hastily exited the study. She could hear the lock latch behind him. Anne fell to her knees and covered her head with her arms on the black lacquered table; she did not silence her cries.

Her stomach tensed with pain, and a wave of nausea sent her sprinting to the nearest trash can. The spasms were unwavering. Feeling weak, she made her way back to the cold chaise lounge, clutching her abdomen.

She watched the light travel across the wall, guessing that afternoon had arrived. Turning to see the newspaper still lying on the table, Anne reached for it. The front page showed a picture of Adam and her. The headline read: **Prominent Minneapolis Attorney Questioned in Disappearance of Fiancée**

Anne read on.

After a missing persons report was filed for Dr. Anne Jamison, the Minneapolis police department received an anonymous tip stating that she had recently ended her relationship with attorney Adam Whitney. Police went to interview Whitney at his home, but he could not be located. They believe he is on the run and possibly trying to leave the country.

"Adam is missing too? No."

The paper fell from her hands. Carter wanted her to read this; it was all his doing. Anne knew Adam was dead and she would be next. There was a knock at the door as a petite brunette walked in carrying a silver tray. She wore a white and grey housekeeper's uniform, with her hair up in a tight bun. She placed the tray in front of Anne, lifting the lid to reveal a large white bowl of tomato soup and a grilled cheese sandwich. The woman nodded and quickly left Anne to eat.

Though she was apprehensive, her stomach screamed for her to eat. Giving in, she gulped down the tomato soup, feeling the hot contents spread through her stomach like a blanket of gratitude.

When she finished eating, Anne walked over to the arched window and saw nothing but green quilted grass with a large bleached marble cherub fountain in the middle. *Where am I?* One thing she did know is that she had to find a way out. Anne rushed over to the door and began banging on it with both fists.

"Hey! I need to use the bathroom! Hello out there!"

She jiggled the pewter handle, but the door was locked. She continued without pause. Finally she felt someone insert a key and unlatch the lock. She stepped back as a bald, burly man towered over her. His tight face was glazed with annoyance.

"I really need to use the bathroom. It's been two days, for crying out loud," Anne demanded.

"Come with me."

The tall gentleman's stride was brisk; she followed closely behind him. The hallway was narrow, layered with scarlet wall coverings and a dark wood wainscoting. Two black iron sconces lit their path down the corridor. A small window was ahead of her, but it did not give any clues regarding her location.

Taking a slight left, she discovered a staircase leading down. *There's my escape.* The frightening man directed her in the opposite direction, toward a rather large powder room. Closing the door and locking it, she leaned against the meticulously crafted wooden vanity. The same dark wallpaper and wood was found inside.

Anne gazed at her reflection, gasping at the train wreck that stood before her. Every part of her was pale and sickly; her lips had even lost their pink hue. She splashed warm water, which felt clean and refreshing, on her face. Her long blonde tresses were riddled with knots.

After relieving herself, she flushed the toilet and washed her hands. Now that she knew which way the staircase led, she would attempt her escape. Opening the door a sliver, she looked up and down the hallway and saw that it was empty. She heard nothing and no one so she cautiously stepped to her right toward the staircase. A sharp agonizing pain tore through her scalp, yanking her off her feet. Screaming in anguish, she reached back to see what was causing such harm. A baseball mitt of a hand had enclosed a healthy section of her hair, pulling her tightly back to her prison.

"No." Anne shrieked. "Carter!"

Anne's feet kicked at the floor as her hands grabbed at the vice grip pulling her hair. She tried to steady herself but his strides were wide and fast. He tossed her back into the study like a rag doll. She tumbled and felt a sting shoot up from her wrist to her shoulder. Anne's weak body was heaved on the Persian rug. The fibers tore through her black nylons, burning her ivory skin. Two large black wing-tips were inches from of her fingers. Anne looked up to see a large hand aiming for her face; she hid her head to shield the blow until she heard a clicking noise. The silence was deafening; Anne slowly looked up and saw a black revolver pointed directly at the man's right temple.

"You touch her again, I'll fucking kill you. Now get the hell out of here."

Wide-eyed, the man nodded. "I'm sorry, sir." He exited the room, shutting the door behind him.

Carter bent down to assist Anne, but she flinched. He was still holding the revolver tightly in his hand. Tucking it back in the waistband of his jeans, he lifted Anne up with one swoop of his arms. Exhausted and miserable, she placed her head against his chest. Her knees were on fire.

"Were you trying to run, Anneliese?

Her lips trembled. "Yes."

He sighed as dark strands fell over his forehead. "Now what will I do with you?"

"Carter, please, I'm begging you, look at me, look what you are doing to me."

His face softened, he glanced over her frail, bruised body. Carter ran his hands up her legs, stroking them tenderly. Twisting herself closer to him, Anne ran her thumb across his lips, feeling the warmth from his breath.

"Remember, Carter, when it was just you and I? No one else mattered—our love kept us alive. Its depth is like no other in this universe. Please remember, Carter."

She kissed his lips and ran her hands through his soft brunette waves. His body was succumbing to her every touch.

"Feel me, Carter. Want me. Love me."

As they arched their bodies into one another, he ravaged her supple neck with commanding kisses. Carter brushed his tongue over her collarbone.

"Oh my love, my Anneliese, together we will rule the world, just you and I," he whispered against her neck.

She ran her hands up and down and his back, digging in her nails, feeling the handle of the gun. Before another word could be whispered or another kiss exchanged, Anne was holding the gun hard against Carter's chest. He looked at her in alarm.

"For someone who is one step ahead, you surely were not expecting this. You see, Adam suggested I learn self-defense, and that included firearms training. My instructor said I was a natural. I do believe Adam was a step ahead of you the entire time."

Anne grasped the gun firmly with her finger on the trigger. Carter's expression turned from lust to disfavor in one tense second. The whites of his eyes were webbed with red, matching the color of his face.

"Are you going to kill me, Anneliese, in cold blood, right here?"

Anne rose from the chaise, continuing to hold his stare.

"I'll claim self-defense. You did kidnap *me*, not the other way around. Plus, I know a great attorney."

Carter growled. She inched her way toward the door, knowing freedom was just steps away; but then Carter dodged from her sight and literally yanked the rug from under her. Anne lost her footing, causing her to drop the gun and fall back against a bookshelf, slamming her spine into the sharp edges.

The gun slid across the hardwood floor and underneath the serving cart. Carter frantically searched the room for the revolver, tripping over the Persian rug and falling on his knees.

"Anneliese!" he charged after her.

She sprinted toward the opposite end of the room. Carter grabbed her ankle, causing Anne to collapse to floor as well. His nails dug into her skin. Kicking her foot that was free, she made contact with Carter's face. He shouted with rage. Only subdued for an instant, he came at her again. Blood seeped from his nose.

"Damn it, Anneliese."

Anne darted behind the mahogany desk but Carter clutched the back of her dress, pulling her toward him. She could feel his heavy breath; his fury seeped out and into the room, tightening its grip on her. Reaching for the weighty antique globe that sat on the polished desk, she forcefully swung it around and struck Carter on the side of the head. Dazed by the blow, he buckled to the floor.

Anne raced to his still body and dug in his pants pocket for keys, pausing for a moment to watch the movement of his breathing. It was shallow but steady. Locating a ring of five keys, she held them tightly in her hand. She wanted the gun, but it was across the room under the serving tray. Anne didn't know how long Carter would be out and wasting a single moment staying in that house wasn't an option.

Listening for any hint of conversation or footsteps, she tiptoed down the staircase. A blanket of grey spread through the window above the grand staircase. Day was ending, which would work in her favor, since soon she would be hunted.

Anne entered a four-stall garage. As she touched the key fob, the Escalade's lights illuminated. Anne ran to the driver's side, sliding onto the leather seat. Because she wasn't wearing any shoes, her feet barely reached the pedals. She tried to pull the seat closer, but didn't want to waste any more time. With a shaky hand, she pushed the garage door opener. Freedom was just seconds away. Once she was confident she could clear the elevated door, Anne slammed the SUV into reverse, squealing black rubber against the asphalt. As she navigated her way down the curved driveway, the iron gate opened. Without hesitation, Anne thrust the gas pedal to the floor. According to the navigation screen, she was heading south and would continue this way until she located a major highway. The twilight engulfed her. There were no trailing headlights. She was in the clear.

For now.

CHAPTER THIRTEEN

Anne's white-knuckle grip caused cramps to radiate through her fatigued muscles. The glow of headlights on Interstate 494 streaked her face, illuminating black in her eyes. She had to find Adam. The urgency of this thought intensified her breathing.

Anne pulled off onto an exit to sort through her next steps for survival. Behind a small strip mall was a gas station. She threw the SUV in park after hiding on the side of the white concrete building out of sight of traffic. She searched in the glove compartment and found a sleek cell phone. Her hands where trembling so violently she could barely dial Casey's number.

Casey finally answered after four agonizing rings. "Hello?"

"Oh God, Casey, it's me." Anne whispered, trying to bite back her sobs.

"Anne, where are you? Are you all right?" Casey yelled.

She knew there was no time for a detailed conversation; she quickly explained what she needed.

"Casey, listen to me. I don't have much time. Have you heard from Adam?"

"No, why? Isn't he with you?" Casey asked.

"No, I don't know what to do. Oh God." Anne began to lose all focus.

"Anne, what is going on? Please tell me."

"I'm in big trouble, Casey. He's going to kill me."

"Who is? Anne? Where are you?"

As Casey began demanding Anne's whereabouts, a beeping noise sounded in the ear piece. Slowly she pulled the phone away to view the screen. An unknown number was calling the phone. Anne already knew who was on the other line. She disconnected from Casey and clicked over, intending to listen quietly but her ragged breath gave her away.

"My sweet Anneliese isn't so sweet anymore."

Anne closed her eyes while her hand covered her mouth to silence her panic. Hearing the roar of an engine in the background, she started the Escalade, speeding through the parking lot and nearly rear-ending a mini-van that was waiting for the light to turn green.

"You can't hide, my love, and you'll never see Adam again."

"Why are you doing this?" Anne shouted into the phone as she maneuvered her way through the dense night traffic, rapidly driving toward the next exit that would get her back onto the interstate.

"I want what is mine. Over the past couple of years, I have come to realize that I was sick and tired of listening to other people boss me around, take advantage of me, and take what belonged to me."

"So you are out for revenge?"

Anne blended into the interstate traffic.

"You know what they say—revenge is profitable. Anneliese, please try and understand." Carter's tranquil voice was laced with insanity.

"This has to end, Carter."

"You're right, and it will not be in a happily-ever-after kind of way."

Swallowing hard, Anne ended the call and tossed the phone on the passenger seat. Rational thoughts seemed like something from a distant era, but Anne needed to find one. Was it possible Adam had known this would happen? He imparted his firearms skills upon her, so what else in their conversations and actions had he left her as a breadcrumb trail to this exact moment?

After parking the Escalade in the darkness of an alley a few blocks from Adam's residence, Anne jogged down the sidewalk and inspected her surroundings. Since Adam was a person of interest in her missing persons case, she assumed there would be an undercover cop hiding somewhere in the vicinity. The smart thing would be for her to run to the car, bang on the window and beg for help, but that would end badly for her.

Hunching down behind a bush that sat near the side entrance of the town home, Anne dug her hand into the unpleasantly cold earth, searching for the hidden key. She had buried it there herself and now, since she was without keys, cell phone, license or even shoes, she needed to locate the key to the house. The bottoms of her feet were numb and sore from the cold pavement.

Pulling the silver metal from the dirt sent relief through her body. She inched toward the door, maintaining her child-size height and inserted the key. Quietly hearing the lock release, she slowly opened the door and peered into the thick black room.

Like a cheetah, she sprinted up the stairs. Surprisingly, Adam's house seemed untouched, which she found odd because the Montgomerys and Minneapolis PD were searching for him. Or maybe they already knew his bleak fate. Anne shook the thought and proceeded to dig in the small walk-in closet for her clothes.

In the darkness, everything looked black and white and out of focus. Finally finding a pair of dark jeans and a magenta shirt, she undressed in the shadowy bedroom. She returned to the closet to find socks and shoes, and began digging through the pile strewn against the baseboard. The warmth of thick cotton felt comforting to Anne's battered feet. She laced up a pair of white canvas shoes and floated down the hallway to Adam's office, where she had once before searched for evidence against him, believing every word that fell from Carter's deceitful lips. She had lost close to two full days of her life, thanks to Rita and Carter. Adam could have been anywhere right now, even halfway around the world, faking his own death like his counterpart. Somewhere burning in the depths of her soul, she knew Adam wouldn't leave her like that, wouldn't throw her to the wolves like Carter had.

Anne shifted a pile of papers sitting atop the wooden desk. She accidentally knocked over a newspaper headlining the Leeds family and a partially torn bank slip. It showed a withdrawal dated yesterday but the amount had been removed.

"Anne?"

She whirled around to find a feminine outline in the doorway as fear traveled down her spine. She squinted, trying to make out who was blocking her in. The figure took a step forward.

"Victoria?" Anne gasped.

Why was the law firm succubus in Adam's house, lurking in the shadows?

"Yes, but I'm actually Agent Victoria Mason."

Victoria flashed a badge at Anne, which she could barely see in the darkness of the office. The only light came from a nearby street lamp.

"Agent…how…when?"

Anne stammered, trying to comprehend this new blind-siding development.

"I've been with the FBI for seven years. Adam was brought on board for intel. I was placed as his assistant to keep him alive and to take down Carter Leeds and his associates. He does a very good job of keeping his hands clean and has made my job quite difficult. Adam took a deal."

"To use me?" Anne snapped.

"No. To gather information about the Leeds and Montgomery families, to possibly lure Carter out of hiding. Adam was instructed to keep you safe."

"Like I said, to use me."

Victoria tugged at her blue nylon coat. "Look, he wasn't supposed to fall in love with you. He jeopardized this case and many lives…." Before Anne could interrupt, Victoria held a hand up, requesting the opportunity to let her finish. Anne nodded. "However, I can't fully fault him. I may be in the FBI, but I don't have a heart of stone. What I'm going to tell you is off the record."

"Okay."

"Adam did what he did to protect you. He couldn't tell you even though he begged to many times, but my superior vehemently denied his request. We knew Carter was alive and unfortunately he has gained some very powerful and dangerous allies."

Anne could barely fill her lungs with enough oxygen to hold herself up. She leaned her trembling frame against the desk. Her mind continued to whirl.

"Anne, are you still with me?"

"Yes," she breathed out.

"Adam is MIA. Do you know where he is?"

"You're the FBI, for God's sake, and you don't know where he is?"

"We assumed he was with you. When we did our sweep of his home, we didn't find anything."

"I was fucking kidnapped by Carter. I've been held against my will for...I don't even know for how long because I don't even know what day it is. Everything is a blur. Isn't that your job to know where he is?" Anne remembered the bank receipt. "Didn't you know he pulled a ton of money from a bank account? I was here five minutes and found a receipt; obviously you didn't look very hard."

She grabbed the paper, holding it up to Victoria whose face scrunched as she read the small print.

"Shit! He probably had an offshore account we didn't know about," Victoria barked.

Anne paced the room, trying to figure out where Adam would go. *What is Carter's plan? To meet Adam? Why the money? Shit.*

"That's why Carter kidnapped me. Ransom money," Anne said, barely above a whisper.

Victoria stared at Anne. "What?"

"He's going to give Carter ransom money for my kidnapping. It's the only thing that makes sense. But why?"

"Leeds Imports and Construction is bankrupt."

Anne's brain was swimming. She had to find Adam, and standing there with Victoria wasn't doing any good.

"I'm going to Leeds Imports and Construction. Maybe they're meeting there." Anne pushed past Victoria.

She gripped Anne's arm, halting her mid-stride. "Carter wants him dead, and Adam's walking right into a trap. You need to stay here."

Anne yanked her arm free. FBI agent or not, she was tired of being man-handled. "I'm going to find Adam before Carter does. This has to end."

"I can't let you do that."

"Watch me."

"Anne. Do I have to arrest you?"

"Only I know what to say to Carter. He'll listen to me. Please, Victoria. I need to do this. I know what I'm doing, trust me," Anne pleaded as Victoria stared at her, gnawing on her lower lip.

"Go. We'll keep trying to locate Adam and will be at Leeds soon with back up. Don't make me regret this, Anne. We all have a lot on the line."

She nodded. Anne swiftly located Adam's spare key for his newly restored 1967 cherry-red Ford Mustang Shelby convertible. The car sat in all its vintage glory under a large black tarp in the car port next to the garage. Anne pulled the heavy nylon covering off the flashy red splendor and slid into the black leather driver's seat. The roar of the engine growled like a lion ready to pounce. The thin, snake-like steering wheel felt peculiar in her hands as she backed out of the parking spot.

Anne was such a fool. She had believed Carter over her own fiancé. Carter had abandoned her, Adam had saved her, and what did she do? She turned around and abandoned him. Her chest flared from rage to sorrow. She wondered if this is how her mother felt when she was driven insane—to the point of no return—by Anne's father. Maybe that's what she needed to finally rid herself of Carter—a little insanity.

CHAPTER FOURTEEN

The moon sat high in the velvet sky, only occasionally covered by black clouds. A few droplets of rain raced down the windshield while distant lightning lit up the city. Silently, Anne prayed that she would make it in time to save Adam. In his own way, he had been protecting her. She had made a deal with the devil the moment Carter held her in his arms and soothed her worries with a lullaby of deception. The very thought of their intimate encounter made her shudder with repulsion.

The drive to Leeds Imports and Construction seemed endless. Flashes of electricity broke through the black clouds, illuminating the large brick building. The parking lot was empty; all was quiet. She pulled around to the back of the building where the barbed-wire fence separated her from the tan metal door. Leaving Adam's prized possession parked in the darkness, she walked along the side of the building where she had noticed a gap between the fencing and brick wall. She slinked through without difficulty and pulled on the door, but it was locked tight.

"Damn it," Anne hissed.

Approaching three two-story dock entrances, she saw that one was slightly open. Lowering her body to peer through the thin slit, she could see nothing but darkness. Hoisting herself onto the damp concrete slab, Anne pushed her body through the tight opening, sucking in her stomach until her ribs grazed the bottom of the massive steel door.

The substantial warehouse was intimidating. Rows of metal shelves stacked with cardboard boxes and pallets filled the space. The reverberation of rumbling thunder echoed through the solid walls. *Inhale, exhale,* she reminded herself while she lightly walked through the open void. She was exposed in the vastness, which sent dread through her bones. Once again, she felt hunted. A set of metal stairs led her to a rickety mezzanine that eventually opened up to the offices of Rita, Steven, and, at one time, Carter. Anne placed her ear to Carter's office door, listening for any type of noise or a voice. A crash of thunder shook the wooden door frame. With an unsteady hand, Anne turned the door handle and eased it open; the office was empty.

It was as if she stepped into a time machine; she had not crossed the threshold into this space since Carter's vanishing act. His taste was very old world; his office was decorated with large, intricately designed wooden pieces and burgundy and bronze fabrics in paisley patterns. His smell lingered; *he's been here,* he was possibly still watching her from a distance, biding his time until she was completely vulnerable.

In the corner of the office stood a cherry armoire. Anne tugged at the black pulls, but it was locked. She yanked on the door again, breaking the latch as she tried to steady her balance. Papers, photos, and letters were stacked in the wooden enclosure. Through the flashes of lightning that flickered through the pane of glass above her, she could see faces of his family, Sam, and other friends.

The glossy photos revealed a time of laughter and smiles. In one picture Carter had hoisted Anne over his shoulder on a beach in the Bahamas. They had just gotten out of the water, his dark waves were cut shorter, his wet hair spiked in every direction. Their faces were scrunched from laughing; she remembered that trip vividly. She remembered all their vacations—Italy, Australia, Brazil. *Was their family business going under then?* She felt the pearls that laid around her neck and drifted back to a time of happiness....

In front of the beautifully lit Eiffel Tower, Carter handed her a blue box. "Merry Christmas, my Anneliese."

She gasped, feeling the cold Paris night air fill her lungs. She took off her gloves to open the gift. The string of pearls reflected the holiday lights that surrounded them. It was magical and enchanting.

Carter lifted the necklace. "Turn around."

Anne did so as she gathered up her hair. She smiled, while watching the pearls come into sight and then land against her skin. The sensation of each pearl trailing her neck as Carter pulled the strand back to fasten them sent excitement through her.

Carter lowered his lips near her ear. "Pearls are powerful, Anneliese. Queen Elizabeth and Cleopatra draped themselves in the exquisite ocean wonders for wisdom and protection."

Anne leaned against him and laughed. "I'm no queen, Carter."

"You are to me...."

A tear trickled down her cheek as she dropped the photos, yanking herself back to the present. Her eyes lowered to the stack of papers. She caught the glint of a something shiny. Anne picked up the gold band, holding it carefully with her index and thumb. Examining the band, her eyes squinted at markings on the inside. *I need more light.* She turned on the floor lamp that stood near her.

It cast a soft glow over her hand as she held the ring closer to the light. The gold was speckled with a rust color. With her nail she scrapped at the markings to see them better. They read: *Love, Lien.*

Anne's mouth fell open. "Oh my God. This is Sam's wedding ring."

The ring fell from her hand, bounced and rolled under Carter's old desk. Anne could hear it finally stop against the wall. That was Sam's blood on the ring. She couldn't feel her legs. *Carter killed Sam, he killed his best friend. He's a monster. He betrayed a man that he called a brother, but why?* Her own blood iced over. *Is he going to kill me?*

Anne's erratic breath burned her throat as she watched sheets of rain pounding the window. A flash of lighting streaked across the heavens, before a hand grasped Anne's shoulder, clawing at her collarbone.

She screamed. The undertones of the darkness and faint light revealed a disheveled Adam Whitney. Scruff covered his face. His dark eyes burned into Anne's. Without another word, she lunged into his chest, and the comfort she once knew so well enveloped her. Silently he laid his cheek on top of her still-damp hair. Pulling back, Anne looked up at Adam for a heartening expression; all that she saw was anger and distress. He softly brushed the bruises and scrapes that lined her face. Flinching as he touched the bruise that had surfaced on her cheekbone after her fight with Carter, she placed her hand over his.

"I know what you've done…and Carter," she whispered, lowering her head. "But I also know you were trying to protect me. Victoria told me everything." Tears trailed down her face, salting her pale lips.

Adam brushed them with his thumb. "I'm not proud of what I've done in the past and whom I've dealt with, but I will never regret falling in love with you. Carter will never take that from me."

The stream of emotion continued down her face. She saw, lying at Adam's feet, two large black duffel bags. "I was a ransom, right? He wants money?"

"Yes. He's in a shitload of trouble and needs money. He knew I would give him anything to get you back alive."

That's all I was to Carter—a bargaining tool. "I know. Victoria told me that Leeds Imports and Construction is bankrupt."

Adam shook his head. "Anne, it's more than that, a lot more than that but I can't explain it all right now."

"He killed Sam, his best friend. I found Sam's wedding band with blood all over it. What makes you think Carter will let us live?

"Sam was an idiot, and he didn't have the money. I do."

Anne wanted to ask where Adam got all that money but was too afraid. *Had he killed someone in his past? Adam had told her he had his demons and that she had saved him, but from what?* Her chest tightened, and the pain flowed out of her like a river.

"Why is he doing this?"

"Carter wants power, not you. He's only doing this because he knew how to get to me. He's not who you think he is. He's not Carter Leeds, he's…"

Something or someone stirred a few feet from outside the office, distracting them. Adam placed his index finger to his lips, hushing Anne. Quietly turning on his heels, Adam started to walk toward the noise. Anne extended her hand to stop him, but she was unsuccessful. He neared the frame of the door and peered up and down the corridor, then stepped out to the right. Blood raced through her veins at Mach speed, her nerves became numb, and her skin tingled with anxiety. The silence was abruptly interrupted by sounds of shuffling feet, followed by two ear-splitting gun shots.

"*Adam!*" Anne screamed.

Illuminated by a bolt of lightning, a sinister shadow appeared in the doorway.

CHAPTER FIFTEEN

"No! Shit, Carter, you shot him! What is wrong with you? Oh, God!" Anne screamed through her tears. Her first instinct was to run to Adam, but before she could Carter had stepped in front of her, blocking her way. He lowered the gun to his side.

Carter bared his teeth. "He deserved to die."

"Who are you?" Fright dripped from her every fiber. She was trembling so hard that her muscles were sore from the barrage of spams.

"I know this must appear disconcerting, but it's just business, Anneliese."

She backed away from him and toward the corner of the room. "You kidnapped me for ransom, didn't you? Were you going to kill me if Adam wouldn't have come through?"

He took a step toward her. "I wouldn't hurt you, my Anneliese. I love you, but I knew he'd pay anything for you."

Anne swallowed the bile that continued to rise. "You killed Sam, your best friend. Why Carter? After everything he had done for you."

"He pissed company money away on some worthless whore he met at a club in Hong Kong. I let that go, but he betrayed me by having a secret meeting with the Montgomerys. He was giving me up to them. This was the only way."

"Sam wouldn't do that! You let me think that it was my fault. You allowed me to feed my own guilt. How dare you? No, no, Sam was loyal to you."

Carter chuckled and drew closer to her. Anne slid her back against the wall, slowly inching to the door.

"Everyone claims loyalty but really, words mean nothing. Believe this, your precious Adam was just as bad as me. When he started working for Richard, he didn't know what he was getting himself into. At first he just sat on the sidelines and took notes, but after he saw the money he could make, greed set in along with the hunger to be number one, to be the big shot. Adam was taking bribes, tampering with juries; he was accepting dirty money under the table." Carter extended his arm. "Criminals walk the streets free because of Adam. Aren't you so proud of him?" He motioned toward the black walkway and then she saw it, Adam's body.

Those were Adam's demons. He had made a deal with the FBI, I helped pull him from that corrupt life. That's how I saved him. Our love saved each other. Saved us from the darkness. Adam's life was fading away from the gunshot wounds Carter had bestowed upon him minutes earlier. Her demons spiraled around her, pulling her back into the darkness the closer Adam drew toward death. She wanted to run to him, scream at him for all the hell he put her through, but also tell him that she needed him and loved him. She wanted to beg him to live, to fight for them. She didn't want to go against Carter alone, but it looked like she had no choice. *Let the demons in, Anne. Let the darkness consume you.*

Pushing down every ounce of emotion was torture but necessary. Turning from Adam's dying body, her hooded gaze locked onto Carter. "You owed the Montgomerys money, you stole the money, not Adam. That's why they wanted him to kill you."

Carter laughed. "They never asked him to kill me. I lied because I knew you two were conspiring together. Granted they wanted me dead, thanks to Adam and his shit scheme in Chicago. When the investment went sour, I had to get out of there but Adam, oh, he decided that he would hide his millions and then snitch to the feds. Thought they could protect him," he smirked. "Guess not."

"Carter, we weren't scheming together on anything. I had no idea this was going on, and I would never be part of something like this. That is blood money. Is that why you did this? Because your family business is bankrupt? Were you trying to save it?"

"No. I'm the one who bankrupted it, with the help of my dear mother. She's just as naïve as you."

Anne's tears evaporated from the heat radiating from her face. "You're sick. Why the hell would you do that?"

"Because I have the power to do so."

Every thunderous crack caused the wall Anne was leaning against to vibrate, pulsating through her from the inside out. Carter lunged toward Anne, pinning her against the wall. His hot breath was unyielding along her neck; her heart thumped through her veins, almost throbbing as he pressed his weight into her.

"My Anneliese, we could have taken over the world, just the two of us, but you ruined it. I come back and see that you're on Adam's side, loving him, trusting him. Do you know how that made me feel?" Carter hissed. "Do you?" His russet eyebrows pushed together.

"You lied to me, Carter. You left me. You killed our baby with your lies. It's *your* fault. Did you really think I would go anywhere with you after everything you've done? You drugged me, kidnapped me, and accused me of setting you up. You murdered your best friend and now you've killed Adam. So just do it already—kill me. I would rather be with Adam in death, than with you alive on this earth."

She could hear his teeth gnashing together; the gun shaking in his hand. He dug his other hand into her dirty blonde locks, as he exhaled hard. A small whimper fell from her lips while her head pressed hard into the wall.

"Why must you push me? I love you so much it exhausts all rational thoughts. I know what I must do and if you won't be with me, you won't be with anyone. I'll grant your request, but a life without you—that will truly kill me."

"Good," Anne seethed.

He lowered the gun toward the floor. She lifted her right knee, slamming it into his groin. He bent over in agony, and his grip on the gun loosened. She kicked it from his hand; it flew back, hitting the opened armoire. Anne dashed toward the mezzanine that led to the warehouse, her feet stumbling beneath her. She was just a few feet from the stairs when her entire body arched backwards, like she was convulsing in mid-air. Her spine crashed into the metal floor. Searing pain shot through her body like an electric shock. Carter hovered over her, his face distorted like the devil himself had just been released. His fingers wrapped themselves around her slender neck. In one swift movement, she was being hoisted off the ground onto her tip-toes. As her air supply lessened, Anne continued to fight Carter off.

She snatched a handful of his wavy mane right from the roots. Carter flinched, dropping Anne against the mezzanine's top railing, her lower back slamming against the unforgiving metal. Ignoring the pain, Anne's survival mode surged through her as she blindly began attacking the man she once cherished more than anyone in the world, the man she would have died for. Her arms flailed ahead of her, landing punches, scratches, and gashes to Carter's face.

Time stopped in the breath of a second, a cry escaped from Anne's mouth. Her hands released the final thrust while Carter's body twisted over the mezzanine's railing. She staggered forward. Carter grasped the top railing with his right hand, clinging to it, white-knuckled from the pressure of holding up his six-foot-three-inch frame with one hand. Anne leaned over the metal and stared into Carter's blackened eyes, searching into the depths of his soul to find any good, any remorse at all. Her hands wrapped themselves around the chipped blue railing.

"Anneliese, please help me. I can't hold on." Carter begged between grunts.

Darkness surrounded them, the spider web of white flashes from outside reflected inside Carter's sapphire eyes. Flashes of their life together, of a love she thought protected her from all the evils of the world tore through her mind. He was her pain, her suffering, her loss.

"Farewell, Carter."

Flinching at her words, his struggle continued, his grip began to slip. Suddenly, his hand flew through the darkness, reaching for her neck. Anne jerked back as Carter's fingers became entangled in her pearls. The delicate strand ripped apart, sending iridescent white pearls flying beneath them. Carter's body began free-falling down into the infinite blackness. She quickly realized, so was hers.

Anne's life halted, and everything happened in an instant. Her memories suspended around her in the warehouse. From out of nowhere, Adam lunged over the railing, reaching for her, screaming her name, but he couldn't reach her in time. She could see his tortured face. He pulled out a cell phone, screaming at someone in the receiver. Anne couldn't hear him, her vision failing as her body crashed into the cold cement below.

An excruciating pain electrified through her, deflating her lungs. A tunnel of black began closing in. Before succumbing to her fate, she willed her eyes to shift to her side. Carter lay beside her, motionless. Relief washed over her with the knowledge that he was dead. She could let go. Silently, she said goodbye to Adam and then, there was nothing…nothing but peace.

CHAPTER SIXTEEN

"Can you hear me, Anne?" Dr. Rasmussen asked. Blinding white light burned Anne's corneas while Dr. Rasmussen examined her. She could hear the humming of machines and feel the cool oxygen being pushed up inside her nose. A metallic taste coated the back of her throat. He glanced at each eye, his own eyes reflecting worry. That was not comforting at all. Her body ached and throbbed. It hurt to even breathe. She willed her voice to come forth but it rebelled.

"Can you feel this?" Dr. Rasmussen squeezed her hand. Anne could see in her peripheral vision that various tubes and wires twisted over her pale skin. She could feel him but couldn't respond, as if the muscles in her jaw were frozen. *Why can't I talk? What is going on?*

"Calm down, Anne, you're all right. It's good that you're responding."

Anne concentrated on the liver spots that dotted Dr. Rasmussen's hand. *Why can't I move? Am I paralyzed? Where's Adam? Is Carter dead?*

"Listen to me, Anne, this is good news. You're making progress."

Anne could feel his warm hand pat hers. A nurse swept in with a syringe and administered the contents into the IV. A wave of euphoria overtook her, calming her muffled hysterics.

"Good morning, Anne, my name is Judy. I'm one of your nurses. This will help you relax, okay?"

She quickly checked Anne's vitals, a cuff squeezing and releasing her forearm. Anne tried to focus her eyes back on Dr. Rasmussen. "Anne, you fell, quite far actually, you've been in a coma for three weeks. You have bruised ribs and a pelvic fracture, and there was swelling in your brain. If you understand what I'm telling you, could you blink for me?"

Anne coaxed her heavy lids to do as she was asked.

"Good girl."

Polaroid flashes of that night lit up her mind. She had found Adam. Carter had killed him then tried to kill her. Carter had clung to the railing before reaching for her. She'd lost her balance and tumbled over the railing, falling toward the concrete floor. She thought she had seen Adam, with grief etched across his face. *But how could that be? Carter had shot him.*

Dr. Rasmussen stepped to the side, revealing her therapist, Dr. Lindsey, standing rigidly in the corner. His face held a look of melancholy, but he gave Anne a smile. She observed their whispered exchange, and then Dr. Rasmussen was gone. Dr. Lindsey cautiously approached her hospital bed. His typical therapist façade was non-existent. He looked like just another middle-aged man wearing jogging pants and a T-shirt.

Come on, move damn it. Scream. Do something. God, please. Please help me. She could feel a tear escape, trailing slowly down her cheek. Dr. Lindsey sat down in a small blue chair, and then he wiped her tear away.

"Oh, Anne, I know you are frustrated. I can see that you want to move and talk so badly but you can't." He paused. "You're in a private facility being cared for by the best doctors in the country. Your recovery will depend on how badly you want retribution. Blink once if you understand what I'm saying."

Retribution? She blinked, leading him to go on.

"Carter survived."

Those two words set her machines off as her blood pressure rose quickly.

"Anne, calm down or the medical staff will come in again. Everyone here is under Carter's thumb. You must stop. Control your breathing."

She tried to focus on Dr. Lindsey's soft voice, just as she did during their many therapy sessions. Her muscles trembled at the thought of Carter still roaming this earth alive. She had survived—why not him? *He never dies. The man had nine lives.* The machines slowly quieted while Dr. Lindsey looked toward the door and back to her.

"He's more mobile than you are, but that's due to the medication they are giving you. They are keeping you incapacitated until Carter gives the go-ahead. He has a plan and, unfortunately, you're right in the middle of it all. I will try to keep you as safe the best as I can because I have a plan of my own."

Anne blinked to show him she understood everything he was telling her. *What plan? What is Carter going to do to me?*

"Adam is alive as well."

Thank God. She *had* indeed seen him. The tears began again. Dr. Lindsey dabbed them with a tissue. She knew

Adam was safe and under FBI protection. Victoria wouldn't let anything happen to him.

"I know you are worried about him, but you need to worry about yourself right now. Once Carter executes his plan, there's no going back. I need you to trust me. Do you trust me, Anne?"

What was she going to do? She had no choice but to trust him. She blinked, but already regretted her decision.

Dr. Lindsey nodded. "Rest, Anne. You're going to need all your strength for what lies ahead."

CHAPTER SEVENTEEN

Nine days had passed since she awakened. Each morning the nurses would scribble the date over on the white board near the door. Through Anne's glazed-over eyes, she watched them inject more medication into her IV. *I don't need anymore. Stop, please.* Her pleas were bound inside of her, so the nurses never heard Anne's cries. As the room morphed into a hallucination of ethereal shadows, her eyes rolled with heavy blinks until Anne was floating away into the medicinal high.

After what felt like seconds, Anne could hear lowered voices over the whoosh of her heartbeat thrumming from the machine beside her. Her temples throbbed. Her lips felt hot. Sheets washed in harsh detergent rubbed against her skin, irritating Anne's ivory flesh. How she desperately wanted to scratch her arms and legs. Anne was disorientated and detached from the world around her, but the voices grew louder.

"I don't want to hear his name from this day on, do you understand me?" Anne heard Carter say.

"I'll put him in a place where Anne can't find him. But, know that Anne won't bend to your will so easily," she heard Dr. Lindsey respond.

"Then I guess you need to manipulate her mind a little bit more than normal, David. I want *my* Anneliese."

She opened her heavy eyes to find Carter and Dr. Lindsey hovering over her. The debilitating medicine continued to drip into her IV, paralyzing all muscle function. Carter steadied himself on crutches, she could see stitches running along the nape of his neck and the skin covering his cheekbones was blotched purple and blue. He locked his wicked irises on hers.

"Good morning, my Anneliese. How are you feeling?"

He knew she couldn't reply. Anne's muscles tensed, but she couldn't move them. Her chest rose and fell as if to build up a scream, but nothing would come out.

"Come now, don't look so forlorn. What I have planned for you is brilliant. Consider yourself lucky that I'm even keeping you alive after what you've done to me."

"Carter," Dr. Lindsey spat out.

"Shut up." Carter shot a glare across her bed. "Since your mother was just as fucked in the head as you, this will work out perfectly."

Tears spilled out of her at the sound of his vile words, but he continued mercilessly.

"It's amazing how readily you can locate certain drugs and medications—for the right price, of course. You are pumped full of so many fucking meds, I'm amazed you're still breathing." Carter moved closer to her, evil rolling off of him. "You will be my puppet, Anneliese. You'll do whatever I say, and your sweet Adam will mean nothing to you. I'm going to suck all the oxygen from your lungs and replace it with mine. Your blood will call out to me." He stroked her wet cheek. "You will belong to me.

"Otherwise, you'll watch me slaughter Casey and her entire family. It'll be your fault. I'll slit their throats and not think twice about it."

She blinked, conceding to his insanity. She had no other choice. The vision of Casey, her husband Tony, and their innocent children's lifeless bodies was her undoing. Internally, her body thrashed from his threats. It convulsed. It screamed. It begged for death. She lay still while the inner war raged, consuming her soul.

"A lot has changed since you've been asleep. You see, Carter Leeds did die all those years ago but Carter Montgomery is alive and well."

Carter Montgomery?

"I've reunited with my true family, a reconciliation in the works for some time. The best thing my mother did all those years ago was spread her legs to Simon Montgomery. Unfortunately, he didn't believe that I was his and walked away from her. All these years, Steven believed I was his but I think he suspected. He always treated me like a nuisance, an inconvenience, until I was making him money. My mother finally confessed her sins, and I set out a course to become a Montgomery."

Carter rose from her hospital bed and hobbled over to the window. *That's what Adam meant when he said that Carter Leeds isn't who he says he is. I thought the Montgomerys hated the Leeds.*

He turned to Anne. "I know what you are thinking; I can see your mind is working hard to piece it all together. While you were playing the doting girlfriend to Adam for the past two years, I've been busy building my own personal empire. With the help of a DNA test, I was able to prove to Simon that I was in fact his son. Montgomery Hotels Incorporated needed new blood, and sadly, Simon Montgomery recently had a stroke and is completely incapacitated."

Carter laughed while maneuvering on his crutches back over to Anne. Her heart pounded against her ribcage. *Like me.*

"Legal documents show that the eldest son, in the case of a medical emergency, becomes acting CEO of Montgomery Hotels Incorporated. I'm the eldest son. My brother Michael wasn't too pleased with the arrangement at first, but he's come around. You see, Anneliese, I have all the power. I snap my fingers, and people do as I say. As will you."

I never will. Anne closed her eyes and took a breath that stung her lungs. She no longer wanted to look at the monster Carter had become.

"There is nothing left for you here. Your apartment has been sold, your belongings are in storage, we are moving to Savannah, Georgia, and taking Montgomery Hotels Incorporated with us. You will be with me." Carter ran his fingers down her cheek and over her lips. "You will stand beside me, you will love me, and you'll never betray me again or one by one, the people you love the most will die. I want *my* Anneliese." He turned to Dr. Lindsey. "Do it."

Carter brought his lips to her skin, brushing them over her, as though she was Snow White and he was breaking some sinful spell that had been cast upon her. However, the opposite was happening. His kiss was poison. He ticked his head at Dr. Lindsey and hobbled from the room.

Dr. Lindsey sat next to her with a grave expression. "This is the only way. You need to trust me. Are you ready, Anne?"

No. I'm not ready for this. How could anyone be ready for something like this? I'll lose who I am, is revenge worth it? Yes, yes it is

because if I don't, I'll lose Casey, Adam, and God knows who else.
Carter will pay for what he's done.

She blinked with tears streaming down her face.

"I'm sorry I have to do this."

She could see his remorse. Anne wanted to reach out to him and tell him she understood, tell him that she knew he didn't have a choice. Just like she didn't have a choice.

"Anne, close your eyes and listen to my voice. Let it take you away, like an ocean current...."

His hypnotic voice towed her deeper and deeper, until his soothing commands breached her subconscious.

CHAPTER EIGHTEEN

Time elapsed in blurred fragments. Minutes bled into hours, which bled into days, then months. It was another world filled with light and darkness but mostly darkness. The city around Anne continued on as she stood still in a hell built by Carter. Every day was orchestrated by him. Robots that resembled humans entered her room, checking her vitals, wheeling her to physical therapy, and bringing her trays of lumpy mashed potatoes and red Jell-o.

A life that she once knew gradually faded, fallen into an abyss of lost memories and recollections. Voices changed, smiles faded, and stories slipped into the air around Anne, evaporating into nothing.

A full season had passed, the summer sun drew further away from earth as Anne watched from her stiff couch the people below slowly start to adjust their wardrobes. She ached for just one breath of fresh air. She scrutinized the blue-on-white walls and beige furnishings, which blended into a suffocating box. Her confinement had nearly driven her to madness. Each awakening day brought stale morning air with the aroma of vengeance, but a sickness also filled her mind. One that seemingly could not be cured with Dr. Lindsey's hypnotic words or a needle filled with euphoric medication.

There was a soft knock at her door, then Dr. Lindsey entered the room. He sat down on the edge of the hospital bed across from her. Her neck muscles pulled as she craned her neck up to look at him.

"Anne, we need to talk."

"Nothing good ever comes from those words," Anne said, as she pulled her hair up into a loose ponytail.

"The only way I can get you released from here is if you are released into Carter's care."

Her spine stiffened and prickled. "What do you mean by 'released into Carter's care'? I don't need his goddamn care. What does he want?"

Dr. Lindsey took in a deep breath. "When we first began our sessions—after your miscarriage—I had jotted down notes about your condition and possible diagnoses...."

"Yeah, yeah, I get it. Skip to the part where I need care." Anne's body was heating like an inferno.

"I need you to understand. Just hear me out. I began your hypnosis to help you cope with the loss of your baby and Carter. You were obsessed with locating him. You would travel to the state park every weekend and I became worried, concerned about your condition. You sank into a deep depression when there was no hope for recovering Carter's body." Dr. Lindsey shook his head and closed his eyes for a moment. "I was so worried for you, Anne. So worried—"

Anne shot up from the couch. Her muscles pulled and ached around her still-healing bones. "You thought I was going to kill myself, didn't you?" Her neuropsychiatric brain kicked into overdrive and put it all together. "Because of my family history. What my mother did to herself." Anne looked down at her wrists. "I wanted to save her, I did. But, letting her go was what I had to do. Her sick mind needed rest, and there was nothing else I could do for her." She looked at Dr. Lindsey. "I would never do that to myself. I would never take my own life."

Her door flew open and caused Anne and Dr. Lindsey to jump. Carter crossed the threshold and closed the door behind him. He gave her a smug look while moving closer to her. Tears pricked her eyes, and the sensation burned deep into the back of her skull.

"You," Anne growled. "What have you done?"

"I'm simply looking out for your mental well-being."

Anne could feel the world falling away from her. Despair swallowed her whole. *Why would Dr. Lindsey be all right with this? Is this his plan? He promised me. He promised he would protect me.* Tears trailed down her cheeks, her legs trembled beneath her.

"You will be released to me, as my wife, and once that is completed, we will leave this God-forsaken city and start fresh."

Her fists tightened. "No."

"No? That's not an option. I warned you months ago what would happen." Carter spoke sternly. "You have a long history of mental issues. Dr. Rasmussen confirmed it as did Dr. Lindsey. You will marry me, Anneliese, or not only will I slit Casey from navel to nose, I'll throw your crazy ass into an institution where you'll rot away. I have the entire legal system in my back pocket." Carter tapped his chin "A certain judge owes me a favor."

What could Anne do? Carter had her trapped, again. He wanted to break her, rebuild her to be what he wanted, what he desired. Carter was power-driven in the illicit corporate world. And now he wanted to own her, to control her.

She glared at Carter with red swollen eyes. "Fine. I'll marry you."

Anne silently cursed her mother, who seemed to be tormenting her from her grave.

~

After her morning shower, Anne stared at her pallid reflection. *This is not my skin, my hallow eyes, or my thoughts that roam inside of my head.* The ends of her hair split and curled under the fluorescent lights. She had the appearance of a mental patient, unkempt and lost.

Anne's memories moved through her brain like an old black-and-white movie. The edges were torn and faces blurred and bled into each other. She wasn't Dr. Anne Jamison; that woman was gone. *Maybe I am like my mother.* Anne's mother had been ill before she became pregnant with her, but it was when Anne's father didn't want to be part of their lives that her mother plunged off the rational cliff. The memory of Anne stroking her mother's matted hair after one of her hysterical fits ripped into her heart.

She ran the palm of her hand over her now-healed rib cage, but winced at the memory of how she received the life-threatening injuries. *He tried to kill you, Anne. He wanted you dead. He has given you no reason to love him.* Anne scolded herself while lifting her hand from her ribs to the raised scar that ran from behind her ear to the base of her skull. *Feel what he has done to you.*

Admitting to herself that Carter was her sickness, her disease, was enough to make her want to throw her body from the roof of the towering building, to plummet to her death and have the people of Minneapolis discover the virus that had overtaken her. Her blood would flow from her broken body and pool around it in a puddle of crimson, and his reflection would be there. Carter's infection played tricks on her mind, forcing her to recall times they had shared together, reminding her of their all-consuming love—a love tainted with lies and deception.

I refuse to be weak and pathetic like her. No man will ever take me down. She allowed the demons to control her. I'm joining mine. They're my allies against the devil himself. Dr. Lindsey walked in, he was fiddling with his silver cuff links. "Carter's on his way." He closed the door behind him and stopped in front of the bathroom door.

Anne shrugged and ran the comb through her long strands, yanking on the last of the snarls that nested near the base of her neck. "I just want you to know that I'm not happy about this arrangement, but I've agreed to it because I have no other choice. He'll either kill Casey or have me permanently committed into a mental institute."

"I know, and I wish there was another solution, but I can only protect you this way. I'm sorry."

"Are you, Dr. Lindsey? Sorry?" Anne tossed the comb in the sink and stormed past him. "I have a hard time believing that, since you have done nothing for months except take your psychiatric hands and dig them deep into my brain and shuffle memories around like a deck of cards. You have taken those memories and the emotions tethered to them and hid them in some dark hole in my mind so I can't find them. But, you're sorry?"

Dr. Lindsey moved closer to her, but she remained still. Her anger had been festering like the infected scratches on her thighs.

"I'm doing this to protect you from Carter. Please understand this is the only way. I have been your therapist for a very long time and Carter needs to see that I'm on his side, but, Anne, I'm always, always on yours," Dr. Lindsey said.

She shook her head. His words were starting to hold little merit with her. "I want to believe you but…" Anne's words scattered around her and crashed into the heavy wooden door that Carter had just thrown open. His domineering presence filled the space between Anne and Dr. Lindsey and halted any further conversation about what brought them to this moment. The man who was walking toward her was not the same man she had fallen in love with all those years ago. Though his outer appearance was still smooth and sexy, with his olive skin and chiseled features, the monster that dwelled behind his gleaming eyes and perfect smile was hidden well.

"Nice of you to dress for the occasion," Anne spat out, as her eyes roamed over Carter's casual attire but pulled the itchy baby-blue hospital gown away from her frame. "Not that my attire is any better."

Carter stood before her and tucked a stray strand of hair behind her ear. He ran the tip of his finger along her jawline. Her immediate reaction was to back away, but something always pulled her toward him. Carter snaked his arm around her waist and pulled her closer.

"Don't start, Anneliese. It's our wedding day. I'll have you know that no matter what you wear, you are beautiful." His fingers splayed over her lower back, pressing her even closer to him. His lips lingered on her forehead. "Don't ruin this occasion. After today, you will be my wife, forever. You are *my* family and I am *yours*."

I will never be yours. Anne swallowed the emotion that was thickening inside her throat.

"Casey's my family," she whispered.

Carter tensed against her chest and she wanted to push him away from her, but she kept her arms limp. He released a deep breath; his lips trailed her hairline and stopped at her ear.

"Not if she's dead."

Tears burned behind Anne's eyes, and a cry slipped from her mouth. *Is this what I deserve for not seeing the evil behind his eyes? Is this my punishment? No. No, I don't deserve this. He has taken my life from me, but I won't allow him to take Casey's.* She tried to contain the tremors that shook beneath her skin.

"You will learn to love me again, my sweet Anneliese," Carter said while he stroked her hair. "Soon you'll be out of this facility and in our new home in Savannah. You'll love it there."

This was the trickery with which her mind would amuse itself. She would lean into his deceptive affections. He showed her pictures of their new home, introduced her to her very own driver, offering glimpses into a make-believe life. A life Carter led to her to think she was free to roam around in but she wasn't. Anne was a brainwashed, caged bird.

Anne sucked in the toxic air that drifted around them; it sobered her. The heated energy surged through her veins.

Carter took half a step back so he could see her face. Slowly, he fished something from his front pocket. With a closed fist, he lifted it to chest level and opened his palm like a rose in bloom, and at the center was a ring with a large, round, black diamond encircled by smaller white diamonds. The diamonds continued down the platinum band and stopped midway.

The ring took Anne's breath away. She couldn't help but be captivated by the large gem; she was drawn to its exquisiteness. She had never laid her eyes upon a black diamond but found it most fitting to her situation.

"Where did you find this?" Anne breathed.

"It was a gift from a dear friend of mine, and it will look perfect on your finger. Perfect for my queen."

The electric red numbers on the clock read early afternoon but also the hour Anne succumbed to the devil. Carter slipped the black diamond on Anne's ring finger while he vowed "till death do us part." The moment the ring came to rest on her finger, it became one with Anne. The darkness webbed beneath it. Anne could have sworn the ring had its very own heartbeat, one she felt thumping hard against her skin. The elderly Justice of the Peace asked Anne to repeat after him. She did as she was told, with cracked lips and a tongue thick as wool.

"To have and to hold, from this day forward, for better, for worse, for richer, for poorer, in sickness and in health, to love and to cherish, till death do us part." Anne spoke but shifted her gaze to look at each man who stood in that room witnessing the corrupt ceremony.

She had been betrayed by Dr. Lindsey and Carter. Dr. Lindsey told her to trust him. He had promised her retribution, but he encouraged this matrimonial union. Anne was an island; she trusted no one. Each one of them had thrust his hands down her throat and ripped her heart right from its chambers. Anne could taste the treachery being pulled up out of her mouth and it left behind bitterness. *I will do to Carter what he has done to me,* Anne plotted behind her flint-green eyes. Her lips curled at the thought. Carter mistook that for approval and bent down to place his lips upon hers. Anne allowed the gesture, but every cell inside her was imploding.

CHAPTER NINETEEN

The sound of a cork being pulled sent giddiness through Anne. She was in desperation to numb her raw emotions. The perky flight attendant poured the merlot and carefully handed a glass to her. "Here you are, Dr. Montgomery. Is there anything else I can get you?"

What a foreign name that was to Anne. Though she had been a Montgomery for nearly two months, it still sounded peculiar in her mind. Oddly, people treated her differently. She was addressed as "ma'am" or "Dr. Anneliese Montgomery," which she found to be a mouthful.

"No, thank you."

Anne took the wine glass in hand. The dark red liquid screamed to her *drink me*. With a tip of the glass, Anne drank down the merlot, releasing a moan. Anne rested her head back against the plush leather headrest, looking out of the private jet window.

Fleecy clouds patched the light blue sky like a quilt. The farmland below looked miniscule as a thin river snaked between the fields. Anne's farewell to Casey had nearly torn her in two. The memory started to fill the small oval with a sea of burnt oranges, golden yellows, and fiery reds....

The brilliant colors swept across the Riverfront District. Autumn crept into the city along with its nippy winds that tickled the vibrant leaves. The mid-afternoon sun felt welcoming on Anne's face as she let the fresh fall air enter her lungs. She had two of her smaller windows open just enough to let the breeze freshen the musty office space. It had been six months since she stepped a foot into her office.

Now that it was time for her to leave Minneapolis, Carter released Anne with specific instructions. She was to travel directly from the rehab facility to her office, pack up her things, and say goodbye to Casey. Carter had sent an entourage with her to make sure his instructions were followed perfectly.

"Anne, what the hell are you doing?"

She exhaled and turned to look at her best friend. Casey's arms were crossed and she looked confused.

"I'm packing up the rest of my office, Casey."

"I'm not an idiot. I can see that but what I want to know is—why? Why are you doing this? I don't see or hear from you for months and then one day you call to tell me you're married and moving to Georgia. What the hell, Anne? I'm your best friend and you get married to Carter?"

"Carter came back for me, this is what I want. We are going to run Montgomery Hotels Incorporated together, as husband and wife."

Casey stared at her like she was an alien. "I don't even understand what you're saying? You're leaving everything behind, your patients, the Mayo Clinic study, me, for Carter? Did you know that Leeds Imports and Construction closed?"

Anne had. Carter had sucked it dry like a vampire.

"I did. Rita and Steven were compensated generously. In fact, they are settling into their new life somewhere far from here."

"Is that what Carter does? Threatens, manipulates, and robs people of their lives, forcing them to start new lives elsewhere?" Casey laced her fingers with Anne's. "What has he done to you? Where's my best friend?"

It was killing Anne not telling her. The agony of it was ripping her apart. Tears pricked her eyes.

"One day you'll understand."

Casey yanked Anne's ring finger up. "I will never understand this."

"Casey, I have to go," she replied sternly and pulled her hand away.

Anne picked up the last box and handed it to one of the bouncer-type men that stood outside her door.

"Meet me in the hallway." They nodded and left the office.

Anne pulled Casey close to her, stopping at the curve of her ear. "I once read that the fastest way to succeed is to look as if you're playing by someone else's rules, while quietly playing by your own."

Backing away she gave Casey a wink, and then walked past her to the waiting entourage.

"Anne?" She heard Casey call out to her, but she was already out the door.

Her stilettos echoed against the tile with an unbridled stride while she tightened the belt on her black trench coat. Once she reached the ground floor, Anne exited the large glass door to the streets of downtown. Ahead of her sat a black Lincoln Town Car; the back door was open.

Before stepping in, she caught sight of an attractive man leaning against the brick wall across from her. His ruffled locks moved with the chilled breeze. And something pulled deep within her. Those familiar dark eyes held her gaze until a baker's truck drove by. The man disappeared once the truck passed. Glancing up and down the dense movements of the street, she couldn't find him. Shrugging, she placed herself gently on the leather seat, and the door was closed by one of the burly men.

Anne fidgeted with the large black diamond that rested heavily on her ring finger while being pulled back to the present. *Casey will forgive me. One day, she'll understand.*

The name Montgomery frightened her at first but now, she planned on taking advantage of the authority it wielded. Slowly she turned her head, resting her eyes on her appointed driver, Robert. He reminded her of what Sam Goodman would have looked like if he had lived long enough to be middle-aged. But Robert's red hair had thinned and revealed a splatter of freckles over his scalp. His formal attire mimicked his demeanor, which Anne found endearing.

A thought brewed in her head. *I wonder if I can trust him?* She had been formulating a plan, what else was she to do while recovering for six months in solitary? Robert raised his eyes from the magazine he had been reading. Embarrassed, she turned back to the window, not really focusing on the vast blue sky but thinking about the obscure entity that seemingly filled her mind. Viewing memories but before she could latch onto them, they would fizzle and disappear. She was truly someone else. Dr. Lindsey had unearthed the darkness that she ran from, and Carter was the catalyst...

Anne's body jerked as the jet hit mild turbulence, effectively releasing her from her musings. The intercom issued a small chime.

"Good afternoon, this is your captain speaking. We will be making our final descent into Savannah, Georgia. Please fasten your safety belts. Thank you."

She fastened her buckle and couldn't dismiss the nausea. *This is it.*

CHAPTER TWENTY

The southern charm had entranced Anne. She took in the beauty that was all around her. It was like she stepped into a tourist brochure as the smell of pumpkin spice spun around Anne, her stomach growling at the aroma. As the sun set behind the tunnel of wiry tree branches that lined Forsyth Park, the glow of orange looked dreamlike, while a saxophone played in the distance.

"Mrs. Montgomery, are you ready?" Anne twisted, Robert held her luggage.

She wiped her sweaty palms on her coat and followed Robert toward the front door of the cornflower-blue Victorian. She tipped her head back at the towering house, three stories tall. Chips of blue paint drifted to her feet. Anne saw it as her haunted, blue birdcage.

The sound of creaky hinges caught her attention as the dark wood door opened, revealing a phantom dressed in Armani. A deep sea of blue fixed on her, before acknowledging Robert.

Carter's fitted dress shirt tightened over his muscles as he walked toward Robert, extending his hand. "Let me help you, Robert." His eyes didn't leave Anne's.

She continued to process her new environment as she slowly walked into the house. Anne's eyes roamed over every wall, corner, and crack. An attack of sneezes overtook her, echoing through the great foyer. Anne covered her face with the back of her hand. She blinked the water from her eyes and sniffed but that made it worse. The taste of dust coated her tongue and throat.

"Carter, this place is filthy." She grimaced while looking at the banner of cobwebs hanging above her head.

Carter and Robert walked past her and over to the staircase that looked more like a deathtrap.

"I've been busy running a million-dollar company, Anneliese. I haven't had time to clean." Carter said while climbing the stairs.

Nice welcome. She huffed and followed them upwards. With each step the wood cracked. Anne was thankful she reached the top without incident. The musty hallway was lined with old wallpaper and closed doors on either side of her. Cracked plaster led her eyes down the passageway and over a line of naked light bulbs. Carter stopped at the end of the hall and opened the last door on the left. Robert disappeared into the room. She swallowed hard. *Dr. Lindsey promised that I wouldn't have to share a bedroom with him.* Her lead feet moved toward Carter.

He stared at her with no emotion, raising his arm. "Here's your room."

My room? She turned and stopped at the doorway. A plain yellow bedroom with antique oak furniture. Opposite of her was a set of French doors that led onto a private balcony.

Carter put his hand at the small of her back, gently pushing her deeper into the bedroom. "Good 'ol Dr. Lindsey instructed me that sharing bedrooms at this juncture of your recovery would be detrimental. But I expect you to fulfill your wifely duties as soon as possible."

Anne bit the inside of her cheek to prevent from cringing.

"Robert, leave us." Carter said with a clipped tone.

Robert laid the last suitcase on the bed, nodded, and left the room. Anne fidgeted with her wedding ring as she turned. She ran her thumb nail over each small diamond, she felt fatigue start to overcome her, but her focus needed to be sharp, especially since she was now alone with Carter.

His lean form stood rigid, his hands hung at his sides. Carter looked at her with a withering gaze.

"I want to discuss some things with you. First, you are my wife; your loyalty lies with me. You will listen to me not only here at home but during business functions as well. Until I can trust you, your access to others will be limited."

Anne firmly placed her hands on her hips. "Trust me?" she laughed. "That's rich. And I do believe you've shoved these expectations down my throat enough. You've made it clear that I'm your prisoner."

His narrow nose flared. "You aren't my prisoner, you're my wife. Do I need to also remind you about the consequences?"

"No." Anne grinded her teeth. "Your threats have been received."

Carter approached her, tracing his finger down her jaw-line. She lifted her chin in defiance.

"May I continue or are you going to make your home-coming unpleasant?"

With a cynical expression creasing her forehead, she took a deep breath in. "Go on."

Carter dropped his hand and walked past her to the French doors. She twisted her body, crossing her arms over her chest.

"Your duties at Montgomery Hotels Incorporated will be to network for the company, reach out to investors and vendors. All correspondence will be monitored. Also, I'm having a business dinner at the Kensington Hotel next month. You are in charge of the entire dinner and arranging travel for our guests." Carter ran a hand through his russet waves. "This dinner is extremely important, Anneliese."

She detected uneasiness from him. "May I ask what this business dinner is about, since I'm in charge of it?"

"Just know that extremely influential guests will be attending. Everything needs to be perfect."

"Who's attending?" Anne asked.

"Marcus Hunt, the controlling partner of Hunt & Williams Law Firm. Magda Alves, CEO of Alves Logistics, and my brother, Michael."

Anne saw her newly appointed position as an advantage. She would be able to research on the attending guests and Carter wouldn't suspect anything, but she would have to be smart about it.

"I can see that your trip has left you drained. I'll go over all the business documents with you tomorrow. I'll be traveling to Atlanta to visit Simon."

"What? Simon's in Atlanta?" He approached Anne, tension breaking the surface. "Yes, I want to make sure my father is as comfortable as possible. He's in a private facility receiving the best treatment possible for his condition."

She knew Carter was behind Simon's stroke. He was Carter's prisoner as well. *Will we all be able to escape or will we die trying?*

CHAPTER TWENTY-ONE

On her first morning in the Victorian prison, Carter couldn't resist humming a threat in her ear before departing to Atlanta, "Misbehave while I'm away and Casey's dead."

His threats set her blood aflame. With a clenched jaw, she complied. But Anne had other plans. She needed to get to Michael Montgomery, undetected. Robert was her only option. Once Carter's vehicle was out of sight, she searched the grounds for her driver.

A footpath led her through overgrown shrubs and grass and to a white shed that was covered with spun webs and ivy. Anne knelt down as she walked, swiping at the unruly landscape that brushed against her leggings. Cautiously side-stepping for fear she would step on a snake or spider, Anne finally reached the shed opening that was shaded by oak trees. She lightly tapped on the termite chewed wood. Robert jerked up, dirt covered his white shirt. What little hair he had left had fallen over his right eye.

Robert brushed the strands away. "Yes, Mrs. Montgomery. What can I do for you?" He stepped over a rusty rake holding a gasoline can.

"I have a favor to ask of you. And you can say no because this favor, I need you to keep secret—from my husband."

He set the gasoline can down and brushed his hands off. "What do you need?"

"I need you to contact Michael Montgomery." Anne picked at the blemished wood frame. "I want to set up a private meeting, and when I say private, I need it to be away from here. Preferably when Carter is out of town. I can't be followed. Can you do that for me?"

Anne was taking a huge risk, but it was one she was willing to take.

"I'll do it right now." Robert spoke without hesitation.

Anne was stunned by his quick response, and though she was apprehensive trusting him with such a secret, she didn't see another way.

"Thank you so much, Robert."

She wanted to hug the dingy man but offered a grin and a squeeze to the arm instead. Before entering back into the house, Anne stopped mid-step. The overwhelming feeling that she was being watched sent the hair on her neck to stand on end.

Anne scanned the road, sidewalks, and trails leading into the park. People roamed throughout the space but none raised a red flag with her. *It's probably Carter's goons watching me.* Her eyes darted around once more; she rubbed the back of her neck. Slowly she crept back into the house, shaking the edgy feeling that she had felt once before when Sam was watching her.

~

A blanket of darkness surrounded the SUV as it went further into rural Georgia. The tires crunched over the rugged gravel road, rocking Anne back and forth in the backseat. With Robert behind the wheel, they arrived at an abandoned schoolhouse that sat on the outskirts of Savannah in an overgrown field of weeds. Robert helped Anne out of the SUV; she grimaced as her feet sunk into the earth.

"When I said away from the house, I didn't mean in a place where they could feed my body to alligators."

Robert quietly laughed. "You're safe, I promise."

An orchestra of crickets and frogs echoed around them in the night. The warped white wooden structure creaked in the cool southern wind while the smell of wet wood and swamp churned Anne's stomach.

She had been surprised that Michael Montgomery had agreed to their meeting so quickly. Anne ran her hands through the cloak of champagne hair that spilled over her shoulders and onto her dark silk blouse. Robert guided her to the dilapidated door of the schoolhouse, which was guarded by a man with heavy stubble and oily dark hair. His stance was stiff and his arms crossed over his bulging chest. The windows of the schoolhouse were concealed beneath layers of dust and grime, but a soft glow flickered through the years of neglect. Anne's heels sunk further into the foul-smelling mud and when she began to fall over, Robert grabbed her arm to steady her. She lifted her mud-covered foot up and groaned as the mud squished between her toes. A screech owl sounded off in the distance. Anne gripped Robert's arm tighter. He couldn't help but chuckle.

"It's just an owl, Mrs. Montgomery."

"I know, but I feel like I'm in the middle of a damn horror film. I certainly didn't dress appropriately for a trek through the swamp. Yuck."

He patted her arm and smiled. "It'll be worth the ruining of your shoes."

"I hope so. I love these heels."

The man at the door smirked and motioned for Anne to lift her arms.

"Raise 'em."

"Why?"

"We don't take chances, sweetheart."

"Right, like I have a rifle hidden up my skirt," she replied, as she placed her hands firmly on her hips.

"Now," the man spat out while he reached forward to yank her arms up.

Anne stepped back. "Don't you dare. I am not about to be man-handled by you."

The man huffed. He was clearly not amused. Anne took a step closer to him. She teetered on the worn wooden steps and raised her hands above her head. He grumbled something and started his pat down. Anne pretended she was at the airport being searched by a trained security guard, not being felt up by a criminal in the middle of a swampy field in Georgia.

Oily strands of hair fell over his forehead while he ran his hands up her legs. Anne cringed at his calloused touch. Once satisfied, he stepped back, opened the rusty-hinged door, and motioned for Anne to go inside. She quickly turned back and looked at Robert, who gestured for her to go in without him.

"I'll be right outside the door," he reassured her.

With a thick swallow, she twisted forward to view the candle-lit school room. The odor of damp, rotten wood and animal decay wafted by her; the plank floor groaned beneath her. She swore she felt the ghosts of children running past her, their little bodies veering close to her in streams of cold air. Four large gas lanterns lit the room, giving just enough light to see the first few steps ahead of her.

Anne saw taut brawny bodyguards dressed in all black standing in each corner of the dim space. They looked like professional wrestlers with their thick necks and shaved heads. The men watched in the flickered illumination as Anne walked deeper into the dingy room. An angular silhouette began to approach her. Anne's heart pounded against her ribcage.

The silhouette morphed into a tall man with tailored black trousers and a crisp, crimson oxford shirt. Anne gasped. *He could pass as Carter's twin.* As he moved closer, she noted a small difference. This man standing before her had fairer skin, but every other feature was the same. Anne was taken off-guard by the uncanny resemblance.

"Are you all right?" he closed the distance between them.

Anne's eyes fluttered. "Um, yes. I'm sorry. It's just that you look—you look like Carter."

"I know. I'm not thrilled about that. Damn DNA." His lips twitched. "It's wonderful to meet you, Anne." Michael Montgomery extended his hand toward her and she accepted it graciously, but she was still in shock.

"Michael, it's a pleasure to meet you, as well. I just can't believe how similar you look to him. You even have your hair pushed to the side just like Carter's."

"I'm going to start feeling insulted soon. Carter and I share a father and he is technically my half-brother, but he's not family." Michael ran a hand through his hair, messing it up a bit. "I have to admit, I was taken aback to hear that you wanted to meet with me in private. Since you didn't contact me directly, I can only assume your husband doesn't know about this?"

"No, he doesn't. I know you have a lot on your plate right now. I do appreciate you meeting with me so quickly, especially since you flew into Savannah yesterday evening."

"Yeah, adjusting to my half-brother's hostile takeover of the family company has kept me quite busy and I haven't been able to see my father, even though he suffered a debilitating stroke, which I am sure you've heard about."

Michael took a few steps away from her. She watched as the flickering light bounced off his body. Anne could clearly see Michael's frustration. *Be careful, Anne.* She reminded herself. She was in the presence of a ruthless man with a savage reputation. Anne needed to tread lightly.

A gust of autumn wind whistled through the rickety rooftop and fluttered around her skirt, swaying the soft fabric against her legs. Her anxiety ticked closer to the surface with each second that passed.

"I apologize, Michael. You know I understand your anger. How is your father doing?"

Michael sighed. "For some reason my dear brother has him tucked away in a private facility in Atlanta. The asshole won't let me see him. Some doctor whose name starts with an *R* cares for him."

"Rasmussen." Anne couldn't help the disdain she attached to each syllable. *Of course Dr. Rasmussen is Simon's*

177

doctor. Anne couldn't reveal the truth about Simon to Michael, not yet anyway.

"Yeah, Dr. Rasmussen updates me via email. The closest I've gotten to him is just inside the door of his room. This whole situation is fucked up." Michael rubbed his eyes with the heel of his palms. "How could my father have been so careless with the company's legalities? He practically handed the company over to Carter on a silver platter. I guess he didn't think his bastard son would crawl out from underneath his mother's skirt to hijack his company."

Anne took two cautious steps toward him. The two of them together against Carter would be her perfect scenario. She didn't care who ran Montgomery Hotels Incorporated, as long as it wasn't Carter. Anne knew how he drove Leeds Imports and Construction into the ground. Anne needed Michael to trust her implicitly even if she didn't return the favor. She no longer trusted a single soul.

"Michael, you'll get the company back. You are the *true* Montgomery son."

"*We'll* get it back."

"No, no, I'm not a Montgomery, just by marriage—if you call this forced arrangement a marriage." Anne gave a small laugh. "And you've just met me."

She felt the weighted black diamond hang on her finger. It was a chain to the devil.

"You mean you didn't marry him out of love, as he claims? Hostile takeover of my company and your life." Michael said, put off. "If we plan on working together, we'll get to know each other in no time. Carter's the enemy. He may technically be the eldest Montgomery son and may have successfully accomplished a hostile takeover, but that's a loophole I plan to close." Michael took a deep breath in. "You know what I want, so what do you want, Anne?"

Her misted eyes roamed every corner of that room. Anne knew if she looked at Michael at that moment, tears would fall and she didn't want her new ally to see her cry.

Anne pushed her shoulders back and blinked the tears away. "I want a life without Carter in it."

"Well, we have common goals then. I can assure you, what was stolen will be returned. I promise you that."

Anne knew very little about Michael and she was placing her trust into his hands, but her instincts led her to believe his promise—a promise she had to believe in. He was a Montgomery, so she knew what he was capable of. He wasn't one of the good guys, but she needed him. What Anne had learned back in Minneapolis about her beloved Carter frightened her to the core. Michael was now her family. Anne's own twisted family tree had long since burned to the ground and was ash beneath her feet.

The only thing she had left of her family was the legacy of her mother's insanity, which Anne feared lay dormant inside of her. The madness pulsed through her veins quietly, phantoms of lunacy waiting to be unleashed. *Am I capable of violence? My mother was.* Anne was snapped from her dark thoughts by the movements of Michael's entourage. The wood cracked underneath their heavy steps. They had moved from their designated corners and now stood near the door. Michael blew out one of the lamps. Wisps of smoke curled in front of him.

Anne walked over to the oil lamp across the room. "When you've spoken to him over the last couple of days, he hasn't suspected anything, has he?" she asked, before extinguishing the light with a puff of air.

"No, our newfound reconciliation has satisfied him. I need to find out why he abruptly moved down here and away from Minneapolis. How is he at home?"

"Decent, and I wouldn't call *that* a home. He has been away for the past two days, but I've kept busy with Montgomery business."

Anne had taken advantage of her Carter-free schedule. When he phoned her, he would ask, "What did you do today, my Anneliese?"

She would reply sweetly, "Networking for the company." Carter seemed pleased by her enthusiasm and proactive demeanor.

"Good. If he believes that you're on board with his scheme, he won't question you. However, I do have a contact of my own monitoring him very carefully."

"May I ask who?" Anne raised her brow.

"Robert. I trust him with my life and now, with yours." Her mouth fell open. That's why he was agreeable in regards to contacting Michael. *What's Robert's plan? Where does he fit into all of this?*

Before Anne could ask more questions, Michael glanced at his gold-banded watch and then motioned to his entourage. Each one lifted an oil lamp. The two left glowing were brought near Anne and Michael. She was thankful for the light. She really didn't want to step on anything dead—or alive, for that matter.

"I have to go. Midnight poker game, twenty-five grand. Want in?"

Anne shook her head. "Oh no, that's too rich for me."

"Not anymore it isn't." Michael smirked.

Anne was smacked in the face with swampy damp air. She raised her hand over her nose and mouth to filter the onslaught of what smelled like decaying reptiles. Robert extended his hand to assist her down the steps.

"Anne, you can contact me night or day. If you come across any information that raises a concern, please contact me and I will do the same."

Anne dropped her hand from her face and extended it to Michael. He didn't hesitate to take it. His skin was hot compared to hers.

"I'm glad that we were able to finally meet and come to an understanding in regards to Carter. I'll be in touch with you soon."

"Goodbye, Anne. Stay safe."

Robert ushered her into the waiting SUV. Once she was secured inside, she contemplated whether or not to ask Robert about his involvement. *Maybe I need to do some digging around on him?* Anne decided to keep quiet, let him come to her. Robert climbed into the driver's seat and brought the engine to life. He cranked the heat on high, and Anne welcomed the blast of warmth.

The little white school house was swallowed up by the night the farther they drove away from it. *My soul was once bright and whole, just like that school house. Little by little it's chipping away, disintegrated by the battering winds. He'll destroy me if I let him.* Anne gazed down at the diamond. It was nearly camouflaged in the black interior of the vehicle, but she felt its presence.

I'll just need to destroy him first.

CHAPTER TWENTY-TWO

The October sunrise crept across the Savannah horizon, sketching the sky in apricot and honey. A breeze of crisp autumn air caressed Anne's face, slowly awakening her from a dreamless slumber. Her body nestled deeper into the plush comforter, protesting, until she heard the crack of the antique rocking chair that was near her bed. Anne's eyes flew open. Without moving, she saw her husband seated in the corner, watching her. Carter rose and moved from the chair to the edge of the bed, but Anne scooted away from him to widen the distance between them.

"Good morning, my Anneliese." He smirked.

Anne's jaw tensed. "What are you doing in here?"

"Do I need a reason to greet my wife in the morning?"

Yes, Anne thought. "I'm surprised to see you. I thought you were returning home tomorrow."

Carter ran his hands through his russet waves, giving off a glint of his platinum band. He caught her glance.

"I enjoy watching you sleep. You look so happy and peaceful. I wish you looked the same when you were awake."

Anne jerked up, letting the covers slide down and puddle in her lap. "How can I possibly be happy when you threaten me every single day?"

"Threaten you? With what?" Carter cocked an eyebrow and leaned in closer to Anne.

"You know damn well with what. You'll murder Casey, or you'll have me committed under false pretenses."

Carter laughed. "Those aren't threats—just reminders of the vows you took and your commitment to me. Speaking of commitments...."

He moved even closer and placed the tips of his fingers at the hollow of her throat. Anne's breath hitched as alarm bells sounded in her brain. She could feel the want rippling from him. His touch sent panic shooting through her and she tried to slip out of the bed, but her legs were tangled in the sheets.

"No, Carter! I'm not ready for that," she said, as she finally scrambled from the bed and backed against the window.

His eyes narrowed. "I need to talk to the great Dr. David Lindsey about that. Not sharing a bed with my wife is bullshit and needs to end. I've waited patiently, Anneliese. We haven't even consummated our marriage yet."

"Jesus, Carter, are you channeling Henry the Eighth? I haven't even lived here for a full three weeks yet. You said you'd give me time. Can I please have my coffee before you start badgering me?"

Carter threw his hands in the air, stood, and walked to the door. Before leaving, he turned back to her. "You and I *will* share a bed, Anneliese, by force if necessary. And that, my love, *is* a threat." Carter smoothed out his black dress shirt and tie. "We need to discuss the business dinner. Be ready in thirty minutes."

Carter and his clipped tone left the room. Anne clenched her fists and ground her teeth; she was tired of his threats. *What am I waiting for?* She shook her head, protesting her thoughts. *Not now. Not now.* What she needed was a shower to wash away his disgusting touch. She walked into the en suite vintage bathroom; the cream honeycomb tile was cold beneath her bare feet. Anne shed her pajamas and stepped into the tub.

Twenty minutes later, she made her way down the forest green hallway. Timeworn yellow, pink, and red wildflowers border stretched along the top of wall. The wooden stairs groaned beneath her black boots while she descended to the main floor of the house. Anne had chosen her skinny black pants and white lace-front top for her meeting with the Kensington Hotel's event coordinator, Natalie Franz, to finalize the menu for the business dinner Carter was hosting.

As she placed her foot on the last of the steps, her peripheral vision caught a hand extending toward her. Anne looked up and in front of her stood Dr. Lindsey, who occupied one of the five bedrooms in the Victorian prison. His once salt-and-pepper hair was now pure salt and he had aged ten years in a mere few months. Carter had that effect on people. He would drain the life from them, leaving them weak and vulnerable. The successful psychologist had left behind his practice and his daughter, Claire. Anne assumed that the same threats were served to him that had been served to her if he did not agree to accompany them to Savannah.

She took his hand. He placed her arm in the crook of his as he led her to the dining room.

He smiled. "Good morning, Anne."

"Good morning, Dr. Lindsey."

"Technically, you are no longer my patient. Please, call me David."

"So, you're here on vacation then?" Anne asked with heavy sarcasm.

"Please. It feels too formal."

"I would rather stick with Dr. Lindsey. You never know—I may need electric shock therapy if Carter continues his morning ambushes. Isn't that why he wanted you to come with us? To keep tabs on his emotionally damaged wife?"

"Anne—" Dr. Lindsey scolded.

"My husband decided to give me a personal wake-up call, badgering me about sharing a bed."

"Yes, I was made aware moments before you came down."

Before they could conclude their conversation, Carter manifested before them.

"Speak of the devil," Anne deadpanned.

"And the devil appears," Carter replied, bowing.

The three of them entered the dining room, where a rustic pedestal table and latticework wooden chairs were gathered underneath a bronzed crystal chandelier. The distressed floral wallpaper from the hallway covered this room as well. Anne hated wallpaper. It looked dingy, covered in dust. Carter held out Anne's chair, placing her between himself and Dr. Lindsey. After sitting down, Carter poured Anne her coffee. She placed the hot porcelain to her lips and sipped the dark liquid. Anne let out a sigh. *Just what I needed.* Her caffeine high was interrupted by Dr. Lindsey's voice.

"I was just talking to Anne about your sleeping arrangement concerns."

"They're more than concerns, David."

185

"As I have said before, hindering her recovery would be detrimental. The last thing she should be concerning herself with is intimacy issues."

"She's my wife."

"She is healing!" Dr. Lindsey raised his voice.

"Anneliese could probably use a good f—"

"Enough!" She raised her hand to stop them. "I am sitting right here and completely capable of making my own decisions." She turned to Carter. "I will share a bed with you when I'm ready, and right now I'm ready for breakfast and ready to end this silly conversation."

This was a boundary she would not allow him to cross. *If he tries anything, I'll kill him right there.* Anne wasn't going to be bullied into sleeping with him. The mere thought of having sex with him again turned her stomach. It was never going to happen, no matter what he threatened her with.

"You are quite feisty this morning, my Anneliese." He stroked her cheek, slowly trailing his hand down to her chin, where his thumb and index finger suddenly dug into her ivory flesh. His fingers pushed harder against the bone and harder still.

"Now that's enough," Carter growled.

She yanked her face away and winced at the sting in her jawbone. Anne's teeth clenched. Her eyes darted to her hand that was white-knuckling a butter knife. Slowly, Anne tried to put it down before Carter could notice, but he already had. Dr. Lindsey sat quietly, but Anne felt his tension.

"Think twice, my love, before doing anything rash."

"A butter knife to the throat would put a damper on my morning," Anne said.

She heard a growl rumble in Carter's chest.

They quietly ate their eggs and sausage, until Carter began talking about the impending dinner. He handed the guest list to Anne, and she skimmed through the prominent and familiar names.

"Why all the fuss over two people, Carter?" Anne asked, as she placed the paper on the table.

"I've already explained to you why. Their power and influence will take me to the top." He rubbed his freshly shaven chin with his thumb as he fell deep into thought.

"To the top of what?"

He grinned. "The food chain."

A shadow passed across Carter's face, but he kept his eyes down on the paper that had the names perfectly penned in black ink. Names that made people quiver and become uncomfortable, names that could erase a person's existence with a snap of the fingers. Anne's throat constricted around the last bite of egg white, but she managed to swallow it down.

"Let's head to the Kensington. They are expecting us soon," Carter announced. He quickly finished his coffee.

The trio stood and exited the dining room while two members of Carter's suited entourage followed behind them. She didn't know their names and had no desire to. They looked like strung-out juice heads who had watched *The Matrix* one too many times; but they carried guns, so Anne kept her mocking thoughts to herself. Anne folded the list and placed it in her black-cherry satchel.

Carter stopped outside the house. "I have meetings after this, so we need to take separate cars. Anneliese, Robert, and David will ride with you."

"Why is Dr. Lindsey coming?" Anne asked.

"I don't want him alone in the house." His eyes moved to where Dr. Lindsey was standing near the SUV.

Anne glanced over her shoulder and then back to Carter, raising an eyebrow to him. "You're acting paranoid, Carter, and besides, you wanted him here."

Without a word but with a disapproving look, he escorted her to Robert. She had noticed some time ago that his demeanor had begun to morph into a crazed paranoid psycho. Well, even more crazed than before, if that was even possible. Anne could see the physical changes in him as well. A mixture of black and purple tainted the skin under his eyes. His skin had lost its olive perfection; it was now dry and taut. Anne suspected drugs.

"I must confess I was almost hoping you would have used that butter knife," Dr. Lindsey said, once they were safely secured in the vehicle.

Anne gave him a sly grin. "I have something so much more gratifying in store for my husband."

CHAPTER TWENTY-THREE

They pulled up to the historic stone hotel that was perched impressively on the banks of the Savannah River like a medieval castle. Robert helped Anne from the SUV. She turned to view the beautiful palm trees that peppered the grounds and surrounded the prestigious building.

Carter approached her. "Shall we, my Anneliese?" He gestured to the hotel.

Anne nodded. Upon entering the lobby, she was immediately absorbed by the gothic ambience. Though it encapsulated the vintage charm of the city, the Kensington's décor was styled in a modern way. The fresh smell of lemons wafted from the recently polished wood furnishings. Anne ran her fingertips over the soft leather that covered the chairs in the lobby.

Carter cupped Anne's elbow, guiding her through the quiet lobby. The echo of their footsteps bounced off the black-and-white veined marble that led them to a tempered glass office suite. A woman with a lean figure, pixie-cut charcoal hair, and plump lips approached them. She extended a welcoming hand.

"Good morning, Mr. and Dr. Montgomery. Welcome to the Kensington Hotel. I'm Natalie Franz, your event coordinator." She spoke in a heavy southern accent. Her almond eyes flitted over Carter, as she bit her bottom lip.

What the hell? Anne stared at this very attractive woman with fluttering eyes who was staring at her husband. She turned her head to Carter, who was oblivious to the entire thing. Anne looked back at Natalie, who was still ogling Carter. She had an overwhelming urge to slap that coy look right off Natalie's fake tan face.

"It's nice to finally meet you, Miss Franz," Anne spoke through her smirk.

Natalie let out a slight giggle and slowly turned her focus to Anne. "Yes, it's nice to finally put a face to the name. Please call me Natalie."

"My wife has the guest list and will be finalizing the menu. I'm here to make sure that the room is adequate in size and that security is aware and properly placed," Carter said, shifting closer to Anne.

"Yes sir, the head of our security team is aware of your concerns, and security will be ready and in place. You will be pleased with the scope of the room." She pointed to her right. "Maria, my assistant, can take you to the room now."

Carter tipped his head and turned to Anne. "I'm leaving right after I check out the room—hey, look at me." Anne hadn't realized that she was still shooting daggers at Natalie. Her skin was hot and blotchy. *What is wrong with me?* Anne shouldn't care if another woman was flirting with Carter. She didn't love him—she didn't want him—so why was she so upset? This was wrong, so wrong. "I love *you*, my Anneliese. Only you." Carter kissed her lips and she willingly allowed it, even though her insides knotted and twisted. *God, we are sick.* This was the mind trickery she battled with daily. A sliver of her wanted his affections to be pure but they weren't. They were for show. Anne was on display for the whole world to see. She was Carter's marionette, his domineered woman, his sick obsession.

Anne heard Natalie huff. Carter pulled away and looked quite satisfied with his performance. He left with Maria by his side while she gave him all the logistics of the dining room and bar area. Anne cringed at the disgusting display that had just taken place. She felt ashamed, dirty, and confused. *Damn you, Dr. Lindsey.*

"Dr. Montgomery, please have a seat. We'll go over everything, and then you can be on your way."

Anne twisted her body toward the twangy request. Natalie had pulled out two chairs at the small conference table. Her plunging neckline revealed a hint of her well-endowed chest. Anne wanted to roll her eyes and then punch her in the face, but she refrained. She walked over to the table, sat down, and placed her purse on the polished surface.

Natalie clicked her pen. "All right, let's go over the guest list first, and confirm who is attending."

Anne pulled the list from her purse and handed it to Natalie. She crossed her arms over her chest, watching Natalie check off the names.

"Have you met my husband before?" Anne blurted out.

Natalie stilled but didn't look at Anne. "No, not really. We spoke briefly on the phone a few times but…" She raised her head and gave Anne a rather odd look. It was one of curiosity and excitement. "But I know *who* he is. Tell me, what's it like?"

Anne tried not to laugh at the Carter groupie. "What's what like?"

Natalie leaned in closer to Anne. "Being married to a Montgomery, of course. The money, the power—oh, I couldn't imagine. When he first reached out to me about the dinner, I knew the name sounded familiar, but I didn't think the Montgomerys lived in Savannah. I knew they were from Chicago and Minneapolis. I'm a sucker for the gossip magazines." Natalie ran her hand down her shiny crown. Subtle streaks of blue reflected the fluorescent lights above. "His brother, Michael, big Vegas gambler. And I was so upset when I read about Simon Montgomery. How so very sad."

This woman is clueless. She was amused by Natalie's delight over the celebrity pedestal on which she had placed them.

"You certainly know a lot about my family." Anne shifted into a more comfortable position in the chair.

Natalie's eyes darted around the room. "I know that up until a few months ago he wasn't a Montgomery at all. In fact, he was supposedly dead but came back from the grave. Oh, how scandalous," Natalie squealed.

"Yes, I'm quite aware of all of that." Anne cleared her throat. "Since I was there."

"Goodness, I'm sorry. I'm such a gossip, look at me—so unprofessional. It's just, well, I'm honored that such famous individuals will be staying here at the Kensington." She tapped at the names on the list with her pen.

"I think the word you mean is *infamous.*"

Natalie let out a high-pitched laugh and looked back down to the papers in front of her. Anne appreciated the silence. This woman was too much. Natalie was in awe of criminals and obviously found Carter attractive. Anger bubbled in Anne's stomach at the thought of Natalie stroking her fingers through Carter's hair. She was baffled by her reactions, her apparent jealousy of Natalie wanting Carter. She knew this was Dr. Lindsey's doing, with his hypnotic words weaving in and out of her memories. He toyed with the emotions attached to them, fiddled with her gray matter like a musical instrument, until she became Carter's "Anneliese." She wasn't Carter's but she believed she was somebody's. Anne belonged to someone.

"Dr. Montgomery? Are you all right? You don't look so good. Can I get you some water?" Natalie asked.

Sweat trailed down Anne's hairline, and she felt clammy and hot. Anne wiped her forehead. "No-no, I'm fine. I'm sorry. Um, are we done here? I have to go." She shot up from the chair and grabbed her purse.

Natalie stumbled as she stood up from her chair.

"Of course. I can take care of everything. Don't you worry. I'll email you if I have any questions." She extended her manicured hand toward Anne. "It was lovely finally meeting you. And please, don't hesitate to call or stop by if you need anything."

"Yes, thank you. I'll be in touch with you soon."

Anne hurried out of Natalie's office and through the lobby. Once outside, she sucked in a deep breath. After a moment of calming down, she raised her hand to shield her eyes from the sun. Her SUV was parked not far from the entrance. Anne walked toward the SUV and found Dr. Lindsey standing outside of it, smoking. That was new.

"When did you decide to give yourself cancer?"

Startled, he turned and looked at the cigarette in his hand. "Old habits die hard."

"Is that a clinical assessment?" She cocked an eyebrow, while Robert opened the rear passenger door.

A billow of smoke left his lips as he flicked the cigarette butt and ground it out with his shoe. Dr. Lindsey slid into the seat next to her. The ghost of his bad habit followed him into the car. Anne opened her window.

"I'm sorry." He pulled a mint from his pocket.

"It's all right. It just reminds of my mother. She smoked like a chimney when she was anxious, but even more so when we drove to Pepin, Wisconsin. The woman would never open a window."

Dr. Lindsey bit into his mint and paused.

"What was at Pepin?"

"It was more like *who* than *what*. It was where she would meet my father."

CHAPTER TWENTY-FOUR

Robert pulled in front of the dreary house, but Anne was not ready to go back inside.

"Dr. Lindsey, will you take a walk with me?"

"Absolutely." He helped Anne from the back seat.

"Robert, Dr. Lindsey and I are going to take a stroll through Forsyth Park. We'll return shortly."

Carter would be checking in, and she didn't want Robert to receive a verbal lashing because he didn't know where she was, even though she was fully aware someone was always watching her. Anne twined her arm through Dr. Lindsey's, and they crossed the street and walked directly into the park.

Autumn was settling into the southern town. Brittle leaves blanketed the walkway that stretched out in front of them. Their pace was slow and lax as the pathways crunched beneath them. They approached the breathtaking Parisian-inspired marble fountain. Its layered spray sent droplets of radiance and color through the air. From a distance, it looked like an arc of diamonds. She motioned for Dr. Lindsey to sit with her at a nearby bench.

The sound of children laughing at the nearby playground turned her lips upward. "I love that sound."

"What sound?"

She ticked her head over at the playground. "Children's laughter. After years of being a child neuropsychiatrist, listening to their stories of abuse and neglect, I always hope that with help I can restore their innocence, their trust."

Her last patient, Stella, came to her mind. The redhaired porcelain-skinned girl had thrust a blade into her arms to release her emotional pain and let it seep out onto the tiled floor of her kitchen. Thank goodness Casey had taken Stella on as her patient. Anne knew she could help the troubled child.

"Anne, you are brilliant at what you do. You've helped so many."

She held up her hand. She didn't want to be reminded of the life she left behind. "We need to talk, and I didn't want to risk Carter overhearing. I need to know what you did to me at in Minneapolis, with the hypnosis. Something isn't right."

A wave of guilt crossed over his face. "What happened?"

"I felt jealousy when the event coordinator gave Carter come-hither eyes. I wanted to punch her out. This isn't the first time I've felt these emotions toward him. Did you pull those forward in my brain? I know how hypnosis works. Is Carter saying trigger words to evoke those emotions from me?"

"I had to, Anne. It was the only way—"

"If you tell me it was the only way to protect me one more time, I may truly lose my mind."

Dr. Lindsey gestured for her to lower her voice.

"Carter's smart. He can see through anyone, especially when they're lying to him."

"How dare you? You aren't God—you can't mess around with my brain like some science experiment. You told me you were going to help me seek redemption and instead, you handed me over to him. I don't want to feel anything for Carter, except hate and rage."

He tried to grab her hands, but she snatched them away.

"I planted subtle triggers that would bring forth those feelings of love and devotion. However, they are very minor. "

"I don't want any of them. My mind is twisted with confusion, and the years of hypnosis have started to unravel me. I trusted you. I needed you to help me and now, I can't—I don't believe anything you say to me."

She began to get up, but Dr. Lindsey grabbed her arm. He looked pitiful. His skin paled even though the heat from the sun was warm.

"Anne, wait. What can I do to make this right?"

Anne pulled her arm away from his grasp once again. She could feel the adrenaline pump through her veins. Chatter from onlookers chipped away at her eardrums. Anne was on the brink of snapping.

"Tell me how to shut those emotions off or tell me the trigger words. Do something to make it go away."

"I'm sorry, I can't do that. It's too risky."

Her eyes narrowed. "Then I suggest you stay out of my way. I'll do this on my own."

Not wanting to hear his protests, Anne turned on her heels and left the deflated Dr. Lindsey to cradle his head in his hands. His betrayal devastated her, but she refused to cry. She refused to show mercy. *Maybe I was wrong. Maybe I don't belong to anyone. It's just me.* With that sobering thought, she walked back to the house. Her plot to gain freedom would be executed by her own hand alone.

CHAPTER TWENTY-FIVE

The next day Anne took advantage of the wonderful morning weather and walked out to her private balcony with her iPod. The tepid breeze moved around her as she sat down on the wicker chair that she had found in the garage last week. Anne pulled out her ear buds, popped them in her ears, and scrolled through the tracks.

Since she arrived in Savannah, Anne kept busy by familiarizing herself with Carter's close business contacts such as Marcus Hunt and Magda Alves. She would document her findings by recording them so she wouldn't forget and not leave a paper trail for Carter to find. Anne thumbed through the tracks, locating the most recent one.

"Marcus Hunt has law firms in the western United States and a few international locations. He has quite the list of prominent clients. Surprise, surprise—Magda Alves is one of his clients. She the acting CEO of Alves Logistics, which is based out of Miami but uses ports in Houston and Jacksonville. I can only assume that is the reason Carter moved Montgomery Hotels Incorporated down to Georgia. A few years ago, she was accused of murdering her husband, but she was never formally charged. Oh, and Marcus Hunt represented her during the police interrogation.

The murder has turned into a cold case. Through my research, I have discovered that three prominent families had developed the term white-collar mafia. *Those three families are the Leeds, Montgomerys, and the Alves. Together, they were part of the mob wars in the nineties. I also discovered that Magda invested in Montgomery Hotels when they opened their first location. I have a feeling she also invested in Leeds Imports and Construction at some point, linking the three families together, indebting themselves to one another. As long as I remain compliant to Carter, I can continue my research without raising too many red flags. I must remain diligent."*

A hand rested on her shoulder, and she jolted up off the wicker chair. Her heart thundered up her throat, leaving her breathless. Anne tore the ear buds from her ears and whirled around.

"Jesus, Carter! Have you ever heard of knocking?"

An annoyed expression registered across his face. "I did, several times in fact."

Anne slid the iPod into her pocket. "I was just listening to music, *trying* to relax."

She sat back down, folding her arms over her chest. His footsteps creaked along the aged wooden balcony. Carter leaned his back against the chipped cornflower blue railing, crossing his arms as well.

"I wanted to know how the meeting went at the Kensington. Everything set?"

"Yes, everything will be perfect, just as you requested."

Something was brewing inside Carter; she could see it in his fake smile and set jaw.

"I had an intriguing phone call earlier."

She gulped down the panic that rose from her knotted stomach. Silently, Anne prayed that he hadn't discovered her alliance with Michael.

"Oh yeah? Well, don't leave me in suspense."

"Marcus Hunt wants to meet with you. Why would he want to meet with just you, Anneliese? Especially since you don't even know the man."

"Carter, stop with the paranoia. There could be a million reasons why. Maybe it has something to do with the dinner or travel arrangements. I am the person putting this little soirée together, remember?"

Anne could see him processing her words. Confident with her explanation, he approached her and crouched between her knees. Her back stiffened like icicles on a bare birch.

"My Anneliese." He laced his fingers with hers, looking at the black diamond. "I know we have less than an honorable past, but we are in this together. 'Til death do us part.'"

Before Anne could respond, Carter's hand moved through the air toward the side of her neck. She felt a pinch and sting. Her peripheral vision could see his thumb moving. By the time she tried to yank away, his hand dropped. Her spinal fluid turned glacial, and a chill spread, causing tiny prickles to erupt through her skin. Anne's body shot up from the chair, knocking it against the house. She placed her hand on her neck. It was tender. Carter stood and backed away from her. He was hiding something in his closed fist.

"What the fuck! Did you just stick a needle in my neck?" she demanded.

Dr. Lindsey burst into the room. Still holding her throbbing neck, Anne was inches from Carter's face.

"Show me right now what the hell is in your hand!"

"Goddamn it, Carter, I told you not to do that without me present," Dr. Lindsey spat out.

Carter towered over Anne, looking down at her unapologetically. He turned his head to Dr. Lindsey.

"Our guests will be arriving any minute. I need her quiet."

Without further explanation, he left the room. Anne marched over to Dr. Lindsey.

"What the hell was that? What did he put in my neck?"

Her white knuckles tightened and her body shook with fury. The deck tilted. She blinked to push away the euphoria that squeezed through her veins.

"Anne, come lie down."

Dr. Lindsey guided her to the bed. Her head hit the feather pillow hard. Tears trailed to her temples and dripped into her ears. Her vision blurred as her eyelids grew heavy. *Oh God, I can't focus on anything.* Anne's thoughts muddled around inside her as the medication flooded her veins.

"Why? W-Why did he do that?"

"Shhhhhh, just rest."

Heaviness slid through her limbs while her body grew cold and weak. She could no longer fight the slowing of her world. Her eyes closed and she tumbled further into the darkness.

CHAPTER TWENTY-SIX

Anne moaned as her body twisted in the sheets, and she rubbed the swollen skin around her eyes. She squinted through heavy lids, and her stomach lurched as the dark room leaned. She swallowed down the bile that was seeping up her throat.

Her throbbing head screamed for pain reliever. Coaxing her legs to lift her from the bed was a battle. After a few minutes, they cooperated. Anne stumbled into the bathroom where she found ibuprofen. *Hello glorious green gel-caps.* She popped them in her mouth. She stripped out of her clothes and threw on pink silk pajamas.

It was nighttime but she needed to eat. She opened her creaky bedroom door and noticed that the house was quiet—too quiet. The cold floorboards squeaked under her bare feet.

She peered inside Carter's office. It was empty. She continued down the hallway, passing two more bedrooms. One was Dr. Lindsey's, and his light wasn't shining from under the door, so she assumed he was asleep. Her limbs still felt shaky. For support, Anne leaned against the wall as she walked down the steep staircase. A soft glow from the fireplace illuminated the front sitting room; shadows danced in the foyer.

Robert sat in one of the floral club chairs in a black jogging suit. *He must be babysitting me tonight.* He was holding a cup of steaming liquid and watching the embers of the fire. The wooden floors gave her away. He looked over and smiled.

"How are you feeling, Mrs. Montgomery? I was told you were in bed with a migraine."

He gestured toward the chair opposite of him. She sat down and rubbed her bleary eyes. "Yeah, something like that. Where is everyone?"

"After Mr. Montgomery's meeting, he informed me that he was going to check on his father in Atlanta, and the good doctor stepped outside."

Anne was sure that Carter did not travel to Atlanta to check on Simon. He had used that as an excuse, but she wasn't quite sure where he went.

Robert gave her a sad smile. "Would you like me to make you a cup of tea and a sandwich?"

"I would love that, thank you."

Anne's adoration for Robert grew even by the day. He had such a fatherly quality about him that drew Anne in. They both stood up and walked to the kitchen. Anne perched herself on a wooden stool and set her elbows on the polished brown granite counter while Robert rummaged through the refrigerator.

"Ham and cheese sound good?"

"Sounds delicious, Robert. I haven't eaten since breakfast." Anne rubbed her stomach.

Robert furrowed his brow. "You should eat more. You're wasting away."

She knew her frame was skeletal, but food was the last thing on her mind. Anne saw this as the perfect opportunity to ask Robert about his involvement.

"Can I ask you a question?"

"Certainly, Mrs. Montgomery." Robert layered the cheese and ham on the bread.

"Does it bother you that I sucked you into this mess? You know, lying about my whereabouts. I know Carter trusts you."

Robert paused while smearing mayonnaise on the sourdough slice. "Mrs. Montgomery, with all due respect, I know you're smarter than that."

Seems that Robert has an agenda of his own.

"How do you know Michael?"

Robert put the sandwich on a glass plate, slid it in front of her, and gently patted her hand.

"I have worked with the Montgomerys for many years. Michael informed me that Carter was seeking a driver for his wife. *I* approached Carter."

"So, you're Michael's spy. He doesn't trust me, does he?" Anne asked as she tucked her hair behind her ears.

"No, he trusts you. Just not his brother. Michael knows that Carter keeps tabs on your every move. I can reach him easier than you can." Robert leaned against the counter. "Mrs. Montgomery, can I give you a bit of advice?"

"Always."

"Never share your secrets with anyone. That will destroy you faster than the secrets themselves." He spoke quietly.

"Understood." She reached over and squeezed his arm.

"Now eat." His words were stern, but he gave her a playful wink.

She ingested his wise words of warning, along with the delicious sandwich. Between bites, she sighed; her stomach was grateful for the food. She was nearly finished when something dawned on her. She looked at Robert who was cleaning up the crumbs with a dishtowel.

"Robert, why do you call me Mrs. Montgomery but you call everyone else by their first names?"

He smiled, his eyes crinkling with amusement.

"I have the utmost respect for you. I'm old fashioned that way."

Anne shrugged and finished eating her sandwich. He took her empty plate, opened the dishwasher, and slid it into the lower rack.

"Are you going to tell me who was here today?"

Robert eyed her. "It's not the right time."

If Anne's brain wasn't still muddled from the medication Carter had thrust into her earlier in the day, she would have argued with Robert, but she didn't have it in her.

"Would you like me to make you a cup of tea before I retire for the night?"

"That would be wonderful, thank you."

In a welcomed silence, Robert made her a cup of soothing peppermint tea with a dash of vanilla.

"Goodnight, Mrs. Montgomery," Robert said as they walked to the foyer where a hallway led to his bedroom.

"Goodnight, Robert. See you in the morning."

Anne decided she needed some fresh air. She opened the front door and stepped out on the wrap-around porch, breathing in the crisp Savannah night. The dizziness had finally subsided. She could walk without stumbling over herself. Anne was fed up with Carter injecting drugs into her. *I need to start thinking like him—be ruthless, cold. If only I could dig into his brain like he did with mine.* Anne had an idea. A sly grin spread over her face. Before turning to go back in, she saw something move across the street.

She could see the dark shape of a man and the glow of a cigarette. Anne squinted. She made out more detail and saw it was Dr. Lindsey. She backed up against the house, nestling into the shadows. Anne didn't want to be seen. A few minutes later, he waved and walked down the stark road. Anne's gaze followed the dimly lit path to another murky shape approaching Dr. Lindsey. By the figure's stance, she could see it was a man. But they were too far away for Anne to make out who it was. After a quick exchange, they both began walking deeper into the night. *Interesting. I wonder who he's meeting with? I knew I couldn't trust him.*

She fumed at the thought. Anne exhaled hard and turned to walk back into the house. She slinked up the stairs toward Carter's office and peered into the dark room where she saw evidence of a meeting. Light-footed, she stepped into the room and flicked on a small lamp. Anne's eyes stopped in front of three empty crystal glasses that lined Carter's desk. She picked one up and sniffed the inside— brandy. The intense aroma sparked a familiarity inside but she couldn't place it. She set it back down and walked over to the other side of the desk.

Anne opened each drawer in the desk, tugging at the copper pulls, sifting through papers and files. Underneath a pile of message pads, she found a small ring of keys. Anne held them in the palm of her hand and scanned the room. She spotted a green metal cabinet tucked in the corner near the fireplace. She tip-toed toward it. Her chest tightened at the anticipation of the contents being kept inside the metal box. Anne knelt in front of the cabinet, inserting each key into the lock to find its owner. After the seventh key, she heard the lock release. She pulled the door open.

"I knew it," she whispered as her knees lowered to the floor.

Bagged pills of various sizes and colors lined the bottom shelf with packaged syringes piled on top of them. On the shelf above that were red-capped vials filled with liquid medication with the name *Diazepam* printed on them. The medication is meant for anxiety, but she knew if it was given in a high dosage it would sedate a person. It was what Carter had stuck into her earlier. Behind the vials was a large white bottle. She popped open the cap and tapped one of the pills out onto her clammy palm. *Why the hell does he have Oxycodone or any of these pills?* Alarm bells sounded in her head, and her face flushed hot as adrenaline pushed through her. Her eyes bounced around the display of drugs.

Anne recognized some of the capsules. She had prescribed them to some of her patients and some Anne had taken herself when her depression had sucked her into a loathing abyss. She capped the bottle and set it back inside. Anne sifted through the small plastic bags and scrutinized one of the bags. *There must be a hundred pills per bag. Is he selling these? He must be taking them—that explains some of his crazy behavior. He has to have more stashed somewhere else.*

A chill hit Anne at her core. *Does Michael know about this little hobby? Is this what the dinner is about? Drugs?* Really, anything illegal that Carter was part of shouldn't surprise her. If Carter was more than willing to murder his best friend and be affiliated with a human sex trafficker, selling black market prescription drugs shouldn't faze her. Anne needed to find out Carter's plan, and she knew exactly how to get under his skin.

CHAPTER TWENTY-SEVEN

The next morning brought thick dark clouds and howling winds. Anne stood in front of the bathroom mirror, her flinty eyes grazing over her pale complexion. The eyes were the windows to the soul, and Anne's soul churned black. *He wants my love? My love will be his disease. I'll creep under his skin and poison him from the inside out.*

Her reflection smiled wickedly. She twisted on her black heels, and sashayed her way to Carter's office. With a deep exhale, Anne knocked softly. At his muffled "come in," she turned the corroded, squeaky doorknob.

Her arm opened the door to reveal her dapper husband. Carter sat behind his gaudy, ornate desk that had a gargoyle head carved into the front. He closed his laptop and peered up at her. The indigo walls complemented Carter's devilish eyes. His dark waves had grown long and unruly. With steepled fingers, Carter pressed his elbows into the desk and held Anne's stare.

She closed the door behind her and pushed out her chest. Carter tilted his brow inquisitively at Anne. She walked with swaying hips and a small grin toward the chipped bookshelf that lined the far wall. Anne could feel his eyes following her. *Draw him in. This is what he wants.* She brought the tips of her fingers to the antique leather-bound books that packed the shelf. Their coarseness against her skin shot tingles through her hand.

She finally spoke. "I forgive you."

She turned to face Carter. He crossed his arms while he observed her.

"You forgive me?"

"I do."

"What are you up to, my Anneliese?" Carter probed.

Anne moved in a way that was deliberate, to show him her need for him, her want. Her fingertips ran over her parted lips and trailed over her chin down to her neck. He shifted in his chair so he could get a better angle. Carter's dark eyes roamed up and down Anne's body. She closed the distance between them. Her peripheral vision caught sight of the metal cabinet that housed the drugs she had found last night. Carter moved his hands to the arms of the chair, his fingers stroking the leather.

Anne stood next to him and leaned against the desk. With hooded eyes, Carter looked at her. Anne knew how to use him, how to get to him. Her seductive demeanor had always been his downfall. A sweet whisper in the ear, a gentle stroke of the hair is all it took. She didn't care if it was the hypnotic manipulations that Dr. Lindsey implanted in her brain or her obsession with vengeance controlling her actions. She carried on.

"I want in. All the way," Anne said in a lowered voice.

"Really?" Carter raised an eyebrow.

"Yes."

Prickles skipped across her rib cage as her heart raged behind it.

"All the way?"

Anne's skin flushed. She swallowed hard. "Yes."

Carter's hand lifted from the arm of the chair, Anne watched his fingers stop at her thigh. He caressed the surface of her black leggings. He trailed toward the hem of her charcoal knit dress. Carter lowered his palm and his heat permeated the thin cotton. Anne's mouth was moist and she licked her bottom lip. Her nerve endings stirred and tingled.

Being touched by Carter was like being smothered by a thousand snakes. Her flesh cringed while his fingers ascended beneath her dress but at the same time her body craved it. *This is my punishment. I'll take the devil inside of me to keep him away from the people I love.* His touch burned her inner thigh. Anne shifted and clutched his hand between her legs. He observed her cautiously and tried to yank his hand free but she tightened her muscles. A slow smile built across his stubbled face.

Anne's fingers explored his crown of thick waves. They were soft and addictive. She then fisted a handful of hair and pulled his head back so his face was in full view. Anne gritted her teeth, and Carter's lips parted. His breathing had picked up. That enticed Anne. She could feel the heat as it spread through every cell in her body and fanned the inferno within.

She leaned in closer. "You need a haircut."

Anne could feel the desire roll off of him, encircling her like black smoke. It was the essence of the demons that resided inside Carter. Anne could sense the smolder from them as she absorbed them one by one. Anne's face was inches from his as a shadow cast over her.

"Is this a truce, my sweet Anneliese?" Carter asked as he pulled his hand free.

"This is a ceasefire but if you drug me one more time, I will fucking kill you, Carter." She moved even closer to him and pulled his hair tighter. "And you were right, I'm not sweet anymore."

She filled her lungs with his scent, that intoxicating mix of sandalwood and vanilla. Carter's eyes widened and his expression was one of lust, not anger. The muscles in his jaw tensed. He brought his hands to her hips and dug into her skin. Anne winced but didn't move.

"No, you aren't. You're *my* love. *My* Anneliese."

In one swift motion, Carter pulled Anne to his lap. She straddled him and could feel his hunger between her thighs. Anne's chest heaved against his, and the thrust of his pull nearly expelled all the breath she had in her lungs. She succumbed to him. Her hungry eyes begged for him to touch her. Carter's muscles shifted underneath his buttoned shirt. His physical power frightened Anne, but she continued to tease him. The weight of her body sank against his, and Carter let out a growl.

Anne had made choices that determined her destiny. Scars she accepted to bear like a scarlet letter. She let go of his hair and knotted her fingers at the nape of his neck and dragged him to her. *Take him, Anne. Take the devil in.* Anne crashed his lips against hers. Carter's tongue plunged inside her mouth. Anne leaned further into him, tasting him, feeding her perverse appetite.

Carter's hands roamed over her. His bittersweet venom soaked into her pores, and she willed it even when the pain and ache intensified within her chest. The edges of her soul curled and wilted the longer his lips remained on hers.

Panting, Carter released his lips from hers. "Say it, Anneliese."

Beads of sweat had gathered at her hairline, and she could feel them slowly start to form down her spine.

With a hitched whisper, she responded. "I will always be *your* Anneliese."

Carter grinned. "Always."

"Til death do us part," she rasped.

Carter's foul ways infiltrated Anne's body each time he touched her and placed his lips on hers. She invited the darkness; it helped block out the light she once knew. Perhaps she was supposed to remain in this obscure haze until her last breath.

CHAPTER TWENTY-EIGHT

Ragged breaths filled Carter's office, and Anne felt the electricity spark around them. His hands slowly pushed up her dress. She felt light-headed and closed her eyes. It felt like she had taken a shot of liquor. The burn jetted through her chest and down her abdomen.

The sound of a throat clearing came from the threshold of the door. Anne and Carter stilled and saw Dr. Lindsey gripping the edge of the door jam. Anne glowered at Dr. Lindsey who looked pale, lifted herself off of Carter, pulled her dress down. Carter glared at him while letting his hands slip off of Anne.

"What do you want, David?" Carter spat out as he stood and smoothed out the wrinkles in his dress shirt.

Dr. Lindsey shot Anne a disapproving look, ignoring Carter's question.

"David. What do you want?" Carter said in a staccato manner.

"Your men are ready to leave for your meeting. I was sent to retrieve you," he replied, still focused on Anne, who returned the criticizing glare.

Carter released a loud and annoyed exhale. "Fine. I'll be down in a minute."

Dr. Lindsey disappeared from their sight. Carter smoothed out his dress pants but stopped when he heard Anne's laugh.

"What's funny?"

"It feels like we were just busted by your dad."

Carter's expression stiffened. He didn't share in her amusement.

Anne leaned against the desk and picked at her cuticles. "Where are you going?"

"A meeting."

Carter walked around her to fetch his suit coat that hung behind the door.

"I gathered that. Can I attend this one?" Anne asked

"No."

Anne threw her hands up. "No?"

"No, Anneliese. This is not your concern." Carter shrugged on his suit coat.

"What the hell, Carter? I thought we had a truce. We're in this together. At least tell me where you're going."

"The ports. Robert knows how to get ahold of me if you need me for anything."

"The ports? Why have a meeting there?"

His eyes narrowed. "Drop it, Anneliese. Now."

Anne huffed. She knew it was pointless to continue to prod him. Carter wasn't going to budge. He placed a soft kiss on her forehead.

"I'm very pleased that we have reached an understanding, Anneliese. We'll finish this later."

She returned his pleased expression, and without another word, Carter left. Anne listened as his footsteps grew more and more faint. She stood stiffly with her heels planted into the floor. His phantom touch lingered over her flesh and her lips grew swollen. The realization slapped Anne in the face, and acid churned up her throat. *I'm losing control. Damn it.* Anne would rather die than be with Carter. She ran her hands through her hair. Her eyes up jerked at the sound of the creaky floorboards. Dr. Lindsey stood in front of her with a hard expression. Anne didn't want to deal with him right now.

"Anne, what are you doing?"

"Standing here." Anne placed her hands firmly on her hips.

"You know that's not what I mean. What did I walk in on?"

Anne leaned away. "Excuse me? That's none of your business."

"Yes, it is. What are you doing?" Dr. Lindsey's voice raised an octave.

"I'm surviving. What are *you* doing?"

Anne brushed past Dr. Lindsey and into the hallway but felt a tug on her arm.

"Where are you going?"

Anne snorted and wrenched her arm from his grasp. "I'm going to follow Carter down to the ports. I want to know what he's doing down there."

"No."

She waved off Dr. Lindsey's disapproval and walked toward the staircase. She could hear his footsteps trail behind her.

"You don't want to go down there, trust me. Stay away from there," Dr. Lindsey said sternly.

The hair on Anne's arms and neck rose at his warning. She stopped and spun on the step.

"What do you know about this?" Anne fired the question at Dr. Lindsey without taking a breath. Dr. Lindsey squirmed at her questions. Finally, he spoke. "Why won't you let me protect you?"

"Why won't you be honest with me? You told me back in Minneapolis that we were going to seek revenge together. How can that happen when you are keeping secrets from me? You've fucked with my brain and emotions. I don't know what's up or down, right or left. I'm so damn confused. Do you know how much it hurts to know what you've done to me?" Anne pointed out the front door. "What you've done for Carter? You're not protecting me. You're killing me." Anne blinked her tears away.

"You talk of secrets, but are you not keeping secrets from me, Anne? It works both ways."

Her eyes widened. *Michael. Does he know? Does Carter know? Oh my God.* A jolt of raw panic surged through her. Anne pushed away from Dr. Lindsey, hurried down the stairs, and swung open the front door. She would heed his warning and not go to the ports but she couldn't stay in that house. She felt suffocated as the lies tightened around her throat.

The Savannah scenery blurred around her as her heels struck hard against the pavement. Anne needed quiet, a place where she could think. She entered the gates of Colonial Park Cemetery. The paths weaved through the crumbled gravestones and offered benches that allowed visitors to sit and listen to the whispers of the dead. The last time Anne had been in a cemetery was when Sam Goodman was put into the earth.

Anne strolled around and became lost inside her own head. *Was this what drove my mother insane? The sick sadistic plague that is love. Can love push a person to madness?* Anne fidgeted with her wedding ring.

Anne had the distinct feeling she was been watched. She assumed it was one of Carter's brutes, but for some reason the sensation felt different. Her eyes bounced around the cemetery. The feeling was…familiar. She wanted to reach out and latch onto the invisible line that was trying to tow her in. *Do I belong to someone?* But there wasn't anyone. After a minute of frantic searching, she found herself alone.

The wind fluttered her dress against her knees, and a shiver zipped through her. Carter's paranoia had rubbed off on her. The feeling was gone. She composed herself and decided to go back to the house. It was time for Anne to speed up her plan. She was done waiting. She needed to meet with Michael. They had much to discuss.

CHAPTER TWENTY-NINE

Anne returned to the empty Victorian house. The ticking of the grandfather clock in the corner was the only noise that echoed through the first floor. She ascended the stairs with winged feet and walked to her bedroom. Once inside her room, her hand covered her mouth and she ran to the toilet. She heaved until she felt such pressure behind her eyes she thought blood would pour from them. The sting of the poisonous acid singed her throat.

Anne grabbed a handful of tissues and wiped her mouth. She pushed off the toilet and grabbed onto the side of the sink. With wobbly legs, she pulled herself up to stand. Lines bracketed her pale lips, and her irises were drained of life. Carter's soul-sucking had started to take a toll on Anne. *Casey would slap me if she could see what I look like.* A small smile graced Anne's lips. Casey prided herself on her glamorous appearance and would scold Anne if she looked the least bit disheveled, but through her dark period, Casey didn't reprimand Anne one time for living in her stained pajamas or only bathing once a week. *I need to get back to her, to my family.*

Anne snapped out of her dire thoughts, splashing a handful of water on her face. *Think like Carter. What underhanded trick would he play?* It came to her with ease. Anne ventured out to locate Robert. She needed to send Michael a message before Carter returned from the ports. Anne found Robert in his small bedroom on the first floor.

He looked up from polishing his shoes.

"Robert, I need your phone to text Michael."

Robert pulled his black phone from his pocket and handed it to Anne without a word. He could see her urgency.

Meet me at the facility where your father is being kept tomorrow. What time?

Seconds passed and he responded:

I can meet you at noon.

Anne instructed him to bring forty-five thousand dollars, in cash, in three separate bags. Ten-thousand in two and twenty-five thousand in one. Michael was the CFO and could arrange to get the money easily. From Anne's digging around, she knew Montgomery Hotels Incorporated had bank accounts strewn over the world.

That's a big number Anne but I trust you know what you are doing. See you tomorrow.

She heard the front door open. Anne quickly handed Robert's phone back to him.

"Delete those," Anne said.

It's time for Simon Montgomery to reclaim his throne.

∽

The morning doves cooed outside Anne's window as she blotted her plump red lips. She tossed the tissue in the trash and smoothed her chignon. Her tan draped knit dress tightened across her chest as she pulled back her shoulders. Anne took wide steps, her scarlet stilettos tapping against the hardwood. She was thankful Carter never came home the night before, sparing her the torture of having to sleep with him. What a vile thought. Anne could only push Carter so far with seduction in order to gain information before he would push back.

Anne walked out to the waiting SUV that would take her to the airport. Robert was accompanying her to Atlanta; otherwise, Carter would question why she was going on a shopping excursion without someone with her. He trusted Robert.

Carter caught up with Anne before she climbed in.

"I'll be at the ports today. I'm managing a shipment for an associate so I'll be late coming home."

"What associate?"

Carter cocked his head. "Anneliese, please. Go have fun shopping, my love. Leave this business to me."

Carter helped her into the SUV and closed the door. She was thrilled that he would leave her alone for the day. She smiled and patted her leather purse, which held her arsenal of damning weapons.

~

The Montgomery jet touched down in Atlanta. Robert had rented a sleek luxury car. The massive skyscrapers towered on all sides of them while they drove deeper into downtown Atlanta.

Anne arrived at the private facility with an unbending attitude and hard features. The dated facility had an eerie feel to it. Water-stained tiles lined the dingy hallway. Robert stepped along with her and guided her through the maze of corridors. A metal door led them to a forgotten wing of the facility. Dr. Rasmussen approached her along with a young male orderly and Simon's private nurse. The nurse opened her mouth to speak but Anne held up her hand.

"I'm Dr. Anne Montgomery. My husband is Carter Montgomery. On behalf of Montgomery Hotels Incorporated, I would like to thank you for taking such good care of Simon Montgomery, but your services will no longer be needed from this day forward. You will both receive generous severance packages. His son, Michael Montgomery, will arrive shortly with your compensation. In cash, of course." The orderly and nurse stood wide-eyed with mouths agape. "However, you understand that this requires silence on your part and if you tell anyone, I can assure you that you will be dealt with accordingly. Do we have an agreement?" Anne plastered a fake smile on her face.

With stuttered words and keyed-up gazes, they agreed. She turned her attention toward Dr. Rasmussen. Furrows bracketed his mouth, and his arthritic frame stood before her. A few strands of silver fell off his wrinkled forehead.

"Dr. Rasmussen." Anne nodded.

"Anne, I'm surprised to see you here."

"I'm sure you are. As I was telling your staff, your services are no longer needed. Michael will be here shortly with your severance package. You will leave Atlanta and stay the hell away from my family."

As the word "family" fell from her lips, it alarmed her that she considered the Montgomerys family. Anne brushed it off and crossed her arms over her chest.

"Does Carter kno—"

"Carter knows nothing and you will tell him nothing. Now, go retrieve the medication needed to wake up Simon, and meet us inside his room." Anne could sense his hesitation. "You owe this to me, Dr. Rasmussen. I would hurry because once Carter catches wind of your involvement, he'll kill you. Maybe try moving to an island in the Pacific somewhere." Anne raised her brow. Dr. Rasmussen kept quiet, turned, and walked away from her.

Anne glanced at Robert. She had a wicked gleam in her eyes. She dropped her arms and walked to the metal door next to her. There was an orange chart clipped to the doorframe. The heavy stench of disinfectant stung her nostrils when she stepped further into the small space. A strip of fluorescent lights hung above the head of Simon Montgomery. She had never laid eyes on him before but she had seen pictures of the vivacious millionaire on the Internet. Ash blond hair hung in his face, his skin was dry, tight, and drained of color.

The fact that Anne appeared the same pallid color as the shell of a man lying before her twisted knots in her stomach. He was a prisoner in his own body, trapped in his mind, clawing and screaming for someone to help him, and coming to the dismal reality that know no one could. *Until now.* She felt the heat from another body behind her and knew who it was.

"He doesn't even look like my father…" Michael rasped.

"He's in there, Michael. Your father can hear everything that is going on around him."

Anne stepped toward the bed-ridden man covered in layers of white cotton as tubes and wires jutted out from underneath the thick blanket. She brushed the errant strands of hair from his face and leaned over just inches from his ear.

"Simon, this is Anne, your daughter-in-law and liberator. I know you are trapped inside your own body, and I know what that's like. Carter did this to you and I'm going to help you escape. You're going to wake up very soon and when you do, remember who set you free," she whispered.

Anne turned to Michael, who looked perplexed.

"What did you say? You're going to help him? How? He had a stroke, Anne. It's up to him when he wakes up. Dr. Rasmussen said—"

"Dr. Rasmussen is Carter's puppet. Why do you think I wanted you to bring the money?" Anne pointed to the bags near the door where Michael had set them down. "We are pulling the strings now, Michael."

Anne moved to Michael and fished the folded papers from her purse that detailed the description of the drugs Carter used to put and keep Simon in a coma. She handed them to him and he scanned them rapidly.

His brow furrowed. "Anne, I don't know what any of this means. It's medical jargon."

"I asked you here so I could tell you the truth behind your father's sudden illness. Remember when I was in the private facility in Minneapolis? Everyone assumed I was in rehab recovering from my *fall*. Actually, Carter was keeping me there against my will. He pumped me full of medication, with a large enough dose to incapacitate me for weeks, like an induced coma. I was imprisoned inside my own body, unable to communicate with anyone. That's what your father is experiencing." Anne looked down at the black diamond ring. "I was forced to marry Carter in order to protect the ones I love. He and Dr. Rasmussen doctored my medical history, showing a pattern of metal instability. I had no choice. I could only destroy him by joining him, by mixing myself into the fold."

Anne could see Michael processing her explanation. His nostrils and the color of his skin blotched crimson. He paced the small room like a caged animal as he crumpled the papers in his hand.

"My God. When my father had his stroke, it was while he and Carter were talking in his office. Carter told me he felt responsible because they were arguing over the fact that he had changed his last name to Montgomery. He told me he would handle everything. I was so preoccupied with the PR shit that before I knew it, Carter had taken over the company."

"What about the board, Michael? Didn't they have a say?"

Michael snorted. "He used physical threats and intimidation to gain leverage. I knew nothing about it until after everything was said and done."

Anne approached him. "Listen to me. I can help Simon, but I need your word that you won't do anything rash."

His stare remained straight ahead.

"Michael, give me your word."

He finally lowered his crystal-blue eyes that bloomed with wrath. "Fine, you have my word." Michael tipped his head back. "That bastard looked me right in the eyes the other day and lied—"

"Wait, when did you see Carter?" *Click.* The light bulb went off in her head. "Oh, you were the one who met with him at the house."

"And Marcus Hunt," Michael added.

A flush of red erupted underneath Anne's pale skin. *Marcus wanted to talk to me. That's why Carter wanted me quiet.* Anne planted her hands firmly on her hips.

"I'm assuming he also didn't tell you about his meeting at the Savannah ports. In fact, he's supervising a shipment for a *friend* today down there. Do you have any idea what that's about?"

Michael's color deepened. He winced as if the realization punched him in the stomach.

"That's why he moved the company down here." Michael tossed the crumbled paper across the room. "Magda Alves is using the ports in Savannah now. Fuck! I knew it. He's entangled the company with her again."

"What does she ship, Michael? Tell me." Anne stood in front of him but he moved around her.

"No, no, you're staying out of this."

Anne threw her hands up. "Jesus, if one more person says that to me, I am going to scream. Carter didn't want me to be part of that meeting, so he decided to stick a needle into my neck to keep me quiet."

"He *what?*" His voice ricocheted off the linoleum and sheetrock like a bullet of fury in the small room. He approached Anne, grabbed at her neck. "Where?"

She pulled away. "It's gone now. Marcus Hunt wanted to meet with me alone and that raised Carter's suspicion. Before you tell me about this meeting, we need to wake up your father."

"How are we going to do that?"

As though his ears were on fire, Dr. Rasmussen entered the room. Michael watched intently as he walked to Simon's intravenous line, inserted a needle, and thrust the medication into the line with a push of his thumb. Simon would soon be released from his private hell.

He disposed of the empty syringe and walked to the door to exit the room. The swish of Dr. Rasmussen's white coat and Simon's monitors created an odd symphony that thrummed through Anne veins. It was control, it was power, and she wanted more of it.

Wide-eyed, Michael approached Anne. "This will work?"

"Yes. Stay here with him until he awakens, which shouldn't be too long from now."

"Will he be strong enough to attend the dinner?"

Anne touched his arm. "Simon will be weak, but he can travel and attend the dinner meeting."

Michael placed his hand on top of hers. "Thank you, Anne. And about the meeting earlier—I know why Carter didn't want you to be there."

Her eyebrows pushed together and lines deepened across her forehead. "Okay."

"Marcus Hunt is bringing a plus one. His new attorney."

"And who would that be?"

"Adam Whitney."

CHAPTER THIRTY

In a shadowed haze Anne could hear her name being called. The soft voice floated along the entrance of her ears, penetrated her brain, and alerted the synapses to respond by sending signals to her mouth. With a brayed voice, a name glided over her lips.

"Adam."

A stabbing pain shot behind her fluttered eyelids and Anne released a cry. *Oh God! Make it stop!*

"Adam!"

It was like a shock of electricity was being forced through her head. Anne was certain someone had shoved heated metal into her ears, seared her brain, and scorched each and every cell. She didn't know what was happening and the overwhelming fear was suffocating her.

A flash erupted behind her eyes. Pictures, memories, a life she had forgotten. A man she had forgotten. *I do belong to someone, I belong to Adam. My angel.* Wisps of fog morphed into Adam's beautiful face. *Is this a dream? Am I dying?* Anne reached out but the fog vanished. It was a mirage. Once Adam's face evaporated, more choppy memories appeared. They chained together through her brain at such a rapid pace that she couldn't focus on them.

I'm falling—why am I falling? The sensation panicked her, but her eyes landed on the figure that stood above her. It screamed her name. Anne fell further from it. Another flash of light enveloped her mind.

Anne was brought back to the chaos around her. A barrage of clattering and voices made it worse. *Shut up! Stop!*

"Anne, hang on."

"Michael, where's Adam? Where's Adam?" Anne sobbed; she could barely catch her breath. Her lungs were burned.

"Dr. Rasmussen is going to give you something, and we'll get you back to Savannah right away," Michael said to Anne as she felt his arms tighten around her.

She didn't want anything. She just wanted Adam. Dr. Lindsey and Carter had kept her away from him. He was her life, her love. Anne felt a warm hand cup hers, then a quick sting and a rush of euphoria gripped her. Anne's head lulled against Michael. Her heart slowed, and the fire that burned in the back of her throat extinguished. The physical torment began to fade away, as did Anne. Then all was quiet.

~

"Anne."

She heard her name in a shaky whisper. With a soft moan she turned her head to see Dr. Lindsey leaning against the edge of the bed, holding a bottle of water out to her. Anne was back in her bedroom in Savannah. The light from a small lamp cast a glow in the corner of the room.

"Here, Anne, drink this."

She sat up against the headboard and took the water. Her hands shook as she lifted it to her dry lips. She then gulped down the water. Tears threaded her long eyelashes and trailed her face as she continued to drink. Anne finished the water and placed the empty bottle on her nightstand. She turned to Dr. Lindsey.

"What—what happened?"

"You fainted, Anne. Why did you go to see Simon? What you did today could have cost you your life," Dr. Lindsey scolded.

That grabbed Anne's attention. "Does Carter...."

"No, he doesn't know anything about your trip to Atlanta and we need to keep it that way."

"How did I get back here?" Anne looked around the dim room.

"Robert and Michael Montgomery took care of everything. I have a feeling your run-in with Michael wasn't coincidental, as Robert has claimed. Tell me what happened."

She ran her fingertips down the sides of her face, feeling the heat trail her touch. Her molten-green irises traced the pattern of delicate stitching on the snowy comforter, and her nails ran against her lips. The angel and demon who split her in half perched themselves firmly on each shoulder, Anne was aware of their weighted presence. Her hand flew to her chest. The flash of light, the memories—everything came back to her sleepy mind.

"I remember everything." With a curled lip, she slowly lifted her rigid eyes and set them right on Dr. Lindsey. "I remember everything you and Carter took away from me."

Anne's ears pounded with a frenzied pulse and, though she had drunk an entire bottle of water, it had evaporated, leaving her mouth dry.

"Anne." Dr. Lindsey leaned closer to her.

Anne slid away from his reach. "No. I remember him, Dr. Lindsey. I remember Adam and our entire life together. When we first met, our holidays together, when he proposed. You took those away from me. I knew I felt something but I could never grasp it."

"Wha—I—*Anne.*"

Anne stood from the bed. "How dare you? You were supposed to be on my side but from the very beginning, you chose Carter over me. Did you think I would never remember? You pushed my emotions toward Carter and took Adam and hid him away." Anne's tears continued to slide down her face. "How could you do such a despicable thing?"

"I needed your memory loss of Adam to be authentic. You are much too emotional when it comes to Adam."

Anne threw her hands. "Emotional? I trusted you. You told me to put my faith in you, but you've been keeping secrets and I want to know right now, who have you been meeting with? Did you know that Adam is working for Marcus Hunt?"

"Yes. I knew because I've meeting with Adam. He wanted to be kept updated on your condition. Adam chose to be on Hunt's payroll so he could be closer to you."

Anne leaned against the wall. "Does he know what you did to me? That you banished him into some dark hole in my mind?"

"I told him that after your fall, you experienced amnesia. He is aware that you don't remember him."

Anne's legs quivered beneath her. Her eyes burned with tears, and the sting webbed through her skull. *He must be heartbroken. My love must be hurting so much.*

Her eyes widened. "You need to get Adam out of Savannah tonight. He can't be here. He can't attend the dinner—once Carter knows what I've done he'll kill him."

Dr. Lindsey moved to Anne. "What do you mean, 'what you've done?'"

"It's not safe, make him go back. He can't know that I remember him."

"Anne, he knows what he's doing."

She launched herself at Dr. Lindsey and clutched the fabric of his shirt with trembling fingers. "No! Make him go away. It's not safe for him here…."

"Anne. You are hysterical. Calm down."

"This is not good. Adam needs to go. He needs to run and hide out some place for a while, just until…."

Dr. Lindsey covered her hands with his warm ones and gently patted them. "Anne, stop. You have to trust him… and me."

She loosened her desperate grip. Anne moved away from him and blinked away the wetness that blurred her vision.

"Trust you? Why? What's in it for you? Why go through all this for me and for Adam?"

He approached her again. "Your safety, Anne. Adam's love for you will save you if I can't."

"Wh-what does that mean—if you can't?"

"It means I've created a plan for you, and it will be executed if something goes wrong. Adam knows the plan. He knows what to do."

A *plan?* This didn't instill confidence in her. The men in her life deceived her all in the name of "love" and "protection." *I'm so sick of this.*

"I'm not seeking a savior, Dr. Lindsey. Allies, yes, but I'm taking Carter down on my own. My game, my rules."

Dr. Lindsey fiddled with his glasses. "What's your game plan then?"

"I'm going to talk in private with Magda Alves. She may be the one to help me. My focus has shifted now that Adam's involved. I know Carter's using drugs. I can see it in his eyes. His behavior is so erratic, but I wonder if he's selling them too." She knotted her fingers, then played with the black diamond ring, then knotted her fingers again. Anne couldn't keep still. Her feet shuffled around the room while her brain plotted a plan. "Selling Magda's drugs? Is that what she is shipping up here?"

Dr. Lindsey scratched his eyebrow. "I believe so, yes." He paused. "Anne, I fear that you're losing yourself in Carter's deceit. These people are dangerous."

"No, I lost myself when you and Carter decided to mess around in my mind. A war rages inside of me daily. My thoughts are not my own. I look in the mirror and I don't know that woman reflected back at me. Anne surrendered to Anneliese, Carter's Anneliese. She's the one who can end this. She's the one to free them both from the binds that tie them to a savage being. I let him into my life, and his evil has spilled out in to everyone else's."

"You didn't bring him in, but Anne it's not too late for you. Don't forget who you are, please…"

Anne gave Dr. Lindsey a weak smile. "It *is* too late. He wants me to be like him—a ruthless, wicked monster—so that's what he's going get."

CHAPTER THIRTY-ONE

Loud voices seeped through the thin walls of the old house. Dawn spilled into Anne's bedroom, where she began to stir. She felt the vibration of heavy steps and then the door flung open, bounced against the wall, and nearly punctured a hole in the aged sheetrock.

"Anneliese, get up."

Anne jolted from the bed, almost falling over from the draped sheets that were twisted around her legs.

"What the hell—?"

"We're going to have a little morning family therapy session. Come downstairs. Now!"

She flinched at the vocal assault. Moments later, Anne's bare feet slapped against the floor. She sprinted toward the raised voices that poured from the sitting room. She froze at the sight of a pale and restless Dr. Lindsey, who sat tautly in the faded floral club chair. A silver handgun sat on the table between him and Carter, whose arms were crossed. Carter's dark gaze targeted Anne when she entered the stifled room.

She shifted her attention back and forth to each man. "What's going on?"

"My sweet Anneliese, you know me the best out of anyone—so you know that betrayal is inexcusable, irrevocable in my book, yes?"

Shit. She slowly nodded.

"Especially when it's someone that I trusted." Carter's manic eyes fell on Dr. Lindsey. "I understand that your memory is quite intact. True or false, Anneliese?"

Anne searched Dr. Lindsey's face, but he kept his focus on his lap. An aura of grimness bound him. A freight train thundered in her chest but she pulled her shoulders back, approached Carter, and lifted her chin.

"True."

"You remember everything?"

"Yes."

Carter's eyes narrowed. "Adam Whitney?"

"Yes. How did you know?"

"Talking walls, my Anneliese. I know everything that goes on."

Not everything, you pompous ass. Still holding her glare, Carter fished his cell phone from his jeans pocket. He quickly texted someone and slipped it back in. He clapped his hands together, and Anne and Dr. Lindsey jumped.

What is he up to?

"Time for some family therapy. Anneliese, have a seat." Carter motioned to the chair near Dr. Lindsey while he moved behind the doctor and placed his hands firmly on his shoulders. "Today's topic will be about absentee fathers, about how they can really screw with kids' heads, making them feel worthless, unwanted, and unloved. You question where you came from, and why that person didn't want you.

Simon didn't want me. He fucked my mother, and she became pregnant but he didn't want her. I mean, yes, I was raised by Steven, but Leeds are beneath Montgomerys. People eat out of the palm of my hand when I tell them who I am. Now the pathetic Leeds are worth nothing."

Anne kept her eyes on Dr. Lindsey but he wouldn't look at her. His leg bounced up and down and he fiddled with his glasses. Anne looked down at the handgun and swallowed hard.

"Most fathers will do anything for their children, protect them, shelter them, and even lie for them. But what happens when you pin one child against the other like my father did? It took some convincing but Michael and I are now a united front. However, you're not so lucky, Anneliese. Your father chose his other child over you," Carter sneered.

The life drained from her veins, leaving her body cold and pale. All the air that once circulated through her lungs evaporated.

"Wha-what do you know about my father?"

Carter laughed and squeezed Dr. Lindsey's shoulders harder. "I know a lot. Isn't that right, David?"

Dr. Lindsey lifted his head, and tears spilled down his cheeks. "Anne, I'm so sorry. I didn't choose Claire over you. It's not as it seems."

Unable to breathe or move, Anne was frozen but in the same moment an inferno rushed over her skin like the demons had been released and encircled her. Her left eye twitched, her limbs tingled, and Carter stood smugly behind Dr. Lindsey. *My father. My father. Claire's my sister. He's my father.* Anne's thoughts were choppy, like the Atlantic during a hurricane. The waves pushed her over and beat her with violent blows.

Dr. Lindsey turned his body to face her. "Anne, please… Carter reached out to me right after he disappeared. He knew I was your father, and that I had had an affair with your mother. I don't know how he knew but he knew your mother was my patient and—when she told me that she was pregnant, I—I couldn't be with her, I couldn't be part of your life. I would have lost my license and—I'm sorry, I know it was wrong and selfish. I did what I could."

Anne had thought she was gaining on Carter, but he was blindsiding her with the one thing that he knew would break her. *This is who my mother was meeting at the lake. He left me with that crazy woman. He abandoned me.*

"Stop! Do you have any idea what I went through with her? Do you? The endless nights of her screaming, cutting into her flesh like it was a piece of fruit with rusty knives. Did you know that she pulled every single piece of hair from her head, one by one? Did you?"

Anne was enraged. She dug her nails deeper into the palms of her hands. Dr. Lindsey shifted uncomfortably in his seat, wiped the tears from his face, and shook his head. Carter moved from behind Dr. Lindsey and now stood to Anne's right.

"Do you know that she tried to stab me with a piece of broken mirror? I was six years old. She blamed me for you leaving. You did what you could? Like what? Send money for new shoes? I didn't need new fucking shoes. I needed a father. I needed a mother who wasn't crazy. How could you do this?"

Tears sprang from her eyes, remembering the torturous memory of her mother coming at her with a piece of shattered mirror….

"You evil little girl! Because of you he doesn't love me. I hate you, you are the spawn of Satan. You drove him away. I should have killed you when you were born."

Her mother barely missed Anne's fingers with the jagged shard. Anne ran and locked herself inside of the bathroom. She sank to the floor crying, her little hands sliding her body away from the door and up against the tub. Anne felt little cuts stinging the palms of her hands. She lifted her hands to see small pieces of the splintered bathroom mirror embedded in her palms...

Anne could no longer speak or relive the memories. Her entire childhood flashed before her, weakening her, turning her into that helpless little girl once again.

Carter moved the veil of blonde from Anne's face and forced her to look up at him. "I'm going to give you the same option I gave your dear old dad. But yours will be a little bit different. Casey isn't blood, per se, but you consider her family, so let's talk about Casey, shall we?"

Panic threaded through her as Anne pressed her fists into her lips. "What? Why?"

Carter pulled his phone back out, quickly scanned the screen and flipped it toward her. "This is real-time, Anneliese, not a recording. I have men there right now ready to pull the trigger."

On the screen, she could see Casey exiting her house with her two young children. The one woman who was more like family to her than anyone was going about her morning business like it was any other day. Her gilded hair shone in the Minnesota sunrise when she tipped her head back, laughing at something her son had said. Anne's chest heaved as if her breath had been sucked right from her lungs.

Anne latched onto his pant leg. "Please, please, Carter, don't. I'm begging you! I'll do anything. Please don't kill Casey."

"My Anneliese, I love you and I know the pain you feel, the betrayal." Carter wiped the tears that hung from her chin. "Your father discarded you like a piece of trash. We are the same, Anneliese. We were meant to be together, not you and Adam. He's lived a privileged life with parents who love and cherish him. That why I know that this will be an easy decision for you." Carter walked around the front of the table where the gun lay. "My love, pick up the handgun, aim it at the man who gave you life but wanted no part of it—until I forced him—and pull the trigger. End his guilt, his suffering. He can't be trusted and he has jeopardized everything. He's betrayed you and he's betrayed me. If you don't, Casey will die. She will be murdered in front of her children and her husband, and Adam will be next."

Hyperventilation began as her vision faded in and out. Carter wanted Anne to commit murder and kill her father. *Could I do that?* She held a life in the palm of her hand. Casey had been her world for so long, had pulled her from her darkness. Both she and Adam had done that. *I just found Adam and my father....*

"Anne, listen to me," Dr. Lindsey pulled her attention to him. "If you kill me, he will hold that over your head for an eternity. You'll never be free."

"Shut up, David." Carter knelt in front of Anne. "He abandoned you, Anneliese. He didn't want you. I love you, my sweet. We are lost to this world but together we will make it ours. We'll dominate everyone and eliminate those who get in our way. You can start with your father."

"Don't be like Carter, Anne. You're stronger than this."
With a heavy blink, she looked at Dr. Lindsey. "Am I?"

"Yes. Look at what you've endured and you've survived."

"No thanks to you. Christ, you knew this entire time that I was your daughter, that I had a sister. I saw Claire all the time—God, how could you do this? Carter's right, I could never choose you over Casey." Her eyes dropped to the gleaming handgun but shifted to Carter.

"How do I know you won't kill Casey anyway?" Anne's lips trembled.

"Trust me, Anneliese. Pull the trigger and all is forgiven. We'll start fresh. David will be gone, Adam will be a distant memory, again, and Casey will live her life in peace with her family. Remember, you said you wanted all in. Give into me, my love. Give into the power I can give you. I'm the only one who can love you. Give in, Anneliese. Pull the trigger." Carter stoked Anne's cheek and gave her a look of promise. Anne turned and looked at the gun. *Should I grab it? Kill Carter right here? What if I don't reach it in time?* A hundred scenarios flooded her frantic thoughts.

"Anne, look at me," Dr. Lindsey sobbed. "I tried to protect you and Claire and I've failed. Please know that I love you, Anne. You are *my* daughter and I'm so proud of you. I won't make you choose. I will not allow my daughter to turn into a monster like Carter. I won't do that to you. It's too late for me but it isn't for you. He'll save you, Anne. Let Adam save you."

Anne felt she was watching the entire scene in slow motion. With her father's final words, he reached for the handgun, placed it firmly in his mouth, and pulled the trigger.

CHAPTER THIRTY-TWO

Anne was covered in her father's blood. It soaked into the tattered floral-patterned fabric and into her nightgown, dripping over her exposed skin. She doubled over, the floor growing closer to her as her knees crashed into it hard, sending a striking pain up her thighs. Anne couldn't hear the commotion around her. It was drowned out by a booming that fractured her hearing. The muscles in her arms stretched as they reached for Dr. Lindsey. She felt something snake around her stomach and lurch her upward. Her insides spun like a hurricane. Anne screamed until her vocal chords ruptured fire and air could no longer invade her lungs.

"NO—NO—NO! OH GOD! OH GOD!"

Robert pulled her flailing body from the scene, dragging her thrashing limbs up the staircase. Anne's heard the words "*hush sweet girl*" uttered repetitively. Her body contorted, unleashing demons and feral screams. Raw pain echoed in the house as she was carried down the hallway. Her subconscious clawed at her insides, shredding every nerve she had ever possessed. *No, not my father, not my father. Please God, no!* Robert held her hands down and tried to control the spasms that rippled through her muscles.

"Let me go! Let me go! I need to go back to him!"

Anne's cries eventually tapered off to silent sobs, as she beat her fist into Robert's chest. In absolute exhaustion, she eventually drifted off into a sleep plagued by dreams of death and memories....

≈

The sparklingly clean office gleamed in the reflection of Anne's green eyes. Casey had recommended Dr. David Lindsey. He had an office in their building and she thought he would be perfect for Anne, who was depressed, lost, and felt out of control after Carter's death.

"Hi, Dr. Lindsey. I'm Dr. Anne Jamison."

Warm blue eyes greeted hers. He had looked at her a bit too long but not in a way that made her feel uncomfortable. "Hello, Anne, take a seat."

Anne sat down but shifted uncomfortably on the white couch and laughed.

"Am I missing the joke?" Dr. Lindsey readied his notepad.

"White couch?" She pointed down. "Kind of ironic, don't you think?"

His eyes crinkled with amusement.

"Yes, I suppose. Let's begin our session, shall we? Let's talk about what brought you here."

She pondered his question for a moment.

"My boyfriend disappeared and is presumed dead. I lost our child while having a nervous breakdown, and I think I'm sick like my mother."

He jotted a few notes and then looked up at her. "Let's start with that, your mother...."

Anne blinked. Dr. Lindsey was grotesque; a cavernous hole twisted from the flesh of his head, and blood poured from the wound like a fountain.

"I'm sorry, Anne. I'm sorry, Anne...Protect your sister. Claire needs you now."

~

Anne jack-knifed up, and a damp washcloth fell into her lap from where it had been placed on her forehead. Her skin was covered in perspiration and her breath remained labored. Robert approached her bedside with worry. He patted her arm and took the cloth from her lap.

"Mrs. Montgomery, it's all right. It was just a dream," he said as he stroked her arm.

Anne rubbed her eyes until she saw stars. Robert was wrong; it wasn't a dream, or a nightmare, but her reality.

"What...what is going on? What's happening?"

A soft knock came from her bedroom door. Robert quickly answered it. A tall, brawny police officer stepped across the threshold, giving Anne a sympathetic look. Robert introduced him as Officer Day and stated that he wanted to ask her a few questions about Dr. Lindsey. Anne felt out of her own body, as if this whole scene was playing out below her. Her biological father had killed himself and tears poured down her face.

The officer observed her blood-splattered clothing.

"Dr. Montgomery, we'll need those clothes for evidence."

Anne looked down to see the red mess. She slid from her bed with the help of Robert. In her bathroom, she stripped out of her tainted clothing and washed her hands and face.

She wrapped herself in her cotton robe and clutched her nightgown tightly until her fingers whined with fatigue. With a deep breath, she exited the bathroom and handed the officer the garments. Another police officer walked in with an evidence bag. Anne sat back down on her bed. Her face was still but the tears wouldn't stop the vision of Dr. Lindsey thrusting the metal into his mouth. Brain matter rupturing across the room—it played over and over in her mind. Anne could feel the acid build in the pit of her stomach. It burned like an ulcer. She tucked a stiff strand of hair behind her ear.

"Dr. Montgomery, my questions will be quick. I know you witnessed a horrific thing today. Do you need to go to the hospital?" Officer Day pulled out a small notepad.

"No." Anne spoke in a voice that didn't even sound like her own.

Officer Day nodded and began his questions. Anne couldn't raise her green eyes to the officer. It took too much effort. She stared down at her black diamond, focused on the small diamonds that encircled the center one. Anne was numb; her lips, teeth, and gums tingled. She knew it was her body absorbing the shock of the situation. Anne's answers were delivered as though she were on auto-pilot; most of the time, she did not fully hear the questions. *Stop asking me these stupid questions. My father blew his brains out. What more do you want from me?* Robert hovered quietly in the corner.

This wasn't the first time she had witnessed a suicide… Her mother had taken a razor and sliced through her veins on the floor of her scummy bedroom. Anne remembered seeing the life rush from the open slits like wine. She'd watched her mother slowly fade away. She hadn't called for help; she hadn't run to the neighbors begging for assistance. Anne hadn't gone to her mother's side and wrapped her wounds with the nearest blanket or towel. No. Anne had watched her mother die right in front of her. The stench of death had filled the room but Anne had stood still. She hadn't wanted to save her mother. Anne had begged for the torture to stop. Either God had answered her prayers or the devil had swallowed her soul. *Maybe I'm the sadistic one...*

The world around her moved in slow motion. Words were drawn out. Movements were sluggish. Dr. Lindsey believed it wasn't too late for her. Right now, she disagreed. *My mother's venom is not in my veins, but Carter's is.*

Anne heard Carter discussing the scene with other officers in the hallway. He wanted to make his presence known, make sure she kept her mouth shut, but he needn't worry. Anne would remain silent. The Savannah Police Department couldn't help her. She wanted this god-awful interview over so she could spiral into nothingness for a while, but the officer kept up his repetitive questions.

"Did Dr. Lindsey reach for the gun? Was the gun in his hands? Did he leave a suicide note?" Officer Day jotted in his brown notebook.

Anne had enough. She slapped her hands on her thighs. "Enough. You've asked the same damn question ten different ways. He took the gun, shoved it in his mouth, and pulled the trigger. There's my statement. Now please leave me be."

The officer scowled while Robert escorted him from the room. Anne kept her eyes down. She could hardly focus. She tried to remain as coherent as possible until the officers left. The noise of people downstairs stirred her insides, but a wave of nausea flooded her when she heard the sound of metal releasing. It was the gurney for Dr. Lindsey's body, her father's body. Robert said it would be all right. *Would it? And if that were true, when? When would it be all right?*

The vision of his lifeless body being shoved into a black bag banished the air from Anne's lungs. She remembered her mother's body being zipped up and rolled into a coroner's van. It was just another day for them. But for Anne, a life was exiled from this world. A life she didn't stop from departing. Anne craved her medication; she would pop each pill and let the medicinal high suck her into the void. *Maybe I can steal some from Carter's stash.*

Anne's eyelids blinked heavy and long. She felt gutted. Carter's voice floated into her room from just outside the door. He talked to an officer about her like she was a stark-raving mad woman.

"My wife is emotionally unstable. She has a history of mental illness. David was her biological father. Her mother also committed suicide."

"I'm sorry, Mr. Montgomery. That's a lot to take on. You must really love her."

"I do, indeed."

Sorry for Carter? Stupid cops. I'm his prisoner. Please let the darkness take me. The darkness never came.

She tumbled over onto the plush comforter, sinking into it like quicksand. Anne had to be patient. Carter's downfall would come soon enough; she had to wait out this torture. Dr. Lindsey was now added to her list of people to avenge. She silently wept for a man she had known and trusted for over three years. A man to whom she had divulged her deepest, darkest secrets, a man who was her father, and who was now dead. How many of those secrets did he share with Carter? All of them? None of them? Someone other than Sam had helped Carter all those years and she was determined to find out who it was.

After the police had left the house and taken their yellow crime scene tape with them, silence occupied the walls. Anne shuffled to her bathroom and disrobed. She turned the shower faucet on and listened to the hot water pipes groan. She stepped in, and the white suds tinged pink while she washed her father's remains off of her. Anne's fingernails dug into her skin, trailing a sting of flushed streaks down her neck and chest. She gritted her teeth through the discomfort of the hot water; she tipped her head back and allowed the pain to become one with her. She leaned against the tile and sobbed her goodbye to her father, Dr. David Lindsey.

CHAPTER THIRTY-THREE

Anne stepped toward Dr. Lindsey's bedroom door and slowly pushed it open to reveal a dim, stale space. The sheer curtains sashayed in the late October breeze, fluttering loose papers on the oak desk. The numb shell Anne's soul currently inhabited crept into the room. She picked up a FedEx receipt that showed a destination of Minneapolis and assumed it was a package to Claire. *Claire, her sister.* She would receive Dr. Lindsey's body, crumble, scream, weep, then choose a funeral home, where the funeral director would suggest a closed casket or cremation due to the nature of his death. She would mourn, float through each step of the grieving process, and be forced to find closure. Anne knew the scenario.

A slender black leather case sat on the second shelf of his bookcase. Anne placed it in the palm of her hand, weighing the heavy enclosure. She opened the case and the hinges let out a small squeak. Inside, a stainless steel letter opener mirrored her red-rimmed eyes. Initials were engraved on the handle:

CMJ & DEL

They were her mother's and Dr. Lindsey's. *She must have given him this as a gift.* Anne picked it up and stroked the smooth metal with her finger over the initials. She trailed her finger to the sharp point and pressed down until a scarlet drop emerged from the broken skin. Anne watched the blood run down the length of her finger. Once it hit the top of her palm, she licked the red trail, placed her finger in her mouth, and sucked at the puncture hole. Anne could taste a metallic sensation on her tongue. *What would it be like to taste Carter's blood on my hands?* The mere image of him dying by her hands sent a frenzy of excitement through her.

She would never know her father, but would she have wanted to? *He left my mother pregnant and alone. He left me with a volatile crazy woman. But he was my blood, my family. Yes, I would've wanted to know him as a daughter knows her father.* Anne felt an urgency to return to Minneapolis not only for Casey, but for Claire, her sister, her family. *Carter will target her next. I need to protect her.*

A light tap on the door drew her attention away from the letter opener. Anne turned to see Robert standing in the doorway. He looked handsome in his black suit and tie.

"Mrs. Montgomery?"

Anne pulled her finger from her mouth. "Yes, Robert?"

"You should change for the dinner soon."

She looked down at her wrinkled pajamas. "I will. First, I need to go to church."

Robert raised his eyebrow. She knew it was an odd request, but when Anne had first arrived in Savannah, her eyes were drawn to the majestic St. Catherine's Catholic Church near Wright Square. Anne had questioned her faith for many years, especially when her mother would lock her inside her bedroom for days without food or clean clothes. God couldn't answer Anne's questions about why her mother was sick, but science could. She immersed herself in every article, textbook, and research study that pertained to neuropsychiatry. Anne would envision herself dissecting her mother's mentally ill brain. It was as black as tar and reeked of sour milk. Throughout Anne's childhood neglect, all she wanted to do was to save her mother, to find a drug or a cure for her sickness but a time came when Anne gave up.

During high school, Anne would sit in church for hours and obsessively study. She appreciated the silence in the sanctuary. The front she displayed as a child made her schools and social services workers none the wiser. Anne knew if they took her mother away, she would be forced into the foster care system, and her hopes to attend college would be snuffed out in a second.

Anne shook off the memories, placed the letter opener back inside the case, closed it, and gently set it down on the desk. Anne motioned for Robert to follow her down the hallway. They were met by Carter, who was ascending the staircase. The whites of his eyes webbed red, and restless shadows hovered underneath them.

"Where are you two running off to?" Carter sneered.

"I'm going to light a candle for Dr. Lindsey."

"Dinner is in a few hours. You need to get ready. Pay your respects later, Anneliese."

A growl vibrated against her ribs. "I'm doing it now."

Talons stung her bicep as Carter yanked her closer to him.

"Be careful, my Anneliese. Be very careful."

Anne heaved her arm from his clutches. She tipped into Robert and held onto his arm to regain her balance. *Another mood swing, great. I wonder what pills he swallowed today?* Her chest lifted tight and her breath was deep. Without another word, Carter stomped down the hallway and slammed his bedroom door.

"I'm going to love destroying him."

Robert grinned at her words.

∼

A kaleidoscope of ethereal beauty surrounded Anne while she dipped her fingers in the holy water vessel. Frankincense and myrrh scented the church. She stepped quietly down the center aisle toward the row of red votive candles that were guarded by a breathtaking marble statue of Mary.

She lit the wick and watched the wax drip around it. She sent up a silent prayer for the man she never knew as her father, the confidante she'd grown to adore, and the hostage who had no other way out of Carter's grip than to put a bullet in his head. Anne would have cried, but those emotions had run dry hours ago. Black ice packed her insides and she wrapped her arms tightly around her stomach.

Anne remembered the minutes after her mother's pulse ceased and all the blood had drained from her open veins. She had called the paramedics and told them she had gone to her mother's apartment and found her dead.

Her voice was impassive while she spoke to the emergency operator. "My mother committed suicide. She's dead."

Anne found it silly that the ambulance arrived with sirens blaring. Corrine Mary Jamison died at 1:47 p.m. on July 17—Anne's twentieth birthday. That year Anne stopped the acknowledgement of her birth. What was the point? She had no connection to the two people who gave her life. What was there to celebrate? Adam always argued that they gave him the greatest gift by bringing her into this world. Anne adored his words. They comforted her, but they were just words. July 17 was just another day for her.

Anne watched the votive candles flicker as a small smile came at the thought of Adam. She would see him tonight at the dinner. *My love, my angel. He can't know the truth, that I remember him. Carter will kill him right there.* She knew tonight was going to get ugly, and Anne relished the fact that Carter would begin to crumble. *Should I ask God for forgiveness for my sins? No, I'm not looking for mercy. I won't repent. I'll never be sorry for destroying Carter.* Anne gave one final look at the statue of Mary. Her marble eyes warned Anne, but she knew what needed to happen. She turned on her heels and walked to the back of the church. Her soul had been damned the second her lips first pressed against Carter's.

CHAPTER THIRTY-FOUR

Anne's thick blonde hair was set in velvet waves that tumbled down her back. Her fluid green eyes were lined with charcoal and her lips were painted scarlet. Her skin was so pale, she looked like an apparition. *Perfect—they'll never see me coming.*

Her strapless raven gown trailed behind her while she exited the Kensington Hotel's lobby restroom. Anne's stilettos clicked against the veined marble. She stopped at the bank of elevators and tucked her velvet clutch under her arm. Carter and his entourage were already upstairs. They arrived early to do one last security sweep. Anne reached out to press the elevator arrow when the follicles on her arms stood at attention and a prickly rawness skated along her ribcage. She knew who was behind her.

"Good evening, Dr. Montgomery."

Her heart leapt into her throat as his baritone voice vibrated her bones. Anne heard the sourness when he spoke her name. *He can't know. Don't give yourself away, not here.* She masked her inner disturbance and slowly turned to see Adam with his perfectly combed chestnut locks and chiseled features standing with one hand in his pants pocket. The dimples she loved so much were hidden by a scowl. It killed Anne to see him so upset. *Pull it together.*

Anne extended her hand. "Good evening."

She needed to touch him. He took her hand and a ribbon of heat fluttered across her hips as he kissed the top of her hand. His lips were soft and God, she wanted them on hers. Her neck, her arms, shoulders, breasts... Anne felt her muscles loosened by the images. Adam released her hand as the world around them slowly dimmed away. Anne's chest knotted and tightened to the point it grew painful to draw in breath. *My heart is breaking. I can't do this to him. Maybe we can run away right now. I'll grab his hand and we'll flee the country.* Anne's eyes clouded over the longer she stared at Adam. His face looked pained and her resolve cracked more.

"You look breathtaking." His dark eyes were steady on hers.

Anne finally spoke. "Thank you. So sweet of a stranger to say that."

It took every bit of self-control to not launch herself at Adam, reveal the truth, and beg forgiveness, but she couldn't. Anne hoped that he could see through her charade, but her skills in deception had sharpened since the last time they had seen one another.

She took a deep breath, Adam's scent of warm cotton and virility was heady. *I need to touch him again, just a quick one.* Her hand rose from her side, but she quickly pushed it back down when a voice boomed near them. Adam's brow furrowed in response to her perplexing action.

The atmosphere shifted around them like it does when a thunderstorm is about to roll in. The air chilled and electrified as Marcus Hunt sauntered through the hotel lobby and toward them.

"Good evening, Dr. Montgomery. I'm Marcus Hunt." The charismatic attorney extended his hand. "And this is

Adam Whitney, my firm's newest attorney—but I'm sure you already knew that." Marcus winked.

Anne accepted his venomous grip. "Good evening, Mr. Hunt. It's a pleasure to meet you."

He stood shoulder-to-shoulder with Adam. His tailored grey suit complemented his espresso skin to perfection. Both men looked dashing in their three-piece ensembles. Anne wanted to roll her eyes at his provocation but she kept them firmly on his. *Stay cold, Anne.* She narrowed her lined eyes to show him she was not intimidated by his haughty attitude. *He may claim to be all powerful but I won't bow to him.* Anne turned and pushed the arrow button to call the elevators. Her close proximity to Adam unnerved her. For a moment, she contemplated taking the stairs.

Marcus stepped next to her. "Tell me, Dr. Montgomery. How are the newlyweds?"

"Fine." Anne flashed a fake smile.

The elevator announced its arrival. Anne led the three of them into the cramped space. Adam brushed against her bare arm; prickles sprinted over her exposed flesh. *What kind of game is this?* Anne pressed the button for the top floor and prayed that the elevator would ascend without any stops.

"What a coincidence, me working with your ex-fiancé and now your new husband. That has to be quite awkward for you."

Adam didn't flinch at the statement and neither did Anne. She was already tired of his provocative behavior. She filled her lungs with fresh oxygen before replying as vaguely as she could.

"Not awkward at all. The amnesia wiped away all memories of my former fiancé."

Oh, my chest. How could I speak such a lie? Anne's soul cried out to Adam like a siren. It begged him not to listen to the lies that tumbled from her mouth. Marcus patted Adam's shoulder. He stood emotionless but Anne watched his smooth jaw tense and his hazel eyes dull. *I'm killing him.*

Marcus leaned against the wall of the elevator. "Interesting. So you have no recollection of Adam here?"

"Mr. Hunt, with all due respect, it would be ill-mannered of me to discuss a previous relationship with you while my husband is in the vicinity."

Marcus nodded, holding his hands up.

"Very well, but we must talk later this evening. I'll buy you a drink."

Adam's lips remained in a tight line and the moment the elevator reached the requested floor, Anne crossed to the bar and ordered a shot. The vodka burned her parched throat but she received the heat while it spread across her upper body. She ordered a second one while a familiar hand glided across the blades of her shoulders.

"Pace yourself, my love," Carter whispered, while he stroked the curve of her back.

She leaned into him and motioned across the polished granite bar to the two men. Carter's hand stilled, then clenched.

"Carter, I just got off the elevator with Marcus Hunt and Adam. Give me a break."

Carter's other hand gripped Anne's waist. "What did they ask you?"

"Marcus Hunt was an arrogant ass, inquired about my relationship with Adam. I believe they suspect my amnesia is a lie. I can't understand why they would think that?" Anne tipped back the shot.

"Don't be condescending, Anneliese. Your father isn't here to save you. You fooled me. I'm sure your performance was just as Oscar-worthy—besides, I'm your husband. Your loyalty and love lies with me."

"I haven't forgotten, but excuse me if I am a bit on edge since my biological father blew his brains out in our home this week."

He pulled her closer, pushing his solid frame against hers. "That's right, our home—don't forget that. Don't forget how I love you so much and I would die without you at my side. Tonight is a very important night. We're going to make millions, and you are going to be my doting wife—or else."

Anne gripped the edge of the bar. "God, can we go one night without death threats? It's getting old."

"You know what's getting old? Your continued defiance."

Anne's face reddened, partially from the liquor and partially from the agitation that spilled over. *I'll show him defiance.* She held up her finger to the bartender for another shot. She watched Natalie, dressed in plum satin, make her catwalk entrance into the bar and stride toward them. Now she would have to contend with Natalie. *Great.*

"Jesus, enough with the vodka," Carter spat out, sliding the shot out of her reach.

She slapped his hand away. "Don't tell me what to do. I need this to even begin to function properly in this fucked situation."

Anne's stare locked onto his while she let the liquid encase her throat in heat. Before he could proceed with the scolding, Natalie approached them.

"Good evening, Mr. and Dr. Montgomery. I do hope everything is to your liking."

"Yes, Miss Franz, everything looks perfect," Anne replied with false pleasantness.

"If you ladies will excuse me, I need to greet our guests."

With those words of departure, Carter walked around the length of the polished bar to where Marcus and Adam stood. The elevator announced its arrival and revealed a breathtaking woman with beautiful skin that was warm in tone whose hair cascaded around her shoulders in a sleek curtain of sable.

Anne watched the woman's curves ebb and flow through the room in a manner that commanded attention and re-spect. Her cinnamon gown hugged her voluptuous figure, which made the men in the room pause.

Natalie gasped. "Magda Alves. Wow, she's gorgeous."

Anne remained silent and watched the small group ex-change pleasantries but felt Adam's pull from across the room. With each glance, her mask cracked. She needed to let him know she was not who he thought she was and she remembered everything. But before she could come up with a plan, Natalie announced that dinner was about to be served.

CHAPTER THIRTY-FIVE

The sleek rectangular dining table seated the five guests comfortably. The architecture of the gothic table enticed Anne to run her stiletto against the turret leg as she sat at one end of the table; Carter sat opposite her. She was grateful for the distance.

Anne eyed each person at the table. Before dinner, Carter had introduced Anne to Magda and instead of being the cold calculating murderess that everyone claimed she was, Anne found her sincere—almost motherly.

Magda cupped Anne's face. "Hello, my dear Anneliese. You are more beautiful than Carter described."

Magda's accent was thick, but Anne could understand most of what she said. On occasion, if Magda couldn't locate an English word, she would say it in Spanish.

"Let me see your wedding ring." Anne lifted her hand toward Magda. "Oh, exquisite and very rare, like you, Anneliese." Anne heard an annoyed huff and could only guess it was from Adam. "Only the strongest of women can carry off a black diamond such as this one and you, Anneliese, carry it very well." Magda stroked the diamond with her midnight-coated fingernails.

Anne felt her heart react to Magda's entrancing words. She could understand why people were charmed by this woman. There was something about her. Anne found herself drawn to every word that Magda spoke.

Anne finished her dinner and drank her glass of champagne.

"Excuse me, Anneliese?"

She put her glass down and turned her attention to Magda. "Yes?"

"Once the men retreat to the patio or bar, we must sit down and talk. Carter has spoken highly of you and I would love to get to know you better."

Anne's nerves simmered and from the corner of her eye, she could see Adam turn his head toward their conversation while he continued to eat. Carter gave her a most pleased expression.

"I would love that, Ms. Alves."

"Please, call me Magda. We have bypassed those formalities."

Anne let out a tight laugh and drank the rest of her champagne. Anne needed to be alert and sober but the train wreck that was about to slam into the hotel forced Anne to flood her frenzied emotions with alcohol. The bombardment of critical conversations would begin once dinner ended.

Anne smiled. "Call me Anne, Magda. My husband is the only one who refers to me as Anneliese." Anne realized that came out a little too harsh, but Carter had that effect on her.

Magda laughed and placed her cloth napkin on top of her mostly empty plate. "I think Anneliese is a beautiful name. I cannot fault him for that."

Dinner ended with chocolate torte and a quick dismissal by Carter. Anne walked to the empty bar and leaned against its smooth edge. A beautiful woman with long, brunette curls stood near the black grand piano singing a sweet ballad. Adam surprised her when he stuck out his right hand.

"May I have this dance?"

Marcus Hunt and Carter were in Anne's peripheral vision. She was not going to pass up this opportunity to irritate Carter. Anne placed her hand in his and felt the burn course through her veins. Carter growled and looked positively homicidal. *Good, serves him right.*

"Oh, let them have a dance, Montgomery. You, Magda, and I have business to conduct," Marcus Hunt belted out.

Carter leaned close to Anne's ear. "Be careful, my Anneliese."

He wasn't warning her of Adam's intentions but of his own. Marcus slapped Carter on the shoulder while he gave Anne a playful wink. The generous gesture confused her but she wasn't going to argue with it right now. She wanted to be in Adam's arms, just for a few moments. Anne allowed him to guide her toward the music.

Their bodies molded together in sweet familiarity and hummed like they had found their counterpart. This was not some stranger she had met on the streets of Savannah; this was a man who held her entire being.

Anne placed her hand in his. "Your intentions are quite transparent."

Adam tried to look offended by her accusation. "Whatever do you mean? I was simply asking you to share a dance with me."

She eyed him. *This is how we are going to play it. Very well.* She was more than happy to indulge him, even though her heart was crumbling inside her chest. Anne's breaths were small and stifled.

"I was made aware of a death in your house."

Anne stiffened. *Why would he bring that up here, now?* She feared if she looked into his eyes she would break down in front of him.

"Yes."

"My condolences, Dr. Montgomery."

"Thank you, but please don't call me that."

They began swaying again.

"Is that not your name?"

She stared right into his eyes. "Not by choice."

"There's always a choice. Some with irreversible consequences."

"I accept that," Anne replied, with a twinge of insolence.

Adam dipped her quickly, then pulled her back up hard against him. "Do you?"

"I have to."

His eyes squinted, Adam tightened his grip around her waist and dug his fingers into her flesh. It angered Anne that her dress separated his skin from hers. Though his anger pulsed through her, she wanted nothing more than to wrap herself around him and never let go.

"I came here for you, but I've seen your intimate exchanges with your husband and I'm second-guessing my reasons for being here."

His statement nipped at her flesh. *He thinks I love Carter. Has he seen me kiss Carter? No! No! It was all for show. How can he think I would do that to him?* Anne knew she had to send him a message to show him she remembered. How would she do that with prying eyes? Adam's eyes shifted above her and before Anne could say anything more, she felt a tap on her shoulder.

CHAPTER THIRTY-SIX

"Excuse me, but I need to talk to Dr. Montgomery," Natalie smiled sweetly as she eyed Adam.

This woman is unbelievable. Anne didn't want to let Adam go, especially not for Natalie. Adam dropped his arms as though they were weighted down and allowed Natalie to sweep her away. She couldn't help but peek over her shoulder at the man whom she desperately loved. The man she needed to feel whole. Anne left him alone on the dance floor, doubting their love, doubting everything that they had ever shared. *Maybe Adam is right—her consequences were irreversible.*

Anne veered toward the ladies room with Natalie prancing behind her. She stormed in and checked each stall to confirm that they were alone. Anne walked back and pressed her palms against the cold granite while Natalie looked on in confusion. Her body shook as tears ribboned her face. Anne felt an arm wrap around her shoulders.

"Oh, what's wrong, Dr. Montgomery? Was it the dinner? Something not cooked right?"

Is she kidding? She would never cry over charred pork, but Natalie didn't know Anne. She didn't know that the man she left on the dance floor was her love, her oxygen, her purpose in this life and after. Natalie didn't know that Anne wanted to destroy Carter because he killed her baby and her father.

She stared at the pale, mascara-streaked woman in the mirror. After a couple of minutes, she regained her composure and shrugged off Natalie's comfort. *Pull yourself together before Natalie runs to Carter.* Natalie handed her a handful of tissues. Anne accepted them and dabbed away the salty streaks.

"I'm fine, thank you, Natalie. Just tired. What is it that you wanted?"

Natalie leaned against the towel dispenser and licked her lips. "Oh, I had heard about the suicide at your house. Tragic, absolutely tragic. I wanted to express my deepest of sympathies."

Anne tried to block out Natalie's insipid voice. *She wants to give the gossip column a juicy insider story. I'm going to kill her, I swear, if she doesn't shut up.* She continued to fix her smeared face while Natalie rambled on.

"Did you see Magda's gown? That is an original Versace, you know, not some knock off from a low-class department store. I Googled it when I saw her walk in. Oh my, and Marcus Hunt, I read this article about him being connected to prostitutes. He hired them to set people up and recorded the entire thing, you know, for blackmail and such. Scandalous." Natalie fanned herself with her hand. "Do you know when Michael is arriving? I would love to sink my teeth into that sexy man. Did you know that he was part of an arranged marriage? So very odd. Who does that in America?"

Anne froze, and her eyes moved to Natalie in the reflection of the mirror. "What do you mean, by *arranged marriage?* When? Where?"

Natalie moved to the other side of Anne and leaned against the counter. "Such a horrible love story. A long time ago it was arranged for Michael to marry Magda Alves's daughter but Michael didn't want anything to do with her— he loved another girl. So when he rejected Magda's daughter, she died—died of a broken heart they said." Natalie clutched her chest. "So sad, I couldn't imagine."

Anne allowed the torrent of information to sink into her brain as she tried to map it all out. *I need to find out when this happened.*

"Natalie, have you seen my husband? I lost track of him after dinner."

"He, Marcus, and Magda are in room 613. I have placed security in the hallway." Natalie smoothed her sleek hair. "Find me when Michael arrives." She winked and left Anne alone in the bathroom.

She freshened up her makeup before she headed back out to the bar. There wasn't any indication of a minor breakdown anywhere on her face. *Where is Michael?* Anne knew he would arrive soon and she didn't want to miss out on the fireworks.

Anne slipped from the ladies restroom and into the cool hotel hallway. She could feel the wisps of late fall air move around her from the open patio doors in the bar area. The brass-plated numbers guided Anne down the L-shaped hall. She spotted the armed entourage once she turned the corner. *This seems a bit much.* Natalie's security and Carter's men saw her coming toward them and stepped in front of the hotel door.

She cocked her brow. "You're kidding me, right?"

The burly men looked at each other and back at Anne.

Anne threw her hands up. "I'll take the blame, okay? Just let me in."

They silently agreed and stepped aside. Anne could hear the whoosh of her dress as she stepped closer to the door. Her lips tingled at the anticipation. *Why the need for so much security?* One of the men tapped the door with his knuckle. Moments later, with the click of the lock, the door opened to another armed guard.

He ticked his head at Anne, instructing her to quickly enter the room. Once she did, her eyes stopped and focused on a circular table. Three opened briefcases filled with money sat staring at Anne. The neatly lined stacks of cash were being covered with a thick plastic by two bodyguards. *What the hell is going on? Is this what the dinner was about? Payment for drugs?* Anne's heart skipped in her chest. What had she gotten herself into?

Marcus and Magda didn't bother to acknowledge Anne's presence; they were too busy examining their money. Carter looked intense and more wild than usual, but oddly, his demeanor emanated a calmness that caused Anne to heighten her inner panic. *He's high as a kite right now.* Carter approached her and took ahold of her hands. She didn't want her panic to seep out. Anne swallowed it down and focused on Carter.

"Is everything all right, my Anneliese?"

"Yes, I was just wondering where you had gone. I wanted to make sure you were alright."

Anne kept up her devoted wife façade but internally she wanted to vomit.

"I see. Well, I was finishing up some business in here...."

"I'm worried about Michael. Maybe you should call him and make sure he's on his way," Anne said, while brushing an imaginary piece of lint from his jacket. She needed Carter distracted so she could talk to Marcus.

"He is quite late." Carter glanced at his watch. "I'm going to head down to the lobby and wait for him. Will you be alright?"

"Of course. Go check on your brother."

Carter pulled out his phone and excused himself. Once Carter exited the room, Anne grasped her opportunity.

"Mr. Hunt, buy me that drink."

He looked up from his Blackberry. "It would be my pleasure, Dr. Montgomery."

Marcus removed himself from the table of scattered drugs. Magda's black eyes bore into Anne's.

"Remember, Anneliese, we need to talk."

"I look forward to it, Magda."

Marcus escorted Anne from the room and back to the bar, where they each ordered a glass of champagne. A train of black fabric cascaded around her while she crossed her legs on the leather stool.

"I had heard from my husband that you wanted to speak with me. I apologize that my schedule didn't allow it."

His brown eyes glinted. "I know that you are an extremely busy woman."

Anne clasped her hands together on the bar. "That I am. Carter has kept me occupied with Montgomery business."

"Yes. He said that you have dived right in."

An awkward silence passed between them while the bartender placed two glasses of champagne in front of them. "What did you want to meet with me about?"

"First, I wanted to warn you about Adam. He shared your story with me and my heart bleeds for him. Second,

I have information regarding your husband and his entrepreneurial dealings."

"Go on," Anne said leaning in a little closer.

"Are you aware that your name is no longer attached to the Mayo Clinic study?"

"No."

"My sources tell me that they dissolved your name on the contract, claiming mental instability."

Carter. He took away from her the one thing that meant everything to her. Anne could barely catch her breath. He was punishing her and would continue to do so until the day she died. The fire roared beneath her skin as it spread up her neck and to her cheeks.

"Does Carter's other business dealings have to do with the piles of cash I saw? I'm not stupid, I know drugs are involved. Are you part of that illegal indiscretion?"

"I appease my clients. I don't ask questions."

"I'm sure you don't. You just collect your money and walk away. Still doesn't leave you with clean hands, Mr. Hunt."

Marcus laughed before he took a drink of his champagne.

Anne tilted her head. "With all due respect, I'm growing impatient with this conversation. What do you want? Why share this with me?"

He shook his finger at her. "Carter said you were feisty."

"Mr. Hunt—"

"Let me be frank with you, I despise Carter. He's a liar and a coward. I have built my empire from the ground up and that prick thinks he can rise to the top with a snap of his pretty-boy fingers? I don't think so. I was more than happy to bring Adam on board; Richard Morris spoke highly of him even with the misunderstanding of him being involved with your brief disappearance." The veins in his neck and temple began to protrude. "Nothing would give me more pleasure than to watch Carter fall."

"But you want me to do the pushing?"

"I gathered you would enjoy that." Marcus clicked his tongue. "You spoke of drugs. You're correct but your husband has taken his fair share and Magda has noticed. That's why she wishes to speak with you. I went to bat for you, telling her that you have nothing to do with it."

"I don't." Anne spoke with an edge to her voice. "We're talking about a substantial supply, correct? Not a small amount that can easily fit inside of a small cabinet."

Marcus belted out in laughter, clutching his abdomen. "You're a funny woman. No, think thousands of dollars gone. Poof." He snapped his fingers. "Just like that. Has he been traveling anywhere specific lately?"

Atlanta. Maybe he's shipping them there? Is that why he stuck Simon there? Anne thrummed her fingers on the bar top. Her eyes narrowed as she lifted her champagne to her lips. The black diamond shimmered from the overhead lighting. The longer the ring sat on her finger, the more the blackness seeped into her skin and filled her veins. Anne was losing herself, just as Dr. Lindsey feared. But revenge had no room for remorse.

CHAPTER THIRTY-SEVEN

Before Anne could respond to Marcus, a familiar pull tugged at her soul.

"Is this seat taken?" Adam murmured in her ear.

Anne spun on the barstool. The man was deliciously gorgeous. A hint of his dimples appeared on either side of his lovely mouth. Anne's heart rate kicked up a notch. Adam affected her in ways that Carter never could.

"I'll leave you two alone." Marcus said, giving Anne a smirk before exiting the bar.

She motioned to the seat next to her. "Please have a seat."

"Enjoying the evening?" Adam asked.

"I am, thank you, but I have a strong feeling it will get even better."

Anne repositioned herself on the stool, gently brushing her hand against his forearm while the tip of her heel grazed his leg. Adam noticed and raised an eyebrow.

"What are you doing?"

Anne batted her thick black lashes. "Whatever do you mean?"

"We need to talk."

"Business or pleasure?"

"Both."

Anne's muscles tightened, her heart leapt to her throat, and a prickle raced along her spine as Adam's hazel eyes darkened like the Savannah night.

"Looks who's flirting now."

Before Adam could respond, she heard a throat clearing behind her. Magda Alves approached them and towered over Anne with her commanding stance. She moved to Adam and placed a hand gently on Adam's shoulder and ran it down his arm. Anne's murderous instincts ignited but she kept still. *First Natalie, now Magda. Good God.* Adam appeared none too thrilled with Magda's playful touch.

"Pardon the interruption but I need to speak with Anneliese before I retire for the night."

Anne rose from the stool and picked up her clutch. "Certainly, Magda."

They excused themselves from Adam, who scowled at the two ladies. Anne led Magda to the empty dining room and they sat down at the table. Magda ran the tip of her manicured black nail along the polished surface in a figure eight. She exuded malevolence. Much more than Carter. Anne quickly built a wall of confidence around her but inside she was shrinking down to a terrified child.

"Anneliese, I will not speak to you like you are a stupid twit. I know you are aware of Carter's business with me. I've known him for years. I've known his family for years."

"Which family?" Anne snapped, but she reeled herself back in when Magda shot her a wicked glare.

"Both, actually. My late husband, Demario, grew up with Simon Montgomery. And there was a time, long ago, when Steven Leeds was close with them both. The eighties were a tough time for us all." Magda's eyes drifted while she spoke to Anne. "Men and their ridiculous egos. They fault women for their emotions but men—men are just as sensitive. Those fools call it passion." Magda chuckled.

Anne folded her hands in her lap. "What happened to your husband, Magda?"

Magda's eyes grew dark and she leaned back against the chair, recrossing her flawless, lean legs.

"Robbery. A bullet to the heart at close range." She sneered. "I was surprised he even had a heart. He certainly didn't have a brain. The man was a worthless tyrant, like my father was."

Anne swallowed the terror that had built up in her throat. She glanced down at the black diamond, recalling Magda's interest in it.

Anne lifted her left hand and set it on the table. "You spoke of strong women being able to wear such a ring. What did you mean by that?"

Magda lowered her eyes to the black diamond, the ink jewel reflecting the flickering candelabras that branched beside them.

"I was born in Coatzacoalcos, Veracruz, Mexico. During the oil boom, my family lived in luxury and my father gave my brother and me whatever we desired. My mother was a beautiful, successful actress but she had a wandering eye. She began an affair with one of my father's business associates who controlled the ports in Coatzacoalcos. My mother and her lover conspired against my father. They wanted to murder him, Anneliese." Anne reminded herself to breathe. Her hand lay flat on the table, and she felt cemented to her chair. "I had noticed that my mother's diamond ring started to change color. Growing darker, until it was black."

"This ring?" Anne whispered.

A sly grin spread across Magda's flush lips. "Anneliese, do you know what Coatzacoalcos means?" Anne shook her head. "It means 'the hiding place of the snake.' My mother, while still holding the gun that killed my father, told me that the venom of their lifestyle, and where they lived, had seeped into her, turning her once pure and unspoiled diamond black and unholy, just like her soul."

Holy shit. Anne stared at Magda in astonishment. She wasn't one to believe in a magical voodoo ring but Anne couldn't deny that she felt like Magda's mother had, years ago. Anne felt the corruption inside of her and with each passing day, the battle continued but the good inside her was diminishing. As she sat there across from Magda, Anne needed the power and deceit to rid her of the snake that coiled itself around her.

"The ring on your finger was my mother's. I would have given it to my daughter, Celesta, but she died some time ago." Magda closed her eyes for a moment.

Anne remembered what gossip queen Natalie said about Magda's daughter dying of a broken heart because of Michael. *Do I dare ask? No. I need to stay focused on Carter. The Michael and Celesta story can wait.*

"Why did your mother kill him?" Anne tilted her head.

"My father was an arrogant dictator who treated my mother like garbage. After his death, she took over the business and when she passed away, she gave it to me. Of course, I became quite popular among opportunist men. Demario caught my attention, but he foolishly thought he could take my money and authority from me because I was a woman. Those serpents from Coatzacoalcos came with me when I arrived in Florida. Anneliese, I see a broken woman before me, but you have strength and brilliance. And these pathetic men want to hold you down. They want to suffocate you. Don't let them, my girl. When Carter explained to me about your accident and how you survived such a fall, I knew that ring would help you. Help you see your potential. Your strength."

Anne tried to process Magda's words. *She's clearly a man-hater. Perfect.*

"Your family business is in illegal product exchanges? Correct?" Anne asked stepping carefully.

"You are correct. I dabble in many product exchanges. I've had to tweak it a bit over the years. Conform. But I remain successful. However, it has come to my attention that someone is stealing from me and that is unacceptable. I am extremely careful whom I bring in, and knowing that people I trusted are biting the hand that feeds them is disturbing."

"You believe it's Carter."

Magda nodded. "I need you to locate my missing supply, and that includes any money he has collected from sales." She fluffed her dark waves. "Anneliese, your husband is sucking Montgomery Hotels Incorporated dry, just as he did with Leeds Imports and Construction. He owes money to very dangerous people and if I know him, he's taking my drugs and selling them on the streets. He's...how do you say in the States?...*fucked*, if he doesn't make good on his word and that includes me. I want my money and supply returned, with interest."

Anne swallowed the growing lump. "He's bleeding multi-million dollar companies dry? How much money does he owe?"

"Anneliese, he was missing for many years. He made contacts, made deals. Carter has bargained too much and he needs to pay. I feel that without my alliance, you could be in danger."

Anne's hands drop onto the table. "Me? Why?"

"People are after you, people you trusted. If you help me, Anneliese, you will be compensated greatly. Not only financially, but I can help you get back your study with the Mayo Clinic. You want to save the innocent, the mentally ill. Let me help you. The FDA is on my payroll." Magda leaned forward, placing her hand over Anne's. "Your poor mother was sick, Anneliese. You can create a new drug without any man's objections. Do not allow another mother to do to her daughter what yours did to you. You can be their redeemer. Carter will disappear forever, my girl."

Anne felt tears weave through her bottom lashes and fall heavily down her cheeks. Her breaths were short. Magda was dangling the illicit carrot in front of her, and Anne was growing more and more captivated. She was becoming overwhelmed.

"How do you know about me no longer being a part of the Mayo Clinic study? Marcus Hunt?"

"I know more than Marcus Hunt knows. I know about the deception before it even happens."

"What if I say no? What if I can't find anything on Carter?" Anne asked toeing the waters.

Magda dug her nails into the top of Anne's hand, and Anne grimaced at the pain.

"The snake will bite, Anneliese. And I will be very disappointed in you."

Anne nodded. "I'll help you."

Let's not provoke the Latin American drug lord. A satisfied curl of the lips stretched upward on Magda's smooth face. The thick black lashes that lined her eyes laced together as she closed her eyes and inhaled deeply. When she opened them, Anne could have sworn that the pupils were elliptical in shape, like a venomous snake. She pulled her hand down into her lap and stroked over the imbedded fingernail crescents, trying to soothe the throbbing.

"I knew you were the right one for the ring. We will be in touch soon, Anneliese."

They rose from their chairs and headed back to the bar. Anne couldn't help but notice the lilies that were sitting on a circular table next to the room's entrance were now wilted and withered in their crystal vase. Turning back now would mean death for them all, and that was not an option for Anne.

Magda said her farewells to Marcus, Anne, and Adam. With a snap of her fingers, her armed entourage escorted her from the bar and to the elevator. Anne's adrenaline chilled inside her, but her ivory skin was flushed. Anne coaxed her emotions to settle down but they didn't obey.

Adam was running his thumb along the sides of his snifter of brandy. His hazel eyes remained focused on the surface of the bar, and Anne could see his muscles were rigid and tight. A light sprouting of facial hair was starting to cover his jaw and cheekbones. Anne perched herself next to him.

"I saw you speaking with Marcus earlier. Was it a beneficial discussion?" Adam's eyes stayed down when he spoke.

"It was."

"And Magda Alves?" Adam still wouldn't look at her.

"Also beneficial." With a furrowed brow and vigilant gaze, she moved closer to Adam. "You shouldn't be here. Go back to Minneapolis. You can't be here."

He guffawed. "I think the Montgomery name has gone to your head." Adam slammed back the remaining amber liquid in his glass.

"Excuse me?"

"You may have the Montgomery brothers and any other man you encounter wrapped around your little manipulative finger, but I don't take orders from you."

His words cut Anne. *He's hurt and I deserve his anger.* He had witnessed the woman who was once his fiancée exchange promises and allegiances with people who were ruthless and cunning. He had seen her share intimate moments with the man who tried to murder him. Adam was probably feeling betrayed, something Anne knew about only too well.

"You don't understand—"

Adam grabbed the hand her black diamond sat on. "You seem quite cozy with this rock on your hand."

Anne wanted to clutch his hand and kiss each finger to show him that she was still his—that her heart was his—but instead she pulled her hand away.

"I can assure you that this is the most unpleasant experience of my life, and I do plan to rectify the situation soon."

A thunderous growl boomed around them. *Finally.*

"Let it begin." Anne whispered.

CHAPTER THIRTY-EIGHT

Carter stormed the bar; rage etched his face and he had an intense, fevered stare. His olive skin was a deep shade of red. He ran a hand through his crown of unruly waves, targeting the man to her right. Carter pointed an accusatory finger in the air and bared his teeth.

"You. This is your doing."

Adam held his hands up. "I would love to take credit for this, but I had nothing to do with it."

Simon and Michael Montgomery entered the room, along with their threatening backup. Simon used an ornate wooden cane to offset his still-weakened muscles. Stubble covered his square jaw and fair cheeks, and shaggy strands hung over his furrowed forehead, yet he still exuded authority and confidence. Michael offered support to his father's lofty frame while keeping his focus on Carter who was ready to launch into a verbal tirade at Adam.

Simon and Michael walked closer. Anne briefly caught Michael's eye, but he shifted his gaze back to Carter. The room was silent. The air grew thick and electrified as the Montgomery men's glares blazed into one another.

"Carter, it's over." Michael stepped into Carter's space.

Anne could hear her heart pounding through her veins. Michael was ready for a fight. And it was one he knew he could win, now that Simon was mobile again.

"I hold control of Montgomery Hotels Incorporated, not you, so this proves nothing," Carter sliced his arm through the air.

"It states that as long as my father is incapable of running the company, you are the acting CEO. As you can plainly see, he is quite capable."

Carter moved closer to Michael. "That's to be determined. *Our* father suffered a stroke that was detrimental to his mental well-being. Do you honestly think he can run a multi-million-dollar corporation while recovering from such a draining ordeal? What will the board say?" Carter sneered.

Simon's authoritative voice broke into the dense atmosphere. "You will discontinue holding this conversation as if I'm not present. We both know it wasn't a stroke, and your vicious threats to the board members are void. You are no longer part of Montgomery Hotels Incorporated, effective immediately, and you are no longer a Montgomery. You aren't man enough to have my name. Go back to being a worthless Leeds." Simon shuffled toward a sullen Carter. He was within inches of his Carter's face. "I'll destroy you. Blood or not, I *will* destroy you," Simon seethed.

Carter leaned in. "I look forward to it, *Father.*"

Carter turned Anne. He looked murderous. "Anneliese, come. We are leaving."

Carter, along with his two brutes, strode toward the elevator. Anne's heels crashed against the tile floor; the force reverberated up her legs. She caught up to them and placed her hands on his arm.

"Carter, I should stay and wrap things up here. Remember, doting wife. I'll do damage control."

"Fine," he growled. "Robert will stay with you. I want you back at the house in an hour. Do you understand me?"

She gave him a fake smile. "Yes, dear. Go cool off before you do something stupid."

"One hour, Anneliese."

Carter placed his lips on her cheekbone. He backed away and entered the elevator, and Anne held his gaze until the doors closed. She walked back to the bar where the men stood silent. The bodyguard who had frisked Anne the night she met Michael at the abandoned schoolhouse leaned against the wall and gave her a leering smirk.

Simon and Michael whispered to each other. Adam turned to Anne with a look of concern that fanned the corners of his eyes.

Adam grabbed her hand. "You need to come with me."

Without argument, Anne agreed. She stretched and reached for her clutch that sat on the bar top. Michael caught their abrupt departure and arched a disapproving eyebrow. Anne gave him a look of reassurance before entering the elevator. Adam's fingers squeezed around hers as he dragged Anne into the hallway and down the back staircase. A car awaited them behind the hotel.

Anne didn't know where they were going and in that moment, she didn't care.

❧

"Would you like a drink?" Adam reached for a bottle of wine from the bar in the corner of his hotel room. "Merlot?"

"Yes, thank you."

Anne looked around the luxurious suite. He had spared no expense. The yellow silk linens and posh baroque décor warmed the vast room. Glossy black chandeliers hung above them, casting a dim light. The historic Le Paradis d'Or Hotel was not far from where she lived. The Parisian-inspired structure sat next to Forsyth Park. The close proximity had been perfect for Adam's midnight meetings with Dr. Lindsey.

She crossed her legs. A hungry ache traveled through her abdomen as she tightened her thighs. She was finally alone with Adam, and the last thing she wanted to do was drink wine and talk. *I need him.* The slit of her dress exposed her slender leg, which didn't go unnoticed by Adam. Anne could see his dimples from across the room.

He walked over to the glass-top table and set down two glasses filled with the burgundy wine. As Anne sipped the delicious wine, Adam sat next to her. Their knees nearly touched, spiking prickles along her skin. She could feel his body heat seep through his clothes.

"Anne?" He crossed his arms over his chest.

Anne put her glass down. "Yes?"

"Was that your doing back there?"

Her eyes held his. "Yes. I'm trying to protect the ones I love, so if that means I make a deal with a few demons, so be it."

"Are you sure you want to make such an arrangement with people who can drag you to hell with them?"

"I'm already in hell," she replied, barely above a whisper.

Adam had already discarded his suit coat. He was now undoing the top two buttons of his dress shirt. Anne's senses were heightened. She watched him pop the white buttons through the eyelets and was mesmerized by Adam's fingers, how they moved with ease. The platinum wedding band that Carter wore should be on Adam's finger. Anne's pulse thrummed in her ears.

Adam parted his perfect lips and that small movement slowly unraveled her from the inside out. He leaned in. His finger scraped her exposed leg, glided over her knee and then reached her thigh.

"So soft." His voice resonated within her chest walls.

His simple touch intensified her want; her body was responsive and craved more. His dark eyes locked onto hers, willing her to break her passive composure. Anne uncrossed her legs and bit down on her lower lip. Adam's hands trailed over the thin fabric of her dress and lifted her hand up as if it were made of glass.

"This ring means nothing. Carter coerced you in to this mockery of matrimony. It doesn't belong there."

Adam slid the black diamond off and laid it between them on the table. It was like a weight had been removed from her chest. He placed the palm of her hand against his warm lips, sending electrical spasms down her spine. A surge of heat radiated throughout her entire being. His arousing caress was her collapse. Tears slipped through her long eyelashes. Adam knelt in front of her, gently thumbing the wetness away.

"You were there…." she choked out. His hazel eyes widened at her words. "The day I left Minneapolis, you were there." *She caught sight of an attractive man leaning against the brick wall across from her. His ruffled locks moved with the chilled breeze. And something pulled deep within her. Those familiar dark eyes held her gaze until a baker's truck drove by. The man disappeared once the truck passed.*

His eyes glistened with tears. "I knew you would remember, Anne. God, I've missed you terribly."

She nodded and stroked his beautifully stubbled cheek. "I could never forget you. You're my angel, my love. Carter could never take those memories from me. He could never take you away from me. I love you, Adam. I will always love you. It will always be you."

Another stream of heavy tears spilled down and Adam drew her into him, tightening his arms around her waist, holding her up as she leaned against his thigh. An eruption of emotion released between them, and Anne shuddered in his arms and buried her face into the crook of his neck. It was the most safe she had felt in months. Anne breathed in his masculine scent as his fingers stroke her shoulder blades and spine.

The memory of seeing his dying body on the floor of Leeds Imports and Construction caused her to cry out with such intensity that she could barely breathe. Adam pulled back, cupped her face, and ran the pad of his thumb over her lips, spreading the salty tears over her quivering mouth. She fisted his shirt, clinging to it like it was her salvation. The air around them morphed into a dense heat. The intensity of their passion awakened something in Anne that had been lifeless for so long.

"I will be glad and rejoice in your love, for you saw my affliction and knew the anguish of my soul," Adam rasped.

Heavy cries echoed from her chest and Adam covered her mouth with his, swallowing each sob. Anne wanted him to absorb all the passion and love that had built up inside her over the bleak months of emotional captivity. Anne plunged her tongue in deeper, wanting more of Adam's sweet taste.

In a swift rush, Adam pulled away, picked her up, and cradled her small frame against his. She could feel the movement of each of his muscles, which she knew so well. Every inch of his skin, she knew. Anne's stilettos slipped from her feet and fell to the floor with soft thuds. He laid her down on the bed, letting her black silk dress sink into the white beneath her like ink on a blank canvas. Waves of blonde hair fanned out around her.

Adam lowered his body and hovered over her. She ran her fingers through his hair. He closed his eyes, relishing her touch. Anne wanted to draw out each second that passed, stretch time to its breaking point, until it shattered around them in a rain of infinity.

Anne pulled Adam down, sucking and nipping at his lips. The intensity of their exchange grew stronger as he swept his tongue inside her mouth. She arched her body into his, practically begging him to rid her of her gown. Adam obliged and stripped Anne down to her ivory flesh.

Each kiss, touch, and stroke was savored. Each moan, cry, and purr was cherished. Tonight was theirs and no one would steal this memory from her; no one would taint it or mock it. Anne would never surrender this moment to Carter. She would treasure it until her last day on this earth.

CHAPTER THIRTY-NINE

The late-night hours stroked past as the moon's light crept in through the silk sheath that swayed from the windows. She listened to his heartbeat as Adam's fingertips traced circles on her damp, naked skin and she did the same to his chest. Her fingers felt two scars. Anne lifted herself to look at them.

Adam covered her hand with his. "They are mementos. Thank God Victoria gave me that bulletproof vest."

There it was—that memory that tightened her chest with terror. She pulled her hand away.

"I thought you were dead. You could have told me that you were wearing a bulletproof vest."

"It didn't come to mind to tell you, and things didn't play out the way they were supposed to." Adam ran his fingers through her mussed hair. "I thought you died that night. I watched you land on that concrete with such force…I thought I had lost you."

Anne sat up and picked at the sheet, avoiding Adam's gaze. "Parts of me did die. All the good parts."

Adam tucked a stray strand of hair behind her ear. "I don't believe that for second."

She jerked away. "You have no idea what I've been through, the emotional torture I've endured, the loss I've had to deal with...."

"I do understand. Every second that went by my soul died a little more. I couldn't get to you and when your father told me about your memory, that you didn't even remember me anymore, I felt helpless. I wanted to kill Carter, make him suffer for all he had done." Adam shifted in the sheets.

"Everyone who I love has lied to me."

"I did it to protect you, Anne."

Anne leaned away and narrowed her eyes. "I'm fed up with people feeding me that line of shit. Look where it's gotten us."

"We've all made choices and with those choices come consequences. I'm not sorry about my choices. I would do it again if it meant falling in love with you. You don't have to fight this on your own. I'm here because I choose to be. Everything I did in Minneapolis I did because I love you. I fell in love with you the minute I met you. I knew I was in trouble. I had an obligation to the FBI and Victoria, but you became my world, my life. I knew Carter would eventually come back. He's had an agenda since before he met you and then you, unfortunately, became a part of it."

Anne picked at the ends of her hair. Adam sat still, waiting for her to say something.

"Dr. Lindsey said that I didn't bring him into my life. He knew what Carter was up to. Why target me?"

His features lined with worry as he took Anne's hands into his. "Carter had his filthy hands in a lot of different illegal pots. I believe your father found the connection, but he refused to share it with me. He had a plan if anything happened to him. What did Magda Alves want to speak with you about?"

Anne plopped down on the edge of the bed. "She believes Carter is stealing her drugs and selling them on the streets. Magda wants me to find the drugs and money. I agreed to help her."

Adam knelt in front of her. "Why would you help her?"

"Carter owes a lot of people a lot of money, and Magda fears that they may come for me. I want him gone, out of my life. If I can't get the information that Marcus has on him, I have Magda in my back pocket."

Adam glowered at her. "Anne, if you cross Magda, she'll kill you. Not kill you, but torture you. She is brutal and ruthless."

"Like a snake," Anne whispered. Rage strained her face as she looked at Adam. "I will help Magda. Carter killed Dr. Lindsey. He may have put the gun in his own mouth, but Carter forced him to pull the trigger. He has taken so much from me. I'm going to destroy him. I'm going to make him suffer. That's what I choose."

Adam closed the space between them and stroked her cheeks. "Where's my angel? Where's *my* Anne?"

"She's lost, Adam—she's broken and lost. You don't want Carter's Anneliese. She's full of hatred and darkness, much worse than before.

"You're wrong. I love you no matter who you are. Look, I'm not innocent either. I have a dirty past, one I'm not proud of, but this is not you. You don't want these repercussions. Your father didn't want them for you either. Please,

Anne, let me in. Let me help. I don't want you doing this on your own. You don't know what you're getting yourself into."

"I do—I want him gone."

Anne wrapped her arms around his neck, digging her fingers into his hair and pulled him closer. "Please Adam, help me forget it. I don't want to remember these past few months. Please…help me forget."

Her voice was desperate, and Adam succumbed to her pleas. He helped her forget until the early hours of the morning.

∽

Leaving Adam was torture. She arched her shoulders back and ran her hands down her mussed hair, trying to smooth it out. Anne snuck through the lobby but ran directly into Robert. She wasn't surprised to see him at Adam's hotel. It was his job to watch over her. Anne could see the worry in his eyes. She felt guilty for not telling him where she was going, but she wanted Adam to rush her away from the Kensington. Take her away from the chaos.

"Mrs. Montgomery, we must get you back to the house at once. Carter isn't home and he can't know you were here."

Robert placed the palm of his hand against her lower back, quickly ushering her from the hotel. He looked up and down the shadowed street and motioned for her to cross. Her stilettos tapped against the pavement as they jogged through Forsyth Park. Anne kept looking over her shoulder. Adam's hotel became hidden by the tendrils of the Spanish moss on the trees and, ahead of her, the daunting Victorian came into view.

CHAPTER FORTY

Out of breath, Anne reached her bedroom. She locked it behind her and quickly removed her dress and shoes, tossing them into the closet. Anne buttoned her flannel pajamas and slid under the covers. Dawn was peeking just below the horizon. *I pray that Robert is the only one who knows where I was. I messed up. I am too emotional when it comes to Adam. Carter's going to know.* She needed sleep, and to dream of a life that she and Adam could live in without the constant burden of Carter threatening their lives.

∾

Blustery, dark clouds rolled through the sky as Anne stared out the window. She had slept a few hours. She squinted at the clock, it read 11:30 a.m. Right on cue, her stomach begged for food. She sat up and stretched her sore muscles. Anne smiled. The memory of making love with Adam strengthened her with resolve.

Anne needed to search Carter's office for anything that would implicate him in the thievery of Magda's illegal merchandise. She would take the drugs, any documents, and financial records and hand them over to Magda. Carter would suffer Magda's justice, and Anne would watch with great satisfaction.

After a quick shower, Anne wrapped her damp locks in a bun and slid on her favorite jeans and red knit top. Gliding down the hall in her black flats, she could hear men's voices coming from the dining room. Curious, she peeked around the corner. Carter sat at the table while the one of his brute bodyguards exited the room. Anne slowly stepped into the dining room. Carter turned in his chair, extending a hand to her.

"Come, sit, my wife. Let's talk."

Her gaze shifted around the room in suspicion. She cautiously stepped into the dining room and immediately noticed his casual attire of jeans, a polo shirt, and sneakers. Recently, he had been donning expensive suits. His clothes looked almost identical to the ones he wore when she first met him at Casey's birthday party.

"What's with the casual ensemble?"

"I figured we could spend the day together, take a little trip."

He rose from his chair and took her left hand; he stroked her bare ring finger. Panic seized her, but he seemed unaffected by the absence of the ring. *My ring. How could I have forgotten it?* Carter would have cemented that black diamond to her finger if he could have. *For him not to notice is bad, very bad.*

Hand-in-hand, they strolled to the luxury sedan. Carter opened the passenger door for her. She slid in, looking around distrustfully. Seconds later, Carter slid in behind the wheel.

"Where's Robert?"

Carter pushed the engine button, and the car roared to life. "I sent him on an errand."

Less than ten minutes later Carter parked the car near Ellis Square. The crowds were thin due to the blustery conditions, and the fountains that shot from the ground were quiet. Wisps of grey threaded through the blue sky as the wind lashed against the buildings. Carter helped Anne from the car and, again, he enclosed her hand in his. They walked the red brick path that intersected the square and made their way over to a row of shops that lined a cobblestone road.

"Do you want coffee?" Carter gestured to a small coffee shop.

"Sure."

After buying coffee, they continued their stroll through the historic downtown. The silence was killing her. He motioned for her to sit down on a wooden bench under a thick canopy of trees. She couldn't tolerate the awkward silence any longer.

"Where'd you go after you left the Kensington?" she blurted out.

"I walked around. Plotted my next move."

"So, what *is* your next move now that Simon is awake?"

Carter sipped his coffee. "I will reveal that to you very soon."

Anxiety erupted from every cell in her. So many dire visions scrambled around in her head. Anne shivered. The hot liquid radiating through the paper cup was not warming her up at all.

"Let's stop pretending, Carter. I'm exhausted. You've threatened to kill my best friend for months and you murdered Sam and Dr. Lindsey. You're cruel and heartless and this whole quality time manipulation thing you have going on isn't working."

A low laugh escaped him. "I figured it wouldn't. You are much too smart for my shenanigans. Let me ask you—where

292

did *you* go last night? I said an hour. I waited for you at the house, and when you didn't show up, I went looking for you. I was told that you left the Kensington shortly after I did. So, where you go?"

"I did go back to the house. I must have just missed you." Anne swallowed the dread that began to clog her throat.

Carter lifted his foot and placed it on top of his knee. "Really? I was told that you left with Adam. When I asked Robert, he said that you returned to the house after a short walk through Forsyth Park. Yet another person lying for you, Anneliese?"

"I didn't leave with Adam. Yes, we talked, but that's it."

"So Robert was mistaken, you didn't take a walk? You went right home?"

Carter was trying to confuse her and it was working. Anne sat silently as the howl of autumn encircled her. Strands of hair fell from her bun and were dancing in front of her face. Carter stood and discarded his coffee.

Anne raised her face to him. "Carter."

In one hasty motion, he was nose-to-nose with her. His hot coffee breaths stirred over her skin. "You seem to have trouble grasping the fact that I am your husband and that I don't tolerate other men coming between us. Now, you have forced my hand. I need to show you how serious I am because the last time I was betrayed, a bloody mess splattered all over the fireplace and ruined one of my favorite chairs."

Carter grabbed her coffee and tossed it in the trash. He seized her hand, pulling her to stand up, yanking her hard toward the car. Anne bit into her cracked lips, fearing their next destination.

CHAPTER FORTY-ONE

A long, polished-white hallway led them to a set of metal double doors. The smell was one of bleach and decay. It churned her stomach. The fluorescent lights burned her retinas. Carter's claw dug into her forearm as he dragged her down the hallway, grinning wickedly.

He knocked on the metal doors that read "Authorized Personnel Only." More than sourness stirred inside her—it was anxiety, panic, and sheer terror. A stout bald man came through the doors; he was wore a white lab coat and blue latex gloves.

After he let go of Anne's arm, Carter handed the man a wad of money. "Give us ten minutes."

"Ten, not a second more," the man grunted as he walked away, counting his cash.

Anne's breaths were growing more erratic. She could barely choke out her question.

"We're at the morgue, aren't we?"

"No one betrays me."

Anne threw her hands over her mouth. "Oh my God, what did you do, Carter?"

"Why don't you have look?" He gestured toward the metal doors.

Her frame shook while he pulled open one of the large doors. The smell of death permeated through the small opening. Anne tried to breathe through her dry heave. She managed to slide her left foot forward, then her right. She repeated the motion until she was fully inside the sterile room. An empty metal slab was to her right but to her left lay a draped sheet.

Blood rushed to her ears; heat ran the length of her body, scorching her. She was steps from the body. *Do I pull the sheet down? Do I really want to know who's beneath this sheet?* She knew if she didn't, Carter would force her. Bringing a shaky hand to her forehead, Anne wiped away the sheen of sweat that had formed. Her body was overheating and she was having difficulty breathing. *If this is Adam, I won't be able to bear it. I won't. I'll kill Carter, right here.*

Anne placed one hand over her mouth and she lowered the other. Her fingertips pinched the thick cloth as her muscles shook under the hesitation. She quickly pulled the sheet down. Anne's chest caved in and she felt the weight of her hysteria suffocate her. An inhuman scream surged from her. It echoed off the concrete walls and could have shattered the exposed glass.

"Oh my God!"

Those were the only words she could coherently form. Her voice choked with tears. Anne touched the body, making it real in her head. Marcus Hunt's skin was icy and taut under her touch. Anne turned and flew at her husband, flailing fists at his chest as an insurmountable rage was freed. She couldn't contain the savage beast that was clawing to come out, wanting to tear her flesh open to ravage the coward who stood before her. His serpentine arms tightened around her, holding her upper body against him. She twisted her body, trying to escape his grasp.

"Get the fuck off of me."

Carter tightened him hold. "Stop it, Anneliese."

Anne crumpled against him and hung in his firm grip while looking at Marcus's lifeless frame through bleary eyes. Sobs fell from her lips. She couldn't breathe. Anne choked on her cries and saliva as her stomach muscles tightened.

"Why would you this?"

"I did nothing. He overdosed. He just couldn't control his drug problem," Carter calmly spoke into her ear.

Her oxygen was depleting the more she looked at him. Marcus had a wife and kids. This was Sam Goodman all over again. Another family ripped to shreds because of Carter.

"You're lying. I know you killed him."

His winding arms squeezed around her, thrusting every bit of remaining air out of her until she could no longer whisper a breath.

"Whatever Hunt told you is dead, just like him. When will you learn, my sweet Anneliese? You'll never win. You'll never be free."

Tunnel vision set in, and the room slowly closed in around her. Her ears rang. *Oh God, what about Adam?*

CHAPTER FORTY-TWO

The car jerked when Carter slid into the driver's seat. An emotion more absorbing than hate ripped through Anne. Revulsion, loathing, spite—they weren't enough— didn't come close to describing the horror exploding within her.

Her hands lay limp beside her until Carter yanked her left one toward him. Plucking out her ring finger, he thrust the black diamond down until it sliced her knuckle and a scrape of red appeared through the broken skin. Anne winced at the sting. The black diamond ring Adam had re- moved before—a wave of cold swept through her.

Anne grinded her teeth. "Where's Adam?"

"This will not be taken off again, do you hear me, Anneliese? You will love *me*, you will trust *me*, and you will rely on *me*, no one else. No man will come between us. I said till death do us part, and death will come to those on whom you place loyalty over me."

Anne yanked her hand away and she clenched a fistful of his shirt. "Goddamn it, Carter. Where the hell is Adam?"

"He didn't want you, Anneliese. He got what he wanted from you and now, he's gone. He saw what I did to his new boss."

Anne let go of him, allowing her arms to go limp while she tipped her head back against the leather seat. All the color drained from her face.

"Why are you doing this to me?" Anne whispered.

"Doing what? I have husbandly expectations, is that too much to ask? Is it too much to ask that you not fuck another man, Anneliese? You seem to not understand the severity of the situation. I will break you and you will be mine and if that means I take away everyone in your life, then I will do just that."

She turned her head, looking at the evil that filled his dilated pupils. "You're sick, Carter. You're a drug addict and you're sick."

Carter flinched at her words. "How does that feel, my love? To know that you fell in love with someone like me? What does that say about you? Do you know what it feels like to know that the one you love despises you? I have been rejected my entire life and to be rejected by you is like dying." Anne's eyes widened by Carter's confession. "Sam, your father, and now Marcus Hunt—they're dead because of you. I enjoy inflicting pain upon you because I want you to feel what I feel. The moment I disappeared, you turned to Adam, of all fucking people." Carter slammed his hands against the steering wheel. "God help me, I love you, Anneliese, but you are really pissing me off."

Anne could have felt empathy for him. She too had felt the sting of rejection from those closest to her, but the hatred she had for him was stronger. Carter's chest heaved, his black eyes burned into her, practically incinerating what was left of her soul.

Carter regained his composure. "I took care of Adam. I hope it was all worth it."

Her body heaved and the tears streamed down, burning her skin. Adam would never agree to disappear. She had to look past the mirage that Carter was laying out before her.

"I hate you," Anne sobbed.

"The feeling is mutual right now, I assure you."

Anne could feel her stomach churn with nausea while he drove them back to the house in silence.

~

Carter was evil, as evil as the flesh that wrapped around his muscles and bones. Depravity filtered through his veins, circulating through his body like oxygen. Anne could clinically diagnose him, but there would be no point to it. He was a sadistic murderer who got off on her anguish.

When they arrived home, Anne stomped to the kitchen. The wine glasses clattered together, as her shaky hands reached for one. She starting pouring the wine but felt the air shift. Anne turned and found Carter standing across from her.

"Leave me the hell alone."

"Did you honestly think I would allow Marcus Hunt to tell you all my dirty little secrets? Really, it worked out perfectly."

Anne corked the wine bottle. "What does that mean?"

"You'll find out soon."

Anne was sick of his convoluted games. Her body shuddered from the fury building inside of her. She turned with the wine glass and hurled it at him, the glass flying across the kitchen, missing Carter's head by an inch before it smashed against the wall. Merlot splashed everywhere and shards of glass erupted around them in a shower of crystal. Carter and Anne shielded their faces from the flying glass. Her arm was soaked with red.

Heavy footsteps pounded against the hardwood floors. Anne moved her arms from her face and saw Robert and Carter's bodyguards standing in the entrance of the kitchen as they surveyed the chaotic scene.

The heat from Carter and Anne's rage toward one another raised the temperature in the room to a stifling degree. Her lungs burned with each breath, and Carter released a deep growl while his fists tightened at his sides.

"Clean this fucking mess up, Anneliese."

Carter stomped from the kitchen, with his guards in tow. Anne heard the front door slam, shaking the walls around them. She let out a scream and clutched the sides of her hair, pulling it from the bun. Robert wrapped his arms around her as she pressed into him, weeping. Anne was exhausted, but she needed time to gather her thoughts, her broken spirit, and to find the strength to finish what she had started.

$\sim$

The following day, Anne dressed in black leggings and a grey cashmere sweater that drowned her shriveled frame. She walked the streets of downtown Savannah, captivated by the bustle of Monday afternoon activity in the historic city. Carter made sure to have one of his brutes trail her at all times.

River Street Market Place was quiet, encouraging privacy. As much as she was given, anyway. The Savannah River rippled blue with the reflection of the vibrant southern skies.

The water lapped against the rocks that rested below her. Anne was no longer associated with the Mayo Clinic study, Carter had made sure to destroy that. Children like Stella would fall into the mental health abyss, never truly receiving proper care. Casey was her only hope. Everything was gone, Anne's faith, trust, and hope. She feared what Carter would do next.

Her head dropped in her hands as a curtain of blonde hid the tears that streamed down her face. Her body shuddered with her silent cries. Her mind was submerged in confusion. *We're all strangers, even Adam.* Anne felt her heart crumbling, deteriorating into ash.

With swollen eyes she looked out at the passing barge. Her entire life had been a lie. No one was real, it was all an illusion conjured up by Carter. *My existence is vapor, a wisp of energy floating around.* She was no longer Anne or Anneliese. She was the darkness, a mere shadow moving amongst the living. And the dead had nothing to lose.

CHAPTER FORTY-THREE

The next day, Anne sat in the third pew from the right, watching the eyes of Christ scrutinize her. *God can't save me now.* A wave of cold air raced up her arm as Robert took a seat next to her. Anne stared straight ahead, showing no emotion.

"How did Marcus Hunt die?" Anne spat out.

Robert hesitated. "You don't want to know, Mrs. Montgomery."

"Tell me Robert. I saw his dead body. Carter claims it was a drug overdose but I know better."

"Carter's men injected him with various drugs until his heart finally stopped. An anonymous tip was called in. Shortly thereafter his body was discovered, his death was ruled an overdose, and he was sent to the morgue."

Anne was surrounded by death. Robert made it sound like it was a simple, every day deed, like raking the leaves or mopping the floors.

"Carter paid the police off, didn't he?"

Robert bent forward, picked up a green leather-bound Bible and thumbed through the thin pages. "Yes. You know, you remind me of my daughter."

Anne was surprised by the change of subject. "You have a daughter?"

"I did…she's been gone for a few years now."

"Oh, Robert, I am so sorry."

"Thank you. She was stubborn, headstrong, and intelligent like you. She actually graduated high school at sixteen. She could have been a surgeon or an attorney, but no, she wanted to stick near her old man. She worried about me. I brought her into a life of murder and corruption."

Robert's complexion was ashen as he stared at Isaiah 48:22: *"There is no peace,"* says the Lord, *"for the wicked."* There would be no peace for Carter.

"What was her name?"

"Gwen Marie Mallen. She was twenty-seven."

"What happened to Gwen?" Anne's voice was just above a whisper to keep from disturbing the parishioners who filtered in around them.

"She was kidnapped and held for ransom in Chicago. Carter, Adam, and Michael were there. Negotiations went badly and before Gwen could blink an eye, she was killed."

Rita had told her a little bit about that Chicago trip, but she had left out an important detail about someone being murdered. Adam never told her that story either, and he had been there.

Robert stared at the Bible. "He executed her and she died alone on the floor of a dirty warehouse."

Anne watched the tension slide down his jaw. Watching him relive the nightmare was too much to bear.

"Who killed her, Robert? Tell me."

"Carter. Magda Alves ordered the kidnapping and killing of my daughter, and Carter carried it out."

Anne lifted her eyes to the angels patched into the stained glass. Her fingertips brushed over her lips, feeling the chill transfer over her sensitive skin. Betrayal: it oozes from pores, it knits through flesh, it fills lungs.

"How awful."

"Michael was devastated. They were in love and wanted to marry. Gwen and Michael paid for their parents' sins. That is why Carter disappeared. Michael discovered who pulled the trigger."

Anne flinched like she had been slapped. "How do you look at him every day? And Michael? Carter should be dead."

"We needed Magda on U.S. soil."

She read between the lines: *Robert is seeking revenge.*

"What happened to Adam?"

"After I brought you back to the house, Carter demanded we return to Adam's hotel room. When we arrived, Adam was gone, but Carter found your ring."

Her body relaxed as Anne laid her hand on top of his. "Look at me." Robert put the Bible back and looked at Anne. "Gwen's death will not be in vain. I promise."

He gave her a small smile, rose, and walked over to the candles. Parents were never supposed to bury their children. It was unnatural. When Anne miscarried her baby, her loss was agonizing. She couldn't imagine losing a child with whom she had shared twenty-seven years. Anne realized now that God knew what He was doing when she lost her baby, Carter's baby. He was saving the innocent.

CHAPTER FORTY-FOUR

Anne walked into the sitting room. She ran her fingers over the flecks of pale pink that stained the white grout holding the crumbling fireplace bricks in place. Remnants of her father would remain in the house forever.

When her mother committed suicide, the priest told Anne that her soul was in hell, that suicide was an unforgivable sin, and that the gates of heaven did not open for those who took their own lives. Anne feared for her mother, but she couldn't believe that God would turn her away. She had been tortured her entire life, tormented by schizophrenic demons—no, God would save her mother. God had saved her father and, somehow, He would save her.

Anne took a healthy swallow of the merlot, feeling it warm her throat. She sat down on the faded green-velvet chaise. A waft of stale perfume expelled from the cushion. The gas lantern flickered from the table near her.

Magda clearly was not a fan of the opposite sex—a sentiment inherited from her mother, no doubt. Anne looked down at the black diamond. *Maybe Magda's blackened soul is trapped inside this piece of stone.*

The evil that was bearing down on Anne felt like a possession. Her soul was being forsaken for her parents' sins.

Children suffer for what the adults in their lives do. Anne had seen it time and time again, and now she was bargaining for her life with the wicked of the world because her mother and father couldn't help themselves. Claire suffered because of her father's adultery. Michael and Gwen were separated by death. Carter, as sadistic as he was, ached as well. He was shunned by his biological father and adopted by another to simply save face.

Why would Anne ever want to bring a child into this world? Would the cycle continue? If she and Adam had a child, would he or she undergo the same fate? Anne couldn't excuse the fact that Magda took Gwen, Robert's only daughter, from him. Anne couldn't understand that mentality. Anne's head throbbed at all the thoughts and questions. *Why would Magda take Gwen away from Robert? Her own daughter died, she knows that loss. Her own revenge? An eye-for-an-eye? Everyone's pasts are colliding right here in Savannah. The ghosts of our sins will roam the streets with haunted wrath.*

Anne's eyes shifted to the staircase. She rose from the chaise and set her glass down on the side table. Carter wasn't home. Anne seized the opportunity to uncover Carter's deceits. With each step she took while climbing the creaking stairs, her heart thumped a little harder. Her bare feet padded down the dim, narrow hallway and stopped in the threshold of Carter's office. The darkness was unsettling. Anne entered the office and flicked on the small lamp that sat at the corner of the desk.

She located the set of keys she had found days ago and walked over to the metal cabinet and crouched down. She inserted the small key, the lock clicked, and Anne slowly opened the heavy door.

Anne stared wide-eyed into the empty cabinet. All the evidence of illegal drugs was gone. To make sure she wasn't hallucinating, Anne placed her hands on the metal shelves to feel around, as though the drugs were hiding under an invisible cloak. They were gone. The bags of pills, the syringes...everything had vanished.

Anne stood, absolutely stunned. She shook her head in disbelief. Her next thought was to start digging through his files. She needed find correspondence or transactions that would implicate him. She remembered seeing Carter's laptop on the desk, Anne took a step back and the pad of her foot landed on what felt like the top of a shoe.

Anne shrieked and leapt forward reaching for the chipped bookcase for balance. She turned to see Carter standing in the small glow of the lamp, or what looked like Carter. The man before her appeared ghostly. His dilated pupils glinted from the desk lamp and stared at her with a glazed menace.

Carter's pale face held no expression as he stood silently. Anne laid a hand over her heart as it slowed.

"Jesus, Carter. What are you doing there?"

He cocked his head to the side as if he was trying to process her question. His eyes lowered to the opened cabinet. Anne took a step toward the window and away from Carter. Her small movements made him look back at her. Anne grew terrified. *He doesn't look human.* This was not Carter. His eyes were glassy; they looked like black burnished marbles. The palms of her hands laid flat against the shelf behind her in case she needed the momentum to push herself away from him.

Carter took two steps forward and Anne launched herself away from the bookcase, but Carter had the advantage with his long legs and arms. His muscular limbs trapped her and his hands grabbed a handful of cotton, hauling Anne's body against him. She cried out, tilting her head away from him, but her chest, stomach, and thighs were flush against him. Carter's hot breath reeked of alcohol and from the glazed look in his eyes, he was clearly high on some kind of drug or a dangerous mixture.

"Carter…stop," Anne managed to exhale.

His grip tightened around her. Carter could easily crack her ribs with one swift move. Anne sunk her nails into his back, but he didn't even flinch. He lowered his head, which was coated in perspiration, and pressed his forehead into her cheekbone. Anne let out another cry from the bone-on-bone contact.

"Why him, Anneliese? Please, tell me," Carter pleaded.

Anne tried again to squirm from his arms, but she finally sagged against him in defeat.

"Carter, you've been drinking and God only knows what else. Let me go."

He opened his mouth and ran his teeth down her cheek and along her jawline.

"When I was gone, when you thought I was dead—" Carter panted. "And you met Adam, did you think of me when you fucked him?"

Anne squeezed her eyes shut. "Stop it, Carter."

"I want to know, Anneliese."

Anne opened her eyes and looked at the monster in front of her. The whites of his eyes were red and his pupils were fully dilated. She could barely see his brilliant sapphire eyes, and his olive skin was taut over his cheekbones. The drugs were taking their toll on him. *Or maybe it was pure madness, like my mother.*

"What do you want me to say, Carter? Yes. Does it matter now? Look at the cruelty you have displayed! Why would I ever love someone like you ever again? You hate me for something that you did. You left. You left me alone. What was I supposed to do? Pine for your ghost for the rest of my life?" Anne could no longer look at him. She turned her head away, praying he would just let her go and sleep off whatever he was on.

Carter unwound his arms from her and pushed her back. Anne stumbled over her own feet. Her lungs were tight and she could barely take in a full breath. He ran his hands through his thick waves and walked over to the metal cabinet where he kicked the door. Metal bounced off of metal. Anne covered her ears.

"What were you looking for? The drugs? While you weep in the corner of your bedroom like a child, I'm plotting my next move. Give up, Anneliese. Whatever plan you and Adam have concocted, it won't work. The problem with you is that you trust too many people." Carter turned and pointed his finger in her direction. "You think you have everyone positioned on their appropriate sides but you're wrong. The innocent can be tainted just as easily. You're the poster child for that."

"Why keep me around? What value do I add to your life?" Anne was exasperated.

Carter tipped his head back and laughed.

"I love you, my Anneliese, and I've stated before, if you won't be with me, you won't be with anybody, especially

Adam Whitney. You will never leave me, Anneliese. I hold all the cards." Carter stepped closer to her. "Someone tipped the police off about a possible prescription drug ring here in Savannah. I believe some junkie they questioned had a torn prescription in his possession. Luckily, the doctor's name was removed or they would have seen it was you, Dr. Anneliese Montgomery."

CHAPTER FORTY-FIVE

"What the hell are you talking about?"

Carter walked to the desk, opened the top drawer and pulled a white prescription pad from under a pile of papers, throwing it on top of the desk in front of Anne. Her eyes widened. There was Anne's prescription pad from her office in Minneapolis.

Carter pointed at the prescription pad. "It's amazing what a drug-addicted low-life will say and do."

"I haven't used this in months." Anne picked up the pad, looking at it closer.

"Naughty, Anneliese, your prescriptions have been seen all over Savannah's seedy pharmacies. Not only that, but you and Marcus Hunt were selling Magda's stolen drugs to local dealers."

Anne was speechless. There was no way Magda would believe Carter's tale. She wanted him dead just as much as Anne did.

"Magda will never buy it, Carter." Anne tossed the pad down.

Carter smirked and dug inside the drawer again. He pulled out photographs, holding them up for Anne to see. It was of a woman, with long blonde hair, like Anne's, but her face was not clearly visible. This woman appeared to be engaging in a drug transaction.

"That's not me. Who the hell is that?"

Carter slid one of the pictures from the bottom of the stack. Anne grabbed it, squinting her eyes. Anne recognized the face.

"Natalie." Anne's face pinched as she stared at the glossy photo. "You made her sell drugs to teenagers. Carter, what the hell is wrong with you?" Anne dropped the photo.

"I didn't make her do anything. She was more than willing. Quite a white-collar crime enthusiast, that southern tart."

He's blackmailing me. Natalie was added to Anne's hit list. The fear that she once experienced in Carter's web of intimidation was not present. Instead, heat surged through her as her body trembled and quaked. She leaned toward Carter, her palms pressed hard into the desk.

"I'm going to destroy you, Carter."

"Don't make threats if you can't carry them out, my love."

"Oh, I plan on carrying them out," Anne snarled.

She swiveled on her heels and left Carter standing there in the dim office, thinking he held all the cards. Anne stalked down the hallway and descended the stairs, looking for Robert. She found him in the kitchen riffling through the pages of the local newspaper. His head jerked up when she entered the room.

Anne motioned for Robert to follow her to the SUV. Once outside in the crisp evening air, Anne felt like she could finally breathe.

"Fuck." She paced the space around the SUV. "Robert, call Michael. Tell him to meet me. Now. I don't care where."

Robert immediately phoned Michael. No more weeping. No more waiting. It was time to end this. Robert fetched the

SUV keys from his pocket, guided Anne into the backseat and placed himself in the driver's seat. The bustle of Bay Street blazed on either side of her. Car horns screamed and motorcycles accelerated, forming a steady hum in Anne's ears. Anne didn't know where Adam was, but she craved his presence. She could smell him all around her.

The SUV rolled to a stop in front of an iron gate. The security guard nodded, and Robert continued down a winding driveway. A yellow house with white pillars sat before her. Palm trees lined the gravel path toward the front door. She didn't realize that Michael had found a home in Savannah.

The stretch of the marsh ran along the side of the SUV as cattails swayed with the breeze. Once Robert pulled the vehicle around the half-circle in front of the house, the front door opened. Anne didn't wait for Robert to open her door; she flew from the automobile. Anne's hair flapped in the wind. Breathless, she reached the slate walkway leading to the door.

Adam stood just beyond the door, a yellow light engulfed him, her angel yelled her name, and ran toward Anne down the stairs. He was there to save her. An ocean poured from her eyes as a magnetic pulse surged through her nervous system. She took off running, flinging her body right into his outstretched arms. They crashed into each other, and her feet left the earth as he swung her around. Her legs wound around him, latching on for dear life. The one who gave her life was here, right now. She knew Adam would never leave her.

Her reedy frame shook against him as every ounce of her soul poured out of her. Adam squeezed her tight and peppered kisses along her neck and cheek. *His smell, God, his smell is home.* Completely immersed with her connection to this man, she didn't hear the conversation ticking back and forth between Adam and Robert. In her own world, she heard jibber and mumbles. Anne shook her head, refusing to move, listen, or respond. She just wanted to hibernate in Adam's embrace.

"Anne, look at me," Adam whispered.

His words were indulgent and sweet. They tickled her ear and coaxed her from her cocoon. Adam cupped her face, wiping her tears away from under her lashes. Her heart slowed as she pulled herself back together. She exhaled a stuttered breath and looked into his eyes.

"I knew you wouldn't leave me." Anne smiled.

"Never. Let's get you inside."

She didn't care why he was there, he was alive and with her and that's all that mattered. Slowly planting her feet back on the stone path, he wrapped his arm around her shoulder, guiding her into the house. Anne stepped into a vast foyer that was illuminated by a beautiful crystal chandelier. She leaned her head against Adam, he rubbed her shoulder and kissed the top of her head. He maneuvered her around the corner into a terra cotta hued living room, where flames crackled and popped in the fireplace across the large room.

Michael and Simon entered the room. Anne walked over to Michael, and he enveloped her in a quick hug. After hearing the story about him and Gwen, her heart broke for him. He had lost the woman he loved—the woman he planned to spend forever with—he was seeking revenge just as much as she was.

"I'm glad you're safe, Anne. What happened?"

314

"Where do I start?"

Simon stepped forward. He still had his cane but his complexion looked healthier. Anne looked at both of them and their scowls.

Anne took a deep breath. "Carter is draining Montgomery Hotels Incorporated dry. He's going to bankrupt your company, just like he did Leeds Import and Construction."

"Why?" Michael looked at his father and then back at Anne. "To settle his debts."

Anne wanted to ask Michael about Gwen, but that was his story tell when he was ready.

"I froze the bank accounts that Carter had access to. He can no longer use Montgomery money." Michael stood stiffly next to his father.

"He's stealing Magda's drugs and selling them here in Savannah and Atlanta, but he's made it look like I'm the one selling the drugs. He has a larger stash hidden somewhere. I need to find it. If I hand over what she has asked, then she'll kill Carter. Right now, he's blackmailing me."

"What about Magda, she gets off, flies back to her compound with her millions and without any consequences?" Michael spat out.

Anne turned to look at Adam, who nodded as if he could read her thoughts. "No." She turned back to Michael and Simon. "There are always consequences."

The silence grew thick, as fire roared behind them. Never in Anne's wildest imagination did she ever think she would be orchestrating the execution of Carter and a Latin American drug lord. But here she was. Seeking redemption for those who had died by their hands. Would it be enough? She could never go back to the life she once had.

Michael stroked his chin. Anne could see his muscles tense.

Simon laid his hand on Michael's shoulder. A shadow passed across his face. "Tomorrow. Tomorrow we end it." Michael's eyes shifted past Anne's. She felt Adam press his body against hers.

"Tomorrow." Adam said.

Anne turned her head to look at him, lacing her fingers with his. "Tomorrow." She looked back at Michael and Simon. "She doesn't get Carter. I do."

CHAPTER FORTY-SIX

Anne and Adam entered the guest bedroom. Scarlet curtains cascaded down the walls, pooling on the dark hardwoods. The velvet pin-tucked headboard mimicked the hue of the curtains, and milky sheets ran the length of the bed. She threw her black cherry satchel on the plush king-sized bed.

Adam's taut, scruffy jaw softened once he caught Anne's gaze and a hint of his dimples peaked through. A breath hadn't passed from Anne's lips before Adam had his on them. She tasted every bit of him and cherished each tease of his tongue. Their frenzied hands pulled buttons, yanked zippers, and discarded each piece of clothing in haste and passion. Their breath filled the room with heat and something sweeter: want, need, desire. There was no time for being slow and gentle. Anne sank her claws in, begging Adam, pleading for him to consume her and the more she begged, the more he wanted to please her. Their bodies moved and twisted; the bedding was soon discarded in a pile on the floor as they made love.

Afterward, lying together, the thought of not being with Adam, not loving him, stripped her soul bare, leaving it raw and exposed. Pain emanated from her chest and before she could control it, choked sobs let loose. Their limbs entwined and Adam leaned his forehead against hers.

Anne's body shuddered. "I can't lose you. God, Adam…."

He cradled her wet, flushed face, stroked the tangled hairs from around her cheeks, hushed her cries, and whispered love and affection while placing kisses over her cheeks and neck.

"I'll never let that happen."

Anne knew that was a promise he could never keep, not as long as Carter was walking this earth. They laid in silence for close to an hour. She watched his chest rise and fall in the soft illumination like waves in the Atlantic.

"How did you know I was coming here?"

Adam took in a deep breath. "I always know where you are, Anne. I told you, we are in this together and I will follow you to the ends of the universe. Are you sure about Carter? That's a burden you must bear each day of your life. Can you live with that? Because I don't think you can."

She knew what he was asking: Would she be able to take a life and still carry on with her own? Anne felt the heavy diamond still on her finger. She sat up in the darkness, a sliver of the moon drew a trail to a set of doors that led outside.

Anne slid from the bed, slipping on Adam's shirt.

"What are you doing?" he asked.

Anne pulled the diamond ring from her finger, sat it on the palm of her hand, and stared at the wicked black gem. The lines in her palm crisscrossed beneath it, as did the scars from the mirror that had embedded into skin all those years ago.

"I'm not theirs anymore," she whispered.

So many had hooked into her soul like a parasite—Carter, Magda, her mother. *Not anymore.* She padded to the doors, unlocked the latch, and pushed them open, revealing tall patchy grass rising from gray-blue swampy waters. An autumn full moon hung just above the horizon. Anne closed her hand, feeling the ring sting her skin as she tightened her grip.

The scenery in front of her reminded Anne of that night when Carter climbed those cabin stairs, unleashing his deception into her lungs, mind, and heart. It seemed like a lifetime ago where a different ring sat on her finger, one given to her by her love, her angel.

Anne stepped out onto the small deck. A shivered traveled through her. She raised her arm, clutching the ring. With every bit of strength she had, Anne brought her arm back and flung it forward. The diamond ring soared through the night air. Though the symphony of frogs played their boisterous melody, she heard the splash of the ring hitting the water.

She felt Adam's arms wrap around her; she turned to look at him. The shadows of the night touched his face, Anne ran her hands down his jawline, his neck, and stopped at his chest. His heart raced under her touch.

"Carter never had my soul—my heart, maybe at one time—but never my soul." A tear streaked down her face. "That will forever belong to you, here and after," Anne whispered.

Adam drank her in. He bent down, kissing the wetness away, then placing kisses on the palms of her hands. "You've held my soul in your beautiful hands, protecting it with your courage and love. I promise, forever will be ours," he spoke against her skin.

She closed her eyes, taking in every bit of him. Anne didn't know what tomorrow would bring but in that moment, in the dark, her soul began to fill with light once again.

ACKNOWLEDGEMENTS

To my husband: Thank you for encouraging me every step of this journey. You are my angel. Scotland or bust.

To my son: Thank you for understanding my crazy writing whims during our schooling time. You are my inspiration.

To my mom, dad, mother-in-law, and grandparents: Thank you for rooting me on, even when I wanted to throw in the towel.

To Maria Gomez and the entire Montlake Romance team: Thank you for your faith in me and your incredible guidance. You work extremely hard and I am forever grateful to be part of the Montlake family.

To Melody Guy: Thank you for being such a fabulous editor.

To Erin: Thank you for being my cheerleader.

To Doreen: Thank you for being "my person."

To my street team and beta readers: Thank you for taking time out of your hectic lives to give me feedback and comments on my books.

To Melyssa Williams: Thank you for being my indie sister.

To my stellar readers: Thank you so much for all your love and support. Thank you for your reviews, emails, and messages sharing your love for *Deadly Deception* and the debauchery that is Carter, Anne, and Adam.

To my go-to person for all my crazy questions about mob activity: Thank you; your secret is safe with me.

ABOUT THE AUTHOR

 Andrea Johnson Beck is a homeschool teacher in North Carolina, where she lives with her husband and young son. Beck vowed to write a full-length book before her thirtieth birthday, which she accomplished just weeks shy of her deadline. *Deadly Deception* is the first in her series of contemporary romantic thrillers. She also writes monthly articles for Homeschool Mosaics and In-Depth Genealogist. Stay in touch with Beck through her blog:
http://andreajohnsonbeck.blogspot.com/
http://andrea-johnsonbeck.com/